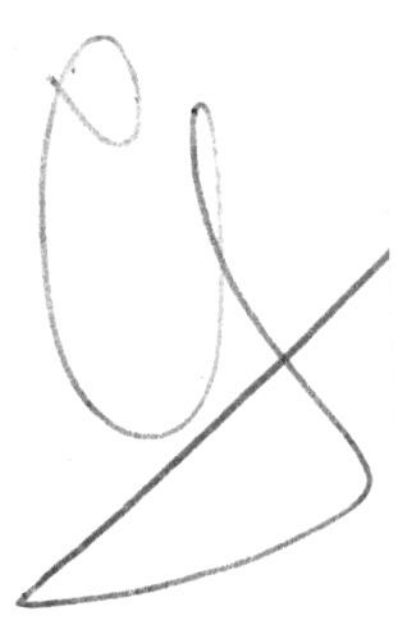

DEADSTREAM

DEADSTREAM

a novel

by

Bradley T. Platt

Library of Congress Number: 2005906002
ISBN : Hardcover 1-59926-018-2
Softcover 1-59926-017-4

This is a work of fiction. Names, characters, places and incidents either are the product of the author's imagination or are used fictitiously, and any resemblance to any actual persons, living or dead, events, or locales is entirely coincidental.

This book was printed in the United States of America.

To order additional copies of this book, contact:
Xlibris Corporation
1-888-795-4274
www.Xlibris.com
Orders@Xlibris.com
27758

CONTENTS

This book is dedicated in loving memory to Dr. Kenneth and Donna Platt—two of the most gracious and loving souls I have ever known. I will see you soon.

bp

Chapter 1

Welcome

My true wish is to confide in you—if only you are so able. I am starting the story from this point with great consideration being given to retrospective. This is one of the few things I can assure you. At precisely this point—I am clearheaded. At this exact moment—I know the difference between right and wrong.

Everything really began that yellow spring morning when I was nothing more than a very green young man. And there he stood quivering on the paper-thin ice like a crazed lunatic—my best friend, Billy Kudray. Poor bastard. His father had moved out of the house less than two weeks ago and I could already surmise his luck wasn't about to change anytime soon. I should have *never* let him hold on to the fucking cigarettes.

"It's the size of a beagle!" Billy says, his fly line dancing in the open water near the narrow blade of ice. "I'm not shittin' ya!"

The thin ice of the beaver pond seemed to take a breath as Billy lurched forward toward the open water. "You need to give that fish some line!" I finally yell.

Billy had indeed hooked a massive brook trout on this half-frozen beaver pond deep within the Deadstream Swamp. We had not expected the pond to still be iced over this late in the year. But after haphazard, "careful speculation," as Billy called it, he decided to make a few casts into the small piece of open water located in the middle of the pond. Billy had the fever of someone who had never landed a decent fish. The fact that it was the opening day of trout season in Michigan would be his only excuse. "Hey! Don't you go near that open water!" I barked again. He sputtered something about "needing a rope" as he crept stiffly and hunched over like a ninety-year-old man toward the open water. Me—I was just worried about those cigarettes. "Let that fish tire itself out and try and flip'em up on the ice," I holler, as my arms flail motioning how to perform the maneuver. "*And*," I screamed at the top of my lungs, knowing full well that yelling would help the situation, "throw me a smoke!"

I began tiptoeing hesitantly while trying to keep at least twenty feet between the two of us. The sun's reflection on the ice was blinding, my eyes began to sting. A massive splash erupted followed by a high-pitched screech from Billy yielded a very large trout flopping on the edge of the ice like a fish out of water. Billy's fly rod lay broken in several pieces at his feet as everything began to revert out of slow motion. He sprinted across the ice toward the fish, and that was it; there wasn't going to be any nicotine in my system for a while.

There was the sound of splashing water, and then Billy disappeared—nothing more than a floating hat spinning among scattered pieces of frothing ice and bright blue water. The fish was nowhere to be seen either. Billy had fallen through the ice before; it wasn't like it was the first time. I had even witnessed one such episode while we were ice fishing last spring. But it is at exactly this moment when things can get a little hairy. When a fisherman's waders suck themselves full of water, it can deliver one to the bottom of a pond very, very quickly. This particular pond happened to be over twenty feet deep. Absolute and utter silence—it was the sound of pure emptiness. Billy's hands finally burst through the icy debris and began grabbing the thin-edge pieces of ice, which began to break immediately.

"What the fuck were you thinkin'?" I bellowed, trying to hide my worry. *My God, he could have died.* I could have lost my best friend right then and there. Knowing Billy, my window wouldn't be open for long. He quickly snapped into formation with his elbows sticking out from his body and placed on the ice. It would be the breaking of the thin ice with his elbows that would safely let him travel to within my grasp. His face was a dull powder blue by now. Damn fool anyway.

"Oh my God! I think I've got hypothermia!" he yells, finally regaining himself awkwardly on the ice. "And I lost my fucking fly rod!" he gasps, managing to get me completely soaked in the process. Our proximity on the ice began to make me nervous.

"This is just fucking great. You could have fucking died!" I yell. "And now we have to go back to the Jeep," I moan, knowing it wasn't even 10:00 a.m.

"You're God damn right we do!" he answers sharply.

"Great! I haven't even caught a fish yet!" I say.

"And hurry the fuck up," he says, scurrying past me toward the beaver dam, which led to the higher ground.

"Oh, quit your pouting!" I answer, as he went past.

"Oh, I'm not the one pouting, Brendon." He stopped and pivoted toward me with his usual quizzical glance. "And don't you worry. I had the Marlboros in a Ziploc bag," he says smiling from ear to ear, knowing full well what was on my mind. I was dumbfounded. "C'mon, let's get the show on the road!" he yells, as he made his way past the beaver house, which stuck awkwardly through the ice. "That was the biggest brookie you have ever seen. Admit it," he says, from the distance he was now creating.

He isn't really a bad guy. Granted, he has been a pain in the ass lately with his father moving out and all. But he is probably the best friend a guy could ever ask for—more of a brother than anything. Unfortunately, in the present day, we just don't talk much anymore. Actually, we don't talk at all. Sometimes far too much can take place in a very short period of time—and sometimes there just isn't much to say.

Chapter 2

Red, White & Blue

Our arrival back to the Jeep was by no means fast enough for Billy as I watched and laughed at him hastily stripping off his wet clothes. "My God, I haven't been this cold since I fell in when we were ice fishing at Pearl Lake!" he stammered through blue lips.

"Yeah, you have a great track record with this kind of thing," I say.

"Well, luckily, I had a rope that time," he answered.

"What kind of idiot puts a life jacket on, ties a rope around his waist, and goes fucking ice fishing," I asked at the top of my lungs, "with less than two inches of ice? You shouldn't even be out there. What the hell is wrong with you?"

"Well, fuck you too," he says.

"You need your head examined."

"Hey, you were there too!" he says, pointing a shaky blue finger.

"Yeah, sitting on the shore, drinking beer," I say. "Someone had to hold the rope."

"You tied it to a tree," countered Billy.

"What fucking ever!" I say back to him—his legitimizations were starting to wear thin.

"Why don't you try and add something positive to the situation," he says, "like letting me put your shirt on or something?"

"Oh no, I'm not giving up my dry clothes just because of another one of yer stupid, fucking stunts," I answer, sharply.

"Well, at least warm up the Jeep, dicknose!" he says, as I laugh.

"You do remember the heating core is out. *There is no heat*." I nod my smug head at the reminder.

"Oh, this is just great!" he moans, realizing that the Jeep wouldn't provide an optimum escape.

"C'mon, get in, let's get the show on the road," I yell. He didn't even seem to have the sense enough to get in the damn jeep. It was as if he were paralyzed.

"I cannot believe you are going to let me sit here half naked like this, man," he says, through chattering teeth, gingerly climbing into the Jeep.

"Yeah," I say. "And maybe you should start using your head when you're out in the woods. You do realize that due to your recent condition, we are going to have to take a shortcut. If we take the road to Reedsburg Dam, we can be in town in half an hour."

"Oh no," he says. "We are not going to drive over that fucking beaver dam again. No way."

"You know that way is quicker; it will save us almost half an hour," I answer.

"Yeah, but that road is closed," he says. "And the last time we tried to do this, the dam collapsed."

"Hey, you're the one sittin' there soaking wet in your God damn underwear."

"This is not a good idea, and you know it. No one has even used that road this spring. I guarantee it."

"It can be done," I answer, nodding my head. "I just need to keep the left set of tires on the old road grade. It's still there; it's just covered by a few inches of water."

"More like a few feet. If we get stuck, I'm not even getting outta the vehicle," he moans.

"Well, that should be helpful," I answer. The rocking vehicle reminded me of my alcohol intake from the previous evening. I was just starting to engage the four-wheel drive as I felt the heavy muddy drops spray across my chin.

"God damn it! Fucking vehicle!" I mutter as we slam into the incline of the dam. Two holes had rusted through each side of the floorboards of the Jeep. Glancing down through the hole, I can see the tangled maze of twisted logs, branches, and mud that made up the beaver dam.

"Hold on!" I scream, as the CJ-7 bounced down the old road bottom with the precision of a slightly retarded jackrabbit. "Did you know," I yell, over the splashing water and the hover of the engine, "that the DNR says there are over ten thousand beaver ponds in northern Michigan?" I say, glancing at poor Billy; he was starting to look dejected again.

"Yeah, and I wish they'd kill every fucking one of them!" he yells, back.

The Jeep rolled up onto the exposed road on the other side of the pond as we headed east into the oncoming sun. I found myself feeling dry, warm, and slightly parched at the same time. God, what a gorgeous morning. "Why don't you make yourself useful and hand me a beer?" I say, smugly, feeling the orange yellow sunlight hitting my face.

"Kind of early, don't ya think?" asks Billy.

"If anything, it'll warm your ass up."

"I don't need a beer," he says, reaching behind the seat for the cooler.

"We have been drunk on beer on the opening day of trout season for six straight years," I say, with a smile.

"Yeah, whatever."

"Probably more than that," I add.

It was true. Billy and I have been drinking beer on the opening day of trout season since we were twelve years old. I was completely against the idea until he decided to steal four cans of Red, White, and Blue beer, relying on Billy's father's drunkenness not to notice. We stole several more beers that evening after quickly pounding the first four. Having been my first-time drinking, it turned into an acutely rough night. I proceeded to throw up a full can of Dinty Moore Stew in Billy's newly bought tent given to him as a birthday present. He was *extremely* happy with me and demanded I leave the tent immediately, which was his explanation when I woke up outside the next morning curled up in a soft bed of red pine needles. I honestly think he would have punched me that day if it wouldn't have been for the colossal piece of grape Hubba Bubba bubble gum that had somehow found its way into my hair that night. I remember eating the gum in order to replace the taste of puke in my mouth, and that is the last thing I remember. I sat in my own tears that morning as Billy roughly cut the gum out of my hair with an extremely dull jackknife, which left a bald patch in the back of my already-pounding head. I vividly remember looking into my mother's large brown eyes and it being a very difficult situation to explain. The sour smell of puke and beer on my breath at the age of twelve probably didn't help the matter either. I couldn't help but giggle at the recollection.

"What are you giggling about? Always fucking giggling," groans Billy, still shivering in his underwear. "Maybe you should realize that I have been going through a lot these days!" he snaps. "With my parents and all," he says, tears welling up in his eyes. "Well, my parent."

Here we go again. His pussy was really sore over this one. "Hey, like I said before, everything will work out. Just give it some time. They need some time," I say, "and have a beer," I add, doing my best to sound concerned. "At least you had the opportunity to meet your father," I mumble under my breath.

"What did you say?" he asks.

"Nothin'."

"Well, I guess I better have at least one—be a shame not to," he says, finally smiling again. "Strictly for medicinal purposes," he says, replicating his father's sentence structure perfectly, unbeknownst to himself.

"You sound just like your fucking old man," I say as he laughs again. Billy's father was a fairly wealthy local illiterate man—he owned one of the largest pulp-cutting outfits in the lower peninsula of Michigan. The only writing he recognized was his own signature. I, on the other hand, lost my father to the jungles of Southeast Asia. My father, by his own choice, joined the Vietnam Conflict at the ripe old age of eighteen and, after three tours, came home a new man—a new man who had inhaled too much of something orange. He died the week of my third birthday, or so I'm told. Considering my age at this loss, I was robbed of even a small blip of remembrance. And *of course*, my mother never speaks of him—it is as if he had never existed. My memories consist of nothing more than off-green, ill-colored photos now. The loss of innocence can come at a very early age for some of us—when those pink clouds turn to gray and there just isn't any coming back. I just hope there is even the slightest chance that I will someday be able to leave this small town—I'm sure my dad felt the same way.

Chapter 3

There Is Nothing Worse Than a Conservation Officer

"Boy, wait till everyone hears about your little antics this morning!" I say to Billy, nodding my head with a smile as I crack open my second beer of the morning. "I can't wait—"

"You can shut the fuck up about what happened this morning," he says. "That fish was huge, and you know it."

"I wouldn't go that far," I say, noticing him staring out the passenger window, doing his best to ignore me.

"Hey," he asks, "how is your mom doing? God, I miss not seeing her every day."

"Oh, she's doing great; she even quit smoking," I say. "Well, yesterday, she quit smoking."

"She's still working at the school?"

"Yep," I answer, remembering how emotional she had been when I had left this morning. *And what the hell was she doing up at 5:00 a.m. on a Saturday morning? She is really starting to worry me these days.*

"Is she dating anyone?" Billy asks, tapping his knee.

I am surprised it took him this long. All of my friends, at one point or another, have had a crush on my mother. Don't get me wrong; she's a very pretty lady, but God, was this always awkward. "Nope, not that I know of," I answer, thinking of the tears that streamed down her face this morning. I don't know why, but her condition this morning hadn't really concerned me until now. She did seem to have tears in her eyes a lot lately.

"I actually heard she was dating that Conservation Officer Frank Pierson," he says, continuing his stare out of the passenger window.

"Don't even fucking say that," I say. "I can't stand that guy; you know that." Billy always knew how to pry. "Besides, they're just friends. She told me," I stressed with each hand in the air. Why the hell was he bringing this up?

"Just what I heard," he says.

"It's not fucking true," I say. The kid always knew how to needle me. I can still remember the day that miserable piece of shit, Frank Pierson, came over to see my mom. He acted like I wasn't even there and hasn't acknowledged me anytime that I have seen him since. They whispered for over an hour in the kitchen, his overly alert blue eyes flicking with arrogance.

"So did you hear about Scotty?" I say, not letting Billy get the best of me. "He flew to London last week! How about that! London! Traverse City to Detroit to London! Can you imagine?" My heart skips a beat at the mention of such a trip. Typical—I have had a passport for over two years and never ventured farther than Canada.

"You just want to go and see that English chick," he growls.

"I just want to get outta here," I say.

"Who are you kiddin'?" he adds.

He was right. Oh my God, that girl. I had been lucky enough to spend one night with her last summer in her parents' guesthouse. We drank beer and talked through the night, and when she awoke in my arms, I calmly explained to her that I had been up the entire night carefully making sure she wasn't harmed. Bright blue eyes and slender golden arms yielded the happiest moment of my life. "I really don't think I ever had a chance with her."

"What are you talking about?" Billy says, mocking me with rolled eyes. "She loved you, you fucking asshole! Jesus, she was hot—I couldn't even hold a conversation with her, couldn't even look at her in the eye. It was that accent," he says. "And you were the one who could have heard that accent in bed, and you didn't do it," he says, wagging his cocky finger.

I looked down at the sight of Billy's skinny, bare legs. They appeared twice the size of my own and reminded me that I have always felt rather deformed from a physical standpoint.

"What a fucking loser," he adds.

"Thanks, man," nodding my head as I answer.

"Her parents spend their summers in a mansion on Higgin's Lake; she's from fucking England, and you don't even call *or* write her back," he says. "Fuckin' homo."

"I can't go to London right now. I'm supposed to sign up for classes this summer, and my mom would kill me, not to mention I'm basically broke."

"You could have called her at the very least," Billy says.

I noticed something out of place in the distance ahead. A metallic object was shining in the sunlight as we approached a bridge. It appeared to be a dark green vehicle of some sort.

"Oh Jesus! It's the DNR," I say, noticing their trademark green truck with the large yellow emblem on each door.

Billy's neck craned in excitement. They were indeed conservation officers, and they were pulled over at a bridge, probably checking opening-day fisherman. There is nothing worse than a DNR officer—nothing. An officer of the Department of Natural Resources has all of the authority of a regular police officer on top of the enforcement of the fish and game laws.

"GREAT!" moans Billy. "This is just great; I haven't bought a fishing license yet. And of course, you gotta bag a weed on ya, as fucking usual," he complains some more.

Anyone I have ever known who has spent any portion of their lives hunting or fishing will sweat a few bullets when seeing a conservation officer—even when following the rules. The last thing I needed was a drunk-driving ticket, and Billy was already the proud owner of one. Turning the Jeep around on this dirt two-track would have simply waived a guilty flag. I began to smell Billy's nervousness in the tiny confines of the Jeep.

"I don't even have any clothes on for Christ's sake!" Billy says, smacking his bare leg, starting to fully understand the situation that lay before us.

"Just put your coat over the twelve pack and—" I say, as my brain starts to rally, "and pour out the open ones," I say, trying to hand him the half-full beer bottle.

"Whhaaattt?" Billy says, looking as confused as ever.

It was always moments like this that the wheels came off in Billy's head. He had seen most of the male members of his family do jail time after altercations with such people.

"Here! Take this! I just opened it!" I say.

"What the fuck am I going to do with it?" he gasps.

"Pour it through the hole in the floor!" I whisper at the top of my lungs. "Are you fucking retarded?" I ask, trying to calm down as we approach the bridge.

"Whatta you going to do?" he asks, on the verge of tears, pouring the beer through a hole in the floorboard.

"I'm gonna keep on goin' . . . give 'em a wave and a smile."

"They'll know something ain't right."

"And drive right on by."

Chapter 4

Tall, Dark, and Parasitic

I hastily down-shifted the Jeep as the bridge that held the conservation officers became larger and more defined. The bridge was fashioned of carefully placed sandbags like the army would use. I was just hoping that it wasn't that asshole Frank Pierson. I'd dealt with conservation officers on several occasions—maintain eye contact, act like you're not the slightest bit rattled, and shake their hand if you get the opportunity. Definitely, and always shake their hand.

"I think you should just pull over!" Billy pleads.

"What? So they can smell booze on our breath at ten thirty in the morning?" I answer, reminding myself never to listen to him in a crisis situation. "Just try and relax," I say, as my eyes focused on the spot of jet-black hair that stood out from the surrounding dull brown April brush.

"It's him," Billy spouts, under his breath.

He was right; it was definitely him. A taut muscle protruded through his shirt on the side of his back as he knelt to talk to the canoeing fisherman. At six foot and four inches, he had a full two inches and fifty pounds on me; I distinctly remember shaking his hand in our kitchen. Upon identification of my vehicle, something seemed to register in his face; strangely enough, it was a smile and a wave. I donned a counterfeit smile and returned the favor—*what a prick anyways.*

"Jesus, that was close!" I say, hoping to calm Billy's nerves, even if for only a second.

"Yeah, Jesus, lucky they're busy right now, or that would be us," he says.

"Waste of good beer is what that was."

"Don't have time for us," Billy says, with a smile smacking his still-bare knee as we bounced toward safety.

"By the way, on a more serious note," I say, "I was really worried about you out on that ice."

"Yeah, I could tell," he says.

"Seriously, you could have died; my best friend could have died," I say, pretending to concentrate on the rearview mirror. "Oh shit! They are pulling out and coming after us!" I say, as he quickly turns his head, laughs, and punches me in the arm—this would be the last time I shared a joke with my best friend, Billy Kudray.

Chapter 5

I Cannot Put What Is in My Heart on My Tongue

The tall tires of the Jeep hummed in a high-pitched manner after we turned onto the two-lane highway. County road M-55 had been the only paved road we had seen in hours. Large tear-shaped raindrops began slapping the windshield as the sky began to darken.

"We'll just pop into my place and get you some warm clothes," I say.

"Are ya sure?" he says, in a nervous tone. The kid seems a little alarmed for whatever reason.

"Well, it is a helluva lot closer than your place, and you need some clothes," I say.

"Think your mom will be around?"

"Maybe, I don't know. Kind of want to check on her anyway. She was a little upset this morning, and I'm not sure why."

"Everything OK?" asks Billy.

"Yeah sure. Knowing my mother, I'm sure everything is fine," I say. We began to enter the gentle and ill-defined entrance of our small town. I sat staring at the slate gray mobile homes that constituted our local community college that I was now being forced to attend. The weather turned quickly, as some spring days do. Rain began to horizontally pummel the line of buildings that lay interspersed like raw knucklebones of the earth.

I do remember engaging the parking brake as we came to a standstill in my driveway.

"You . . . ah . . . mind getting me some dry clothes so yer mom doesn't have to see me in my underwear?" He smiles.

"No problem," I say, shutting the car door and heading toward the house and up the stairs of the porch. *I knew something was wrong the second I opened the door of the house. It was a familiar smell in a very unfamiliar place. It was the pungent aroma of gunpowder. I stepped into the unquiet darkness of my home that morning and the white noise that is still there today began to ring in my ears. I yell, and I yell loud, "Mom, are you here?" I listened as the frantic nothingness answered. "Mom,* ARE YOU HERE?*" I scream. My life changed forever that morning. I begin to run as I round the corner of our dismal hallway and see the brownish green streaks of gray matter sprayed upon the crystalline white walls of our bathroom. I step and slip in the substance before it became exactly clear what I am looking at—my mother had taken the business end of my sixteen-gauge shotgun and pulled both triggers—the gun had been loaded. When I awoke this morning, I felt as though I had the entire world on a downward pull; this was supposed to be the day that couldn't offer me more. And now, at noon on the last Saturday in April, exactly four days after my nineteenth birthday, there she lay. The gums of my teeth went numb, tears that morning—she was wounded, and I didn't even have the time to properly take notice and ask why. And to know now that I someday will see through it all.*

I lunge through the storm window on the aging screen door and stumble onto the porch, gasping for a breath of fresh air that will not come. I feel the glands of my throat begin their liquid movements as the morning's beer resurfaces hotly down my arm and chin. Billy's alarmed face stares at me through the rain as the railing catches my shins hard, and I topple forward. The ground feels wonderful and cool as I stare up at the dissipating pinprick of white blue sky above me before the blackness rushes in and engulfs it.

Chapter 6

My Audience

Lawrence Vintage's reedy voice creaked over the PA and into the dark paneled walls of Sheriff Trenton Mayfair's office.

"He ate the fee'ish," he says. "*They ate* all the fee'ish."

"What fish, Lawrence?" asks the sheriff impatiently. *Get on with it, you southern fucking hillbilly*, he thought. *Lawrence always had a way of getting on my nerves when I was hung over with his slow southern way of explaining everything.*

"Out here at the country club. I'm here now," Lawrence says. "Clifford Stoink and Lance Pierson ate all the tropical fish—right outta the God damn aquarium!"

What? What the hell is Lance doin' outta prison already? That is one name I will never forget. Talk about the nightmare of my life, and who would have thought that he would have kept a handcuff key on his necklace anyway?

"Theyz as drunk as sailors in here last night," Lawrence continues. "Melvin's pissed, wants to press charges this time, Sheriff. They scared some people outta here last night, on account of their behavior; this is a golf course and all," he says. "He even wants ta give 'em a lifetime ban from the premises."

Jesus Christ, what's next? Trent thought as he peered out of the window, watching the day begin to darken, rain smacking the windowpane. *Gotta wait and meet that federal agent from Detroit who is up here for God knows what reason. That's great, just what I need. He'd better make it soon. He's fifteen minutes late already.* "Lawrence, tell Mel about those charges. Tell 'um I'll be out there for lunch today, and I'll personally sort this one out myself," the sheriff says, rubbing the gray hair around his temples in disgust. *Why the hell didn't I receive a notice that Lance Pierson was released from prison? The son of a bitch threatened my family—for Christ's sake!—after we arrested him. Not to mention he cut me up with a carpet knife after he escaped with the handcuff key on his necklace maneuver. Ten years already. Ten years. What a bullshit sentence that is.*

"I'll tell 'um, Sheriff," Lawrence says.

Sheriff Mayfair didn't notice the unmarked car towing the silver Airstream trailer pull into the restaurant across the street as he hung up the phone.

Special Agent Joseph Deacon was on his first assignment after having completed his mandatory stay in a drug task force in a major city. Making sure his vehicle was not seen in the parking lot of the police post was a very small part of his careful plan. He had never seen the likes of a town like Houghton Lake; it just seemed like an endless stretch of cottages and scattered business strung out along a perpetual shoreline rimmed with giant white pine trees. It was as if there were no true town and felt as though he had left the confines of the city and had dropped into the Midwest's version of Alaska. He was enjoying the new scenery and the fact that he was finally solo and away from his first training assignment. As a new recruit, he had heard about the city of Detroit, but the horror he had witnessed there in the past six months was indescribable. The Motor City had certainly lived up to its reputation.

A voice boomed simultaneously as Special Agent Deacon opened the doors into the small brick police post.

"Sadie, what time is that J. Edgar supposed to be up here today, anyway?" the sheriff says.

"He just stepped into the lobby, Sheriff," she says, trying to hide the fact that she is cleaning her dentures.

"Good, send him in," the sheriff says.

Chapter 7

Poor Billy

The rain poured from the bruised sky, slapping at the top of the Jeep as Billy sat shivering in his goose bumps. *Brendon couldn't have known about what happened. My God, he'd better not. And if he did know, he sure didn't let on today.* The insecurity about his drunken blunder several months before had turned into a never-ending nightmare that kept replaying in his head and would not stop.

That day he had quickly downed a six-pack of beer and stopped by unannounced to see if Brendon was around to provide a drinking partner. Upon his arrival, he gave Maddie, Brendon's mother, a much-longer kiss than needed when greeting your best friend's mother. An instant hand on the curve of her upper thigh did not help matters either. Her almond-colored eyes flicked awkwardly as she quickly put distance between them. The words slipped from her mouth immediately. "That wasn't necessary, Billy," she said. "And Brendon's not here." Billy's anxiety increased and then quickly subsided at the sight that was unraveling on the front porch in front of him. Brendon's body twisted in a retarded manner as he lurched through the screen door—my God, he was puking! Billy watched in awe as the limp body began to tumble over the railing of the front porch and slide lazily to the ground. *What in God's name is he doing? How in the hell can he be that drunk? He'd only drank three beers. And here I sit in a pair of fucking white underwear, and he is screwing around and pulling another one of his stunts. Typical,* Billy thought. *He had to get back at me for this morning's incident on the ice.* Billy's head quickly checked for oncoming traffic as he made his way out of the Jeep and across the muddy lawn to the now-limp body of his best friend. The mud was greasy and slimy and began to squirm between the spaces of his toes.

"Jesus Christ, man! What the fuck!" he says, shocked at the sight of the whites of Brendon's eyes rolling into the back of his head. He knelt down. *Thank God, he has a pulse. Thank fucking God, he is breathing. Jesus Christ, he's cut his arm on the broken glass from the door. He isn't fucking around. Something is wrong. Phone. I need a fucking phone.* He ran up the stairs of the porch and stepped into the void of the home, his olfactory system quickly catching something that wasn't right. "Maddie?" he yells. Silence. Perfect silence. "Mrs. Castleman?" he says lightly, realizing just how serious the situation could really be—eggshells. He tiptoed toward the dining room, slipping quietly past the only bathroom in the house. As he glanced left, the realization registered immediately. *Oh God, oh God, no. This can't be right. This just hasn't happened. I'll go sit in the Jeep now. Oh no.*

The back of her head was touching her face held only together by a light membrane of skin. It was Mrs. Castleman, and it was Brendon's mom—and she was gone.

Chapter 8

Good Afternoon, Gentlemen

Special Agent Deacon examined the tiny room in the small brick building carefully, acknowledging that it probably wasn't worth over twenty thousand dollars. *Well, this should be interesting,* he thought. *First undercover assignment, and here I am meeting with a genuine Barney Fife. They tried warning me before I left Detroit about these small-town Podunk sheriffs. J. Edgar my ass. I can't believe he has the nerve to call me that. It's not my fault the guy turned out to be a cross-dressing homo.* He glanced at the secretary with the seemingly sucked-in mouth. *Maybe I should have stayed in the city and not had to walk in here and meet this small-town hick of a sheriff and explain to him that I will be working in his county, and he doesn't need to know why. And I don't even really know why. Is this what promotions are all about? The only information I was given was the fax I received, and that didn't exactly explain what the sheriff's role was. The meeting had better go well was all that the paper had really said. Well, there she sits, and there he stands. At least, she's smiling.*

"Sadie, for Christ's sake, put yer teeth in," are the first growling words that pass through his mouth—nothing like kicking the dog when you're angry.

"Nice to meet you, sir," Deacon says, trying to gain eye contact. "I appreciate your taking some time out of your busy day. I just wanted to stop by and introduce myself."

"Well," the sheriff says, lackadaisically, "I'm sure there's more to it than that."

"I won't be taking much of your time," Deacon says.

"Good, cuz I don't have much," the sheriff says.

"Well," the special agent says, nodding his head in disgust. *Oh, you must be busy,* he thought. *Which was it this time, Sheriff, the local town drunk or the kitty in the tree?* "You have a very pretty town up here, Sheriff."

"Yeah, if you like nothing but trees and water. Fortunately, I kind of like both," he answers, motioning for the special agent to have a seat.

"I'll stand, thanks," Deacon says, as the sheriff remains standing as well. *Why did they want me to meet this man? Who is to say that the sheriff isn't involved?*

"First off, why don't you tell me why you're here?" asks the sheriff gruffly.

Joseph Deacon found himself stroking his unshaven beard at the comment as the first small wave of insecurity began to form in moist beads of sweat on his forehead. "We are doing some work in the area," Deacon says. "I am the person you would come to if you had any questions," he continues, trying to maintain equilibrium. Deacon hadn't gone unshaved since first joining the academy five years prior and had never quite realized just how much confidence a standard black suit had provided.

"Again, what are you doing here?" the sheriff asks impatiently.

"I was just stopping by to let you know that I will be working undercover in Roscommon County," continues the special agent. "Your county, sir." *For God's sake, I don't even know why I am really here.*

"And?" the sheriff asks, lowering his chin.

"And that's it," he says, breaking eye contact noticing the framed master's degree from the University of Michigan on the wall. *Maybe he isn't the person I thought he was. Here I am dressed like a local, and he's busting my balls. They told me to dress like I was from northern Michigan, try and fit in. Dressed like a fucking lumberjack is what I am.*

"Where ya staying?" the sheriff asks.

"I actually brought my own accommodation, and I will be staying in a campground just west of town. I think it's called Redsburg or something."

"It's pronounced *Reedsburg*, and that seems like an awfully strange place for a federal agent to be staying," the sheriff says.

"Well, I'm expecting to be quite mobile," he answers.

"So where are you from?" asks the sheriff.

"Detroit."

"And you're camping," he asks quizzically, "in a motor home?"

A motor home full of surveillance equipment, thinks the special agent nodding his head with a smile.

"So essentially you've interrupted my day to tell me that you will be working in my county, and you can't tell me why."

"Sir, I was instructed to make you aware of my presence out of respect, not to explain the nature of my work. Nothing more," he says. "I was just on my way to Traverse City, I didn't have to do this, you know."

"Geez, thanks for the favor," answers the sheriff.

"Well, I know how busy you are," Deacon says with outstretched arms, rolling his eyes at the quiet and empty office. *Damn, I may have gone too far.*

"Are you naturally a dickhead, or is that something you actually have to work at?" asks the sheriff as their eyes meet again. *Don't say a word,* the sheriff thought. *If he expects an ounce of my help, he'd better cough up something about why the hell he's here.*

"My boss thought it would be a good idea if I popped in. That's all, sir. Again, out of respect. After all, we may need your help."

"Relax a little, Mr. Deacon. I'm just doing my job. You know that," the sheriff says. "By the way, who ya meetin' up in Traverse City?"

"Sheriff!" bounces the high-pitched squeal from the intercom on the sheriff's desk.

"Not now, Sadie," he says, nodding apologetically at Special Agent Deacon, both still standing. "Sadie, you know I'm busy," barks the sheriff, holding the button on the intercom.

"Sheriff," her voice now begins screeching over the intercom, "I know yer busy, but this sounds like a right old mess," she says, as the sheriff begins to again massage his temples.

"Billy Kudray called," she says, "I mean the young one."

"I know the young one, Sadie," the sheriff says impatiently.

"Called in here 'bout five minutes ago all flustered and cryin' and carryin' on," she continues. "I didn't want ta bug ya, so I sent Deputy Lawrence over there ta check on him. Lawrence was only a couple a minutes away, ya see," she says. "Lawrence said it's real bad over there; you need to come over ASAP, Sheriff," blasts the intercom. The sheriff pointed to his ear and to Joseph Deacon while motioning through the wall to Sadie.

"I can hear ya, Sadie. Now speak. Get it out," he says.

"He says, well," she hesitates, "he said Maddie Castleman has gone and shot herself. With a gun. She's dead."

Are you fucking kidding me? thought the sheriff. *Beautiful, brown-eyed Madeline Castleman? I've had a crush on that woman since the age of sixteen. She always seemed a bit troubled, but this can't be. No, this can't be true.*

"Lawrence told me to call a doctor immediately. Apparently, Brendon, her son, is in pretty rough shape too."

"Sadie, you tell Lawrence not to touch a God damn thing!" the sheriff barks. "And I will be there in two minutes. You hear me, Sadie?"

"Yes, sir," she answers. "I'll go ahead and call Dr. Jury."

Oh God, anyone but her, thought the sheriff, causing him to freeze in mid stride. *She's neurotic on a good day.* "Isn't there someone else you can call?" he says.

"Not on a weekend, Sheriff."

"For God's sake, Sadie, Dr. Jury and Maddie are good friends," he stammers. "Oh, go ahead and call her. And tell her to hurry. God, this is going to be a mess. Special Agent Deacon, I gotta go," the sheriff says as he shuffles rigidly around the small room gathering his belt and gun. Special Agent Deacon smelled the stale smell of alcohol for the first time leaking from the sheriff's now-active pores.

"My God, how can I help, Sheriff? I mean this sounds pretty bad. I'm sorry, did you know the deceased?" Deacon asks.

"Yes, I did. We graduated high school together as a matter of fact. And no, you are obviously very busy," the sheriff says. "Well, actually, yes," he says, "you can help. Next time you're working in my county, you can tell me why the hell you're here."

"But, Sheriff—," Joseph Deacon says.

"Listen to me," interrupts the sheriff. "Take my card. Use it if you need to," the sheriff says, hastily shaking the young man's hand, making his way out of the small office. "And I mean that. Sadie, can you see Mr. Deacon out?" he asks. "I gotta go."

Chapter 9

Cliffy and Phyllis

Phyllis Stoink hovered nervously near the small paint-chipped space heater in her dingy double-wide trailer with the dark red shutters. The hair on her chubby pink arms stood at length as she noticed the Cro-Magnon forehead tilt slightly in the bed before her. She was always used to the nervousness in her husband's presence. After all, he was starting to move, and he had been drunk last night. And she had also stolen a few handfuls of marijuana from his closet that he used to prove that he had a full-time job. The cute summer boys at the country club had always been so impressed with her easy access to weed, and they gave her money on top of the attention. Her hands flattened in the air as her chin dropped submissively.

"You want some coffee, Cliff?" she whispers. "I even made you some tator tots—"

"Jesus Christ!" he moans, rotating the eyes that are deeply set into his skull. "Those fuckin' kids!" he barks. "I can't get no sleep. Shouldn't they be in school?"

"It's Saturday, Cliff. Anyway, thar with yer brother's kids today. Beatrice picked 'em up again."

The whiskey thumped heavily on his head. The evening before was beginning to filter through in small bits and pieces. *How did I get home last night?* he thought. *That's right. Lance Pierson. That no-good Canuck gave me a ride home from the bar. Haven't seen him in over ten years, and there he is, drunk as hell, talking about the connection of a lifetime. Told me to just wait—this was the big one. Last I heard he was headed to prison. Always was a shady fucker, and his brother is a conservation officer. Isn't that typical, one on each side of the law?*

"The kids are gone, Cliff. Do you want some coffee or not?" she says, nervously.

"Of course I do." He sighs, his own noise makes his head throb. "Shut the fuck up already!"

"It probably isn't the right time," she says smelling him look in her direction, "But the rent is due tomorrow."

"So?" he answers.

"So what are you doin' with those checks from the government?" she says, again testing the water.

"None of yer fuckin' business what I been doin' with those checks. Whatta ya been doin' with yer tips from the golf course?" he says, mocking her every word in a high-pitched voice.

"The country club ain't technically really open yet, Cliff," she says.

"Well, ya been there, ain' ya?" gasps Cliff.

"Yeah, cleanin'! How do ya think the kids been eatin' lately?" she says, already feeling the foul breath upon her as he rears out of bed.

"Woman," screams Cliff, "don't you ever talk to me that way! And don't you ever call that stupid brother of mine for money either," he says as she begins to whimper. "I know ya did."

"Please calm down, Cliff," she begs, carefully taking a step backward into the narrow hallway of the trailer home. "We'll make ends meet. We always do. I was just hopin' ta get ahead, ya know. Get a house, get a real house, like we talked," she says as Cliff finally gains his balance after stumbling from the bed. He makes his way toward the hallway, causing Phyllis to begin the careful stare at her feet.

"Roll me a joint, God damn it," he says.

"I already did, honey," she whispers. "Cliffy, darlin', where is yer moped? I didn't see it outside."

"Oh yeah, I'm gonna need a ride," he says.

"Where?" she asks.

"Ta get the motorcycle."

"The moped?" she asks.

"How many times I gotta tell ya it ain't a fuckin' moped!" he says, groaning as he grabs his first beer of the day and makes his way to the bathroom.

"There better be some God damn hot water left," mumbling as he speaks. "Fuckin' kids." The water sprays off Cliff's elbow, helping the large patch of moss-colored mold grow in the corner of the small shower. *I wonder if that shady Canuck was being serious, swearing me to secrecy about some shipment of drugs he was going to get. Said he'd be supplying Detroit and Chicago. I could definitely use the money, and he did sound serious enough to carry a loaded pistol underneath the seat of his car.*

Chapter 10

Flashpoint

What in the world would possess that beautiful specimen of a woman to put a gun to her head? This is just unbelievable! What a way to leave this world, not to mention leaving a teenage son. Something just isn't right. Sharon Jury is going to have a nervous breakdown when she realizes what has happened, and she is on her way right now. They're practically neighbors for Christ's sake! God help me. The sheriff's sedan roars up to the quiet neighborhood in a screeching halt as his car door slams. He quickly notices Dr. Jury walking down the quiet sidewalk toward him with her bag in hand as he runs up to the house.

"Jesus Christ, Lawrence, how long ya been here?" yells the sheriff as he closes the gap.

"Long 'nuff," answers Deputy Vintage in his slow talk, standing over Brendon Castleman's limp body that lay awkwardly in the dirt-encrusted flower bed.

"My God, Lawrence, what happened to him?" the sheriff asks, looking down at the now-muddy, unconscious body.

"He's in rough shape; he's been passed out since I got here," says the deputy. "But he's breathin'."

"And poor Billy, for Christ's sake, why is he in his underwear?" asks the sheriff, staring at the ghostlike sight of the young man sitting and crying at the end of the porch. The sheriff notices the glass lying on the porch from the broken metal door. The light sprinkle that remained in the air begins to pick up.

"I'm . . . ah . . . not sure about that one, sir, but they both smell like booze," Lawrence says, nervously eyeing the quickly approaching doctor. "I am glad yer here, Doctor. I checked everythin' I could. I mean he's a breathin' and stuff, but his eyes is kinda rolled back inta his head, ya know."

"Oh my God, what happened?" huffs Dr. Sharon Jury. "Sheriff, what happened here?"

"He is in rough shape, Doc," continues Lawrence, "smells like he's been hittin' the booze this morning too. But the real problem is with his mother."

"Sheriff, what is he talking about? And what's wrong with Maddie?" she says, struggling in the mud trying to check Brendon's pulse.

"Dr. Jury, it sounds like there's been an accident," says the sheriff.

"More like a tragedy," says the deputy.

"Sheriff, what's he talkin' about? Lawrence, what are you—"

"It's a tragedy on account a who found her," continues the deputy. "Billy says that Brendon's the one that found her," he says. "She's in the bathroom; she's left this world now, Doctor."

"Lawrence, give Dr. Jury a hand and—," says the sheriff.

"Where's Maddie?" shudders Dr. Jury, tears slipping down her face as she lightly pries the limp body in front of her. "Sheriff, for God's sake, tell me," she says, beginning to sob. "Tell me what happened!"

"Sharon," the sheriff says in a raised voice, "I need you to relax. I haven't even been inside yet. Lawrence, you help her with Brendon. I'm going inside. Call an ambulance already, for God's sake!"

"There is one on the way," answers Deputy Vintage.

"Good. Keep an eye on Billy. And get him some clothes to put on immediately. I have a coat in my car," the sheriff says, climbing the wooden stairs of the porch and approaching the blank stare of young Billy who sat shivering on the opposite end of the porch. The sheriff felt the dampness in his shirt and the heavy beat of his heart as he knelt down next to the half-naked stark white body. "You gonna be all right, Billy?" he says, holding Billy's arm. "Everything is goin' to be OK," he says reassuringly. Billy's glazed-over, soaked eyes seemed to barely register at the words. "Deputy Lawrence is gonna get you some clothes, and I'm going to need to talk to you very soon. Understood?" he asks, into Billy's unbroken stare placing a hand on the young man's shoulder. "I'll be right back," the sheriff says, making his way carefully down the porch and to the now-broken front door. He tiptoes around the broken glass and opens the screen door with his shirtsleeve. *My God, please tell me this isn't true. Not her. Not Maddie Castleman.* "Lawrence, tell me, did you touch anything in here?" he yells.

"Not a God damn thing," answers the deputy.

"Good," answers the sheriff. "Deputy, Dr. Jury, listen to me. Stay here and help get Brendon into the ambulance. Billy should probably go too just in case," he says, as all eyes meet. "I'm going inside."

Chapter 11

Spider Bite

Wavelets of fine gunpowder hung in horizontal slats in the air of the small house. The sheriff's breathing began to slow as he approached the bathroom, knowing half well what he would see. *She had always been the shy, coy girl that never initiated conversation. And my God, you could get lost in those eyes. Large almond-colored beauties that commanded a room with life and emotion—the kind of eyes that could create a car accident or cause a man to stumble while exiting a building. I've often heard them referred to as the windows of the soul, and with Maddie Castleman, I honestly believe that. Brendon always had his mother's eyes, and now he owned them to himself. As we grew older and everyone married and began raising children, I distinctly remember those eyes as they began to turn to a dull haze that always seemed to be concealing an impending problem. Whether it was losing her husband after Vietnam or just the everyday rigors of life, who knows? And considering the incidents of this morning, none of us will ever know. I could always get lost in those eyes. And here I stand—in her bathroom, as the sheriff of this town—examining just how exactly she managed to get both barrels of her son's twenty-gauge shotgun into her mouth and pull the trigger. Poor kid is hardly twenty years old, and he had to walk into this horror. Now I understand why that young man is lying in the flower bed. My God, from the look of what little is left of the back of her head—she may have pulled both triggers. Her shoulder seemed to be the only portion of her body propping her up against the toilet as if she were praying.*

The smell of burnt hair immediately hit his nose as he began to take in her position more closely while squinting at the seemingly perfect set of teeth biting down on metal. *There was no more pain after you pulled that trigger. Was there, Maddie?* Blood dripped slowly off her chin and down the metallic barrel of the shotgun. *For God's sake, woman*—recognizing the shotgun as Brendon's from several duck-hunting trips taken over the past few years—*did you have to use your own son's gun to get the job done?*

"Share-iff," says Deputy Vintage through the broken portion of the storm window on the screen door.

"Yes, Lawrence," the sheriff says, kneeling.

"I think the doctor," Lawrence says, trying to whisper, "I think the doctor is having a nervous breakdown or something. She just kinda realized why Brendon puked and is passed out in the front yard."

Jesus fucking Christ, thought the sheriff. *This is just perfect—just perfect.*

"She knows what Maddie did, and she just gave Brendon a shot in the arm; his eyes are flippin' back and forth. I'm worried, Sheriff."

"A shot?" asks the sheriff.

"Yeah, Trent, a shot?" says the deputy.

"What kind of shot?" he asks.

"I don't know. I just don't," says the deputy.

"This is just fucking great!" interrupts the sheriff. "And God damn it, Lawrence! This could be a crime scene for all we know! And there you stand with a cigarette."

"I know. I'm sorry. She's makin' me nervous," answers the deputy.

"Where's the fucking ambulance, Lawrence?" says the sheriff in his most monotonous and calm voice.

"I don't know, Sheriff, but I sure don't appreciate you takin' that tone with me," says Lawrence.

"I need you to focus, Lawrence," says the sheriff.

"I was just trying to help. You know the doctor and Maddie were friends and all," says the deputy.

That is precisely why I didn't want Sharon Jury called on this one. "I know they were good friends, Lawrence; I graduated high school with both of them. I'm obviously busy in here. Now listen, what exactly is she doing?"

"She's lyin' in the front yard sobbin' and cryin'," says the deputy.

"I knew it, that fucking woman," says the sheriff, interrupting the deputy.

"She's lyin' right by Brendon, and he seems kinda awake right now. I just don't know what to do," says the deputy.

"Where's Billy?" asks the sheriff. *And why the hell did I have to get so drunk last night? Of all the mornings to be hungover. Oh, that God damn Sharon Jury. I can't even move Maddie's body without a doctor pronouncing her dead. God help me.*

"He's right here," says the deputy, quickly looking to his left. "Oh my God, he's . . . he's not," says Lawrence as the clip-clop of his boots fades down the wooden porch.

"What?" the sheriff says, hastily flipping open the screen door, which causes more glass to fall to the porch. The sheriff watches the deputy carefully make the three-foot step off the end of the porch, where Billy had been sitting less than five minutes before. It was true—Billy was nowhere to be seen. And there lay both Brendon Castleman and Dr. Sharon Jury. It looks like a mass murder took place, for Christ's sake. The scream of the ambulance only escalated his already-pounding headache. It was becoming very obvious—this just wasn't going to be a good day.

"Dr. Jury," the sheriff yells, scrambling down the stairs of the porch toward the two bodies. He hesitates as to which body he should attend to first. "Dr. Jury," he says, noticing the small bloodstain on the interior of the boy's elbow, "Sharon, wake up and pull yourself together. Did you give Brendon a shot?"

"Yes," she sobs. The poor woman is lying in the fetal position with her hands tucked under her head. She looks like a child.

"What did you give him? The ambulance is here, Sharon." *If you hadn't noticed the fucking siren. Come on, woman, speak.*

"I gave him morphine," she whimpers.

"Morphine? Why?" asks the sheriff.

"I just came from Jeffrey Stoink's place. It's all I had. I thought it would help calm him down," she says, trying to move her head toward the direction of the large white vehicle with the flashing lights.

"Oh, I heard Jeffrey was real bad off," says the sheriff.

"Yes, he is," says the doctor as she sits up. "Sheriff, Maddie killed herself, didn't she?" asks the doctor.

"Yes, Sharon, she did."

"We were still very close, you know," she says, trying to regain her footing.

"I know ya were, Sharon. Let me help you up," he says.

"Most people don't know this, Sheriff, but I treated her. She was my patient."

"I didn't know that. Since when?" asks the sheriff.

"I've been treating her ever since Brendon's father died from the war—she's deeply depressed."

"*Was* depressed, Sharon, *was*," says the sheriff. "Well then, we're going to need to talk. First, we need to get this young man into the ambulance," he says, noticing the doctor seeming to snap out of the haze she had been in. The two men quickly approached with the stretcher.

"And then, Dr. Jury, I'm going to need you to gain your composure, and we need to go inside and see the body," says the sheriff as their tangled eyes met.

"Sheriff, whatta we got here?" asks the out-of-breath medic.

"Don't ask. Take this young man to the hospital immediately. I'm going to need a body bag for his mother. I want him out of here now," the sheriff says, lowering his chin and looking at Dr. Jury with his head cocked to the side.

"And I gave him a shot," she sputters. "It was morphine. It should help calm him down, but now, I'm not sure it was the right thing to do," she says through a face full of tears.

"Morphine? Why would you do that?" asks the medic as Sharon begins to cry harder. The two men in white had Brendon's body on the wooden platform and mobile within seconds.

"Just make sure the doctor at the hospital knows about that, OK, guys?" interrupts the sheriff. "And where the hell is Lawrence?" he says. Lawrence's fatigued figure rounds the corner simultaneously wearing his most bewildered face.

"Sheriff, he just up and disappeared!" gasps the deputy.

"Disappeared! He was only wearing fucking underwear, Lawrence," says the sheriff. "Now listen, you find him, and you find him now. I don't want to see you without him. Call Sadie and let her know what has happened. Put out an APB. He's probably in the same state of mind that Brendon is in; only he didn't lose consciousness. Do you understand me? He's in shock, Lawrence. When you find him, you call me AND an ambulance," says the sheriff to Lawrence's back as the deputy scrambles to his squad car. The two men lifted Brendon's body as Sharon Jury's sobbing began again. "Dr. Jury," the sheriff says, "you feelin' a little better now?"

"Well, this isn't exactly a joy," she answers, as both of their eyes meet.

"We need . . . I need you to go in there," he says, pointing to the house, "and we need to determine the time of Maddie's death. Do you understand?" Her head lowers at the diction. "C'mon, Sharon, we're going to get through this." She stares at her feet as he holds her trembling arm and they slowly climb the four steps of the porch. The sheriff watches both vehicles hurriedly depart from his slightly elevated view of the porch. "Sharon, you don't have to do this. I can have another doctor called," says the sheriff. "I realize that . . . that this is a personal matter for you." *Oh God, let this wacky woman snap out of it. I have never even had a suicide in this town, not exactly something that can help my career.*

"I don't want to do it," she says, raising her chin high and looking at the sky through soaked eyes.

"OK," answers the sheriff, closing his eyes. "I understand," he says, nodding his head.

"You know," she continues, "Brendon is going to need some very special attention in the next few months."

"Yes, you're right," he says, awkwardly stroking her arm.

"No sharp objects. He needs to be in a controlled environment. He doesn't have much to live for right now," she says, looking at the sheriff directly in the eyes over a trembling chin.

The sheriff nods his head in agreement.

"Are you ready?" she whispers. "Let's go see Maddie."

Chapter 12

Hand in Hand

Glass begins to crash to the floor of the porch for the second time in the last fifteen minutes as the sheriff feels the hair on his neck stand on end, the sound sending shivers again up on his spine. "God damn it! We gotta clean this up," he says out loud. *Speaking of cleaning up,* he thought, *that bathroom is going to need a serious washing down.* He felt the doctor's hand quickly grab his own and clamp down hard as they carefully closed the broken door of the house. *Well, isn't this professional; here I am, hand in hand, walking into the scene of a suicide with a religious fanatic psychiatrist who just so happens to be a deputy to the medical examiner. Boy, can't wait for this one to make the paper. Not to mention she was a good friend of the deceased. I hope she has what it takes to at least pronounce Maddie's body dead, for Christ's sake.*

Their bodies began to inch toward the apparent bathroom in the dim house. *Keep an eye on her,* thought the sheriff. *She might lose it again, and if she does, I'll be calling the medical examiner directly for this one. I can't believe this shit; even if it is Maddie Castleman's body, you still need to do your job.*

"Sheriff," whispers the doctor through the dull haze of gun smoke.

"Yes, Doctor," he says.

"We should have gloves on, especially if I decide to call an autopsy," she says.

"Well, I agree with you about the gloves, but why an autopsy? I've already looked at her, Sharon. This is a typical suicide."

"Have you ever seen a suicide?" says the doctor.

"Well, no," says the sheriff.

"I'm sure you are right, but I'm just saying what we *should* be doing. I have only done three or four of these, and it has always been a case of old age. But shouldn't we at least have gloves on?" she adds.

"She is still connected to the fucking shotgun, Sharon."

"Don't swear at me, Trent," she says.

"Sharon, this isn't a crime scene. It's a suicide. All I need you to do is declare her dead. And believe me, she is such," says the sheriff.

"OK," says the doctor.

"And after you do your job, you can leave," says the sheriff. "Now, if you're really worried about wearing gloves, just don't touch anything." He again felt the intense odor when they peered around the corner.

There she goes again. She's starting to tremble. I need a drink, he thought.

"Oh no," the doctor says and begins to whimper.

"Sharon," interrupts the sheriff, "do you declare her dead?"

"Who's gun is that? It looks like a hunting gun," she asks.

"As a deputy of the medical examiner of Roscommon County, do you declare her dead?" barks the sheriff.

"Yes, of course," she whimpers.

"Now. Yes, it is a hunting gun. It's Brendon's shotgun," he answers. *She's gonna lose it again. Gotta get her outta here.*

"I can't believe she left him this way. I mean he's the one who found her!" she bellows in realization.

The sheriff nods his head. She was right. Maddie's body lay propped up to the toilet with the barrel of her son's shotgun still carefully placed in her mouth. The sheriff once again winced at the stinging smell of burnt hair as Dr. Jury began to say a short prayer.

"Oh, Lord, please be with her," she says, whimpering. "Oh, Lord, this is just awful. She almost looks as though she were—she were praying. I can't believe she's gone," says the doctor through a face of tears.

"I know, Sharon. Now let's get you out of here. We need to go and find Billy. You understand?"

"I understand," she says, slowly turning her back to the bathroom. "Just please don't tell anyone of my behavior earlier. I am so sorry. I just thought so much of Maddie. And Brendon, for that matter. I just lost my composure when I realized what had happened. I know it wasn't professional of me; it'll never happen again, Sheriff. She'd been doing so well in treatment over the years until recently anyway. She seemed very down as of late."

"Everyone thought a lot of both of them, Sharon. Now follow me. I need to find out if they have found Billy yet. I want to speak to you about your treatment of Maddie as soon as possible, OK? But now is not the time."

"She acted like she kinda given up, you know. I should have known. I should have seen it coming," says the doctor.

"It wasn't your fault, Sharon. Don't even go down that road. Please try and focus."

"Sheriff, you go and find Billy. I'll go and check on Brendon at the hospital."

"Well, I really don't think there is much you can do at this point," he says.

"You're probably right, but someone has to be there for him when he wakes. He doesn't have anyone right now. Think about it. He needs to be watched. The next few days are going to be very rough."

"You do that, he probably won't be there for long. Give the post a call in a few hours and let Sadie know what's going on if I'm not at the hospital yet. I want to see the boy too," says the sheriff.

"Sheriff, the next few months will be critical in his life. I've studied these kinds of things like this. Do you realize that the odds of Brendon now committing suicide have quadrupled?" she says as they carefully make their way around the shattered glass.

"Don't talk like that. We'll keep an eye on him, Sharon. I promise you that," he says.

"I know I mentioned it earlier, but he will need to be in a very controlled environment," she says.

"Sharon, listen to me. I have another boy to find here, OK?" he says. *She is going to drive me over the fucking edge. What a day for a splitting headache.*

"I will, Sheriff. Speak with you soon."

"OK, Sharon, you run along now."

Chapter 13

Gone

Sewing my own armor, I will concentrate only on my next breath. That is the farthest space my mind will take me. It's been only three somber days since my mother's accident, and I am still very high off of the fumes that hung in the air of our small house that nauseous day. Gunpowder and brain matter have a tendency to have a lasting effect on the olfactory system—especially when it is your own genetic sprayed across the walls. The inside of my left elbow throbs nicely, and here I lay in the most Godforsaken place I could imagine—Billy's bedroom. Maybe this bed is the only place for me at this point in time. I can't stomach the thought of emerging into this town after what has taken place over the last three days. I can already feel the eyes upon me. *Oh, that poor boy. Can you believe what his mother did? Can you believe the manner in which she left him? Can you imagine how fucked up he must be over this? I even heard she used his gun.*

That poor bastard Billy had to be with me that day, his usual stumbling and stammering self. He always maintained the charade that I didn't realize nor consider his feelings toward my mother. He was wrong, and so were they all. No one but me will ever absorb what transpired when I found my mother that morning; they all thought I was asleep in my front yard. My body weighed at least a thousand pounds, and my lungs rendered me useless, but I remember everything. And I mean everything. Poor Billy. He fell through the ice that morning when we went fishing and then ended up slipping and sliding around our front yard clad only in his underwear. I will never forget that fleeting moment for as long as I live—him standing over me, hoping that I would wake. I tried to explain to him what she had done. I tried to speak, and I tried to breathe. I was successful in neither attempt as he began to cry and scream for help. And then he began to sob and cry harder, and then he began to shake. He left me for at least five minutes—the bastard. Who would leave a dying, bleeding man who cannot breathe? Who? Please tell me who. Certainly, not a best friend. Certainly not. And then we have the emotional wreck who wears the name tag Dr. Sharon Jury, who relies on a simple, misguided need to try and help people who are almost as fucked up as she is. She even tried to treat my mother, and they kept it their own little secret. Like everyone my mom associated with, there was always a secret. They whispered in the kitchen just like my mom and that asshole DNR officer. That psychiatrist wanna-be doctor gave me a shot of morphine because I had been sick and was shaking having just found my mother's body after her accident, and this is why I love Sharon Jury. My skin begins to itch at the thought of the needle entering my arm and the brown liquid that made my feet lift off the ground and into the gray sky. She was here yesterday, "checking in," as she calls it, whittling away as if nothing had even happened, preaching to me about the fact that time heals and how she is going to teach me how to smile again.

And it wouldn't be fair to forget the well-meant sheriff with his traditional hangover stretched across his face in a worried smile. He was stressed and did his best to maintain a sense of control of the situation. I remember the dizziness and the hot liquid running down my chin and the sharp pain of the railing catching my shins. And that stupid, fucking deputy standing over me chain-smoking cigarettes. I know one thing now if I know anything—this will be the last situation that I don't have complete control over. Sitting here, rotting away in this bed that isn't even my own, patiently waiting for the shot in the arm that will never arrive. And if I would have had only a semblance of control over that fateful day, I would have only asked for one thing. One simple request really. I just want five minutes alone with my mother—that is all I ask. I want five minutes to hold her and hear her voice. I want to smell the first five seconds of her newly lit cigarette and to see the look in her eyes when I used to leave for school. I want to see her lip curl when I feel like disagreeing with her, and I want to see her smile and raise her shoulders slightly when I say something that makes her proud. Five minutes is all I ask. It would give me time to apologize for getting drunk when I was twelve years old and having a piece of Hubba Bubba bubblegum in my hair, and it would also give her sufficient time to apologize for wearing a fucking mask for the first nineteen years of my life. When I left that morning, she was crying. I saw her crying, and I did everything within my power to leave as soon as possible. Large pearl-shaped tears slipping gently down my mother's face. It is hard to smile when there is so much to hate.

Chapter 14

I Was in a Place

I was in a place one time, a place where no one knew my name for I knew no one. I walked alone among thousands, and more importantly, I looked everyone in the eye—this is the place of my dreams. There will never be a passing day that I won't consider my mother's accident, and that is the reality that I will now deal with. I know in my heart there is a reason for her actions, and it is almost as if the truth is right around the corner. There is talk of funerals and rain tomorrow as well as power of attorney. A thin layer of clear plastic covers my only window, and I watch it breathe every time a door is opened and closed in this thin house that isn't my own. I have had several visitors since my mother's death, and I will tell you this: they all truly seem to care about my well-being. They care about my fate in this calamity. Oh, what a generous token of the human consciousness. I can see the true pity in their eyes, just as they read the genuine pain in mine.

Dr. Jury visited again last night and asked me what I wanted to do with my life and where my future was going to take me and that I must never lose hope. *What kinds of questions are these, Doctor? How would you answer that question, Doctor, after your mother used your shotgun—the only gift from a father you never knew who died from the Vietnam War—to blow her head off and leave you with nothing? Don't worry, Doctor; seriously, everything is going to be OK. You just have to learn to smile again. Her and all her banter.* Her nervousness made the room vibrate slightly, and she always looked a bit distraught. But then again, Billy's mother's face wears this same expression as she enters the room with a soft knock. Her nervous eyes peer around the door as usual. *What is this? A fucking museum?*

"Are you hungry, Brendon?" she says, making a meal out of her bottom lip. "Thirsty maybe?" she asks.

You know what, Shirley, as a matter of fact, I am a little parched. How about a Jack and Coke on the rocks? Easy on the Coke. I'll just sit here and stir it with my middle finger.

"Brendon, you have a guest," she says, and judging by the expression on her face, I must be quite a specimen.

"Really? How special?" I answer.

"Sheriff Mayfair is here. I'll just leave you two alone so you can talk," she says with an artificial smile.

Gee, Shirley, thanks for leaving me alone with the sheriff.

"Hi, Brendon," he says awkwardly with his hat in his hand and slight bow to his walk, "I've been thinking about you. Sorry I haven't stopped by until now."

Sheriff Trenton Mayfair hasn't had a good week, I notice, getting my first good look at his face. A worn face of hard miles of drinking with long lines surrounding his eyes and if I were a betting man, my money would be invested in the fact that his wife absolutely hates him. Or at least, that is what my mom used to insinuate.

"I'm not going to ask you how you've been, son. You . . . you've been through a lot for a young man," he says, sitting down. "But please do listen," he says as his eyes began to water. "I will say that time and only time heals. Never forget that. I graduated high school with yer mother, you know. She was a beautiful person."

"Well, there's a new one. She's beautiful. Well, I'll tell ya what, Sheriff, she wasn't beautiful the last time I saw her. How about you?" *Handle that one, old man. Look at him squirm as the lines around his eyes begin to define themselves. He's a bit too agitated to be fair. Poor guy.* "You know, I was awake that day in the front yard," I say, trying to change the subject. "As a matter of fact, I was awake the entire time. I was even awake when you showed up at my home. Did you know that?"

"No," he shifts his weight toward the door. "I didn't, Brendon. It was a rough day. I thought a lot of your mother. I am really sorry that this is the way everything turned out. I really am." He shakes his head and mumbles something while staring off through the clear plastic of the window.

"So, Sheriff, I need your help. Where's the note? I mean they all leave a note, don't they? I mean, right? They all leave a note, and this was my mother . . . and I want to read it."

"I am really sorry to say this, but she didn't leave a note, Brendon. But I know she loved you. I do know that," he says, looking as sober as a nun.

Well, fuck you, you fucking prick. She didn't leave a note, did she? Well, isn't that something? She wasn't thinking of me anyway. Fucking cunt anyhow.

"How do you know? What if she left it somewhere? What if she put it only for me to find?" I ask.

"I don't know, Brendon. All I know is we didn't find a note," he says.

It must be true—the fucking bitch didn't leave a note.

"When is the funeral?" I ask.

"Well, we can do it tomorrow like we talked if that's OK with you. I spoke to your aunt Mary. Unfortunately, she said she can't make it," he says.

Typical. Aunt Mary hasn't been home in over ten years. Why would she come now? The black sheep of the family outlives the white.

"I'll be there, of course, and I know Dr. Jury wants to be there. Billy and his family will be there, and I am sure there will be a few others," he shakes his head trying to gurgle another sentence.

"You know, Sheriff, I am starting to feel as though I don't belong here. But then again, I suppose I don't really belong anywhere at this point," I say, as our eyes meet.

"Well, don't say that," he says.

"I mean this house, Trent. I need to get out of here. I really do."

"Do you want to go home? 'Cause we'll have the place as good as new by tomorrow if you do."

"No, I don't want to go there, for God's sake, at all. I want to go somewhere where I can be alone. I just want to go somewhere that isn't here. Simple as that. I want to travel or something. Get away, ya know," I say as he nods his head as if it were a good idea. "I don't have any money, but I want to go see Scotty—he's in Europe, ya know."

"I know he is. Maybe that can be arranged. We'll see what we can do," he says, finally looking relaxed in my presence. "Sounds like maybe you want to go see that pretty English girl that spends her summers here."

"Yes, Sheriff," I say, "I would." *You have no idea, Sheriff. There is nothing I would rather do than witness that girl glide across the room. Now that would numb the pain.*

"Well, let's see what we can do about that, and I'll see what I can do about gettin' you outta here. I'll see you tomorrow, and I'll be the one to pick you up. Call me if I can help with anything, and I mean that," he says, standing up to leave, nodding his head, just as they all did. Come look at the boy who just lost his mother; come see the body that shouldn't be moved for fear of hurting oneself. They all came, and they all left—all except Billy. He was there when I found my mother and is now a changed man I am sure. His father moved out of the house; his best friend's mother decided to take the business end of his best friend's shotgun and killed herself. He hasn't had what it takes to face me, although I am sure he will be there tomorrow. He'd better be there tomorrow.

What an immensely selfish move on her part. And I'll tell you—if on earth as it is in heaven, I'd rather not go.

Chapter 15

Grand Traverse

Well, I certainly hope this goes well, and I obviously only have one chance to make a good impression with Special Agent in Charge Thomas Hayward. The guy has a colorful reputation at the academy, but he is known for getting the job done no matter what it takes. Let's hope there wasn't much riding on the meeting yesterday with that sheriff. Jesus, was that a train wreck. Mr. Hayward seems taller in person than the pictures I've seen.

"How ya doin', Joseph? Or do you prefer Joe?" he asks, through white teeth and a tan face. "Welcome to beautiful Traverse City, Michigan. Nice to be outta that city, I imagine?"

"Yes, sir. More importantly, it is nice to finally be assigned to something," I say.

"Oh yeah. Whatta ya assigned to?" he asks, with a smile. *Is everyone fucking with me this week, and is every meeting I have going to be this cryptic?*

"I don't know, sir. I just assumed that is why I was told to leave Detroit and why I met with that sheriff in Roscommon County. I assumed that I was here on assignment."

"Don't assume anything in the FBI, Joseph—ever," he says. "You'll make an A-S-S outta *U* and *ME*, you understand?" he says, spelling out the letters to the word *assume*. "Now, how did your meeting go yesterday with the local yokel sheriff in Houghton Lake?"

"Not well, to be honest. He was a little pissed off that I couldn't tell him why I would be working in his backyard."

"Yeah, well, can you blame him? I would have been too," he says.

"He actually referred me as a J. Edgar to his secretary. He didn't realize I was standing there," I say.

"Sounds like about par for the course. So why didn't you just tell him why you were there?" he asks.

"Because I was never told the nature of the assignment. I received your fax, and it said I should introduce myself to the sheriff out of respect and that we really, really needed the meeting to go well."

"And why, Special Agent Deacon, do you think I put that in the fax?" he asks impatiently. "And more importantly, why do you think I purposely didn't tell you what you would be doing on this assignment?" he asks again with a quizzical glance.

"Honestly, sir," I answer, "I don't have the slightest."

"Because I wanted you to learn how to think on your feet and quit calling me *sir* for fuck's sake! Now listen, you are a special agent of the FBI; you need to know how to act at all times. And if you listen to one thing I say and if only one, you need to learn how to lie. Never forget that. Nobody needs to know why you're doing shit. You need to put people like that sheriff in their place, period," he says. "Understood?"

"Yes, I understand," I say. *I got it, loud and clear. Lie to these people and put them in their place. What a philosophy. I must have missed that class at the academy.*

"You keep everyone you meet on a need-to-know basis, especially while working on a case of this magnitude," he says.

A case of this magnitude. Holy cow, this is it. This is relevant.

"Now, sit down. Let's get down to business. One thing you will learn about working with me and especially working for me, I am pretty fucking candid," he says, "And first off, I'll tell you something. You're too green for this job," he says, shaking his head back and forth. "But if this is all the great people of this country's tax dollars have for me, then so be it," he says, approaching the Midwestern section of the map of the United States on the wall with a gleam in his eye. "Here's the deal. There has been a flood of the purest heroin known to man hitting the streets of Detroit every six to eight weeks for just under a year now. Detroit's got enough fucking problems without this shit. Our buyers have purchased the same brand as far as Cleveland and Chicago as well, but by the time it gets there, it's been cut, which doesn't yield as many casualties and headlines. Anyway, the trick is, how are these cocksuckers getting it into the country? *That* is the million-dollar question. From week one, when Detroit had seventeen different overdose cases dropped at various hospital emergency rooms within a forty-eight-hour period, all signs have pointed to an internal. And I am now fully sure that it is an internal."

"I didn't know this was about drugs. And what is an internal?" I ask, almost out of breath.

"Drugs? Who said it was about drugs?" he says, with that stupid smile again. "Now, let's talk about the internal. This is someone on the inside, a cop, someone heavily affiliated with law enforcement. See? It's just too seamless not to be. And that, my new friend, is why you are here."

"Please, continue," I say, practically begging him to keep speaking.

"I, very recently, received a series of court-ordered wiretaps," he says. "This is the key. We can now monitor our target, for the first time, may I add," he says. "You get all the gravy, kid. I have wanted to figure out how these assholes are pulling this off for almost a year now. But something else has come up that I need to take care of."

"But how are they getting the drugs initially, and how are they getting the drugs into Detroit?"

"Hell if I know. It's almost like it might be coming from the north or something, but we just can't figure out how. It's not the usual Miami or Texas groups. I do know that. As a matter of fact, if the usual cartels knew who it was, they'd just kill 'em, competition and all. Basically, one of these guys thought of something new. The drug's genetic content has been traced to Asia, so your guess is as good as mine," he says, staring at his beloved map. "You're coming in on the tail end of an assignment that's been going on for too long. You fuck this up, kid, and your ass is back in Detroit. Now listen to me; for reasons you will never know, we think and, more importantly, I think we got our man."

"And?" I say.

"And that's what your wiretaps are for."

"And he's a cop?" I ask.

"Oh no. He's actually more powerful than your average cop. He maintains all the parameters of a police officer, and he protects the fish and game laws; he's an officer of the Department of Natural Resources," he says with a trace of smugness in his voice. "His name is Frank Pierson, and he grew up in Sault St. Marie, Canada. His brother did time for drug trafficking in Montreal. He was a slimy bastard too. Met him once, but that's a different story. But anyway," he says, as I interrupt.

"Well, he should be easy to monitor at the very least. What kind of vehicle does he drive?" I ask.

"Standard issue, big green pickup truck with a gold emblem on the side. He seems to have a fondness for a pay phone right next to an exit on I-75. I find that kind of odd personally, don't you?"

"Why yes, of course. I mean why not use the phone at home or at the office? He is either up to something, or he's having an affair, right?" I ask, quickly.

"Maybe both? I like the way you think, young Joseph. Frank's territory is a large one simply because he has worked there for fifteen years. He's based outta Roscommon, and he handles everything north of M-55 all the way up to Mackinac Bridge. Now, here's where things get a little more interesting. He's also involved in an off-the-radar task force called SANE. That stands for Straights Area Narcotics Enforcement."

"Well, isn't that convenient," I say.

"Yes, Joe, it is," he answers, "and if it wasn't for his brother doing time in a federal prison for narcotics, we still wouldn't have a clue at this point."

"So why did I have to meet that sheriff?"

"Because you will literally be working in his backyard, and I want you to stay in that campground with the pull trailer and surveillance equipment. Basically, no one but the sheriff should know you are there. Anyone asks or approaches you, you're just on vacation fishing for a week or something."

"And how do you know that the sheriff isn't involved in the . . . the illegal substances?" I say.

"Because we checked him out, that's why. There's history there, and we also learned that he and Frank Pierson don't really get along. That could be advantageous, you know."

"I see," I answer. *It's finally happened. This is a case. This is a real case.*

"The sheriff's apparently a fairly heavy drinker and all, but who am I to talk? Anyway, I want the wiretap installed at the pay phone within twenty-four hours, and here's the paperwork that will get you there. You can handle that, can't you?"

"Yes, sir, of course," I say, realizing my mistake of calling him *sir*. At least he's smiling this time.

"No one can see you. Do it under the cover of darkness if you have to and don't let anyone see your vehicle," he says.

"OK," I answer.

"He seems to visit that phone every fourth Thursday around 4:00 p.m. for whatever reason. The Thursday in question is tomorrow," he says.

"And one more thing. When do I approach the sheriff again?" I ask, realizing that the hair on my neck is standing on end.

"When you need to use him, that's when. My mobile phone number is on my card. You call me when you need to. Obviously, make sure the tape is on when you get him live. We will need it in court. Now, I am outta here. I have a more pressing matter to attend to. I have a four thirty flight to Metro, back to Detroit."

"Oh yes, Detroit—where the weak are killed and eaten," I say, answering the man confidently for the first time.

"Exactly," is his answer as he strolls out the door.

CHAPTER 16

Dr. Sharon Jury

Well, this is it, she thought as she drummed her fingers on her oak desk. *Funeral day. Three awful days of worry since I lost control in Maddie Castleman's front yard. I still can't believe I lost it. Gosh, darn it! That was so unlike me. I have always been so good in crisis situations. The realization of Maddie taking her own life . . . it . . . it just hit me like a freight train. I can't even imagine being in that state of mind again; I was utterly and completely uncontrollable.* The doctor's fingers continued to strum as her head began to shake in disgust, and her eyes began the gentle and comforting gaze toward the ceiling of her office, the very office where she had treated so many other patients in need. *I couldn't help it, Lord,* she thought. *I was the first doctor on the scene. I couldn't keep my composure. And what about the sheriff? He must think I am a right old loon. A friend and patient commits suicide, and I will never live down the embarrassment of my own behavior. Help me, Jesus, help me if you have ever helped me before. This poor young man needs our help. And if he doesn't receive our comfort, he may soon join his mother. I warn you now, my All-knowing Savior. Just please help me through this day.*

The ringing of a phone brings her eyes back down to her desk. "Hello," she says.

"Doctor, your 10:00 a.m. is here. Martha Gladstone," says the receptionist.

"Oh no, Cindy, I told you to cancel everything today. Today is Maddie's funeral, and I have to go see Brendon beforehand. I told you that," she says impatiently. *Not to mention I'm supposed to meet with the sheriff before the funeral.*

"I'm sorry, Doctor. I don't remember you telling me that. Martha is here the first Wednesday of the month—every month."

"I know that. Just tell her that I had an emergency and I can't see her," says the doctor. *My God, what can I do to help Martha Gladstone anyway? That hapless woman drives to my office and lives less than five hundred yards from the building. She needs to go on a diet. That's what she needs to do. Four hundred pounds and rising. And she gets so uppity when I mention the importance of her physical health.*

Good thing she's a librarian. She couldn't walk across the room without pushing that cart full of books to hold herself upright.

"Doctor, are you sure you don't want to tell her yourself? She is trying to get up the front stairs right now," says the receptionist.

"No. Please tell her I am not available, Cindy. I really need to get out of here. I am running late as it is," she says. "And call Sheriff Mayfair and confirm that we are still meeting at noon please." *That is a meeting I am not looking forward to,* she thought. *I haven't seen him since that dreadful day. I'll bet he has a few choice words for me. I won't even be able to make eye contact with him. I can feel it already. That man has never acted as though he liked me for as long as I have known him. It probably doesn't help that I find him attractive. Oh well. And that shot I gave to Brendon—what was I thinking? I could lose my license . . . over something like that.*

"Dr. Jury, I caught Martha on the steps. She said it's OK, and she will rebook and hopes everything is OK."

Thank God, I need to get out of here, thought the doctor.

"Oh, and I forgot to mention," continues Cindy. "There was a message on the machine when I got in this morning; it was from Dr. Ray. He said the clinic must have been left open last night. He sounded kind of alarmed. Said they were going to check and see if anything was missing. Apparently, the door was unlocked when he got to work this morning."

"OK, um . . . I'll call him later," says Dr. Jury. *So that's why he left me a message last night; that is impossible,* she thought. *I was there late last night, and I locked up. Oh, God, not now. I still have to go visit Brendon before the funeral. I am positive I locked up, almost positive. I wonder if I did forget to lock the door. Maybe one of the doctors showed up after me. But that's not likely. I didn't leave until after nine. There are only three of us with keys to the place. What else is going to go wrong today?* she thought as she pulled into the Kudrays' driveway. *Oh, God, please be with me on this visit. I need to be strong in front of him. I must let him know that there is hope in this world.* She walked into the house after a soft knock and received a quiet hello from Shirley Kudray.

"It's so nice of you to check in on him. We all know this is going to be a rough day. It's not going to be an open casket, is it?" she whispers.

"No, Shirley, it's not," says the doctor, lowering her voice and making sure the bedroom door was closed.

Shirley quietly points at the bedroom that had become Brendon's home since that fateful day. Sharon nods and opens the now-familiar door. And there he sits, with his mother's eyes. "Hi, Brendon," she says.

"Hi, Doctor," he says.

"How are you today?" she says. *My God, he sure does look pale. Poor guy needs to see some sunlight.*

"Oh, about the same, I guess," he says. "So tell me, Doc, why am I in bed? I mean my mom blew her head off, but it's not like I got hit by a car or something. Everyone acts like if I leave this room, I will break or something."

"Well, Brendon, we just wanted you to be, at the very least, comfortable. As comfortable as possible. You took a nasty spill off the porch, ya know. You probably don't remember that, though," she says, nodding her head.

"Oh, I remember everything, Doctor. You'd be surprised how much I remember," he answers.

Oh, God, no. He remembers, she thought. *For heaven on earth, how can I help this young man? I treated his mother for almost fifteen years, and today we put her in the ground from her own hand. Do I even know what I am doing right now? I knew I should have given art school a chance.*

"But more importantly, Doc," he continues, "I need to get out of here, for God's sake. Lying in this bed all day is making me sore. But I do have a question. Sharon, you're a psychiatrist. Why didn't my mother leave a note? Isn't that standard with a suicide? The sheriff told me that she didn't leave anything that he knew of, other than the mess in the bathroom, of course."

"Well, I don't know, to be honest. There's a lot about this world I don't know about, Brendon. I know the sheriff has always thought a lot of you and your mom for that matter. Not to mention your father; he knew both of them well from high school," she says, wiping the beads of sweat from her forehead and continuing the nervous pacing around the bedroom. "I want you to remember your mother's actions are not your fault, and you must remember that. If anything, please remember this," she says, stopping to see his reaction. *Oh no, he looks almost as if he is smiling,* she thought. *I must be starting to sound like a broken record again.* The silence was beginning to make her uncomfortable. "You must have faith—faith in life," she continues.

"Please don't tell me what to do," says Brendon, pointing his finger. "You have no idea."

"I'm sorry. It's just that your mother—she was such a darling, but she did suffer greatly from depression. You deserve to know that. I tried, Brendon. I really did, and I thought we were on the right path for her recovery. But I was obviously wrong. Quite frankly, I don't think she ever got over losing your father after the war."

"Tell me about my father. I dare you," he says.

"What do you mean you dare me?" she says. *Oh my God,* she thought, *where is this going? Am I going to have a hand in damaging another soul? This boy is far too young for this sort of mental trauma.*

"Well, my mother refused to speak of him and raised her upper lip whenever I broached the subject. She didn't have what it takes to enlighten me of my own father. You're a devoted Christian and a psychiatrist. What do you make of this?"

"Please don't mock me, Brendon. I'm only here to help," she says as tears began to flow once again.

"Oh, I'm not mocking you. I'm just being genuine; I want to know about my father, and no one has the balls to tell me. The sheriff doesn't seem comfortable with the subject as long as I have known him. I have asked him many times over the years, and I could see the worry in his eyes immediately."

"Your father was a very nice man, and that fucking war ruined him," she says in disbelief as she felt the words blurt out. *Not now, Sharon,* she thought. *I mustn't swear. Keep it together, Sharon. This is going to be a long day considering we still have a funeral to attend.* "I just mean," she says, "they were kids when they left for that war—all of 'em. It was a crime—some of those boys still had baby fat on them. And no one, including your mother, knew what to expect when they got home. All of those boys were so troubled when they got back from Asia. And then, they just got married. It's what civil people did."

"So they got married and had kids, or a kid, in my parents' case?"

"Yes, that is exactly what they did," she says. "Maddie could have made it through the hell, I promise you. She just didn't give it time. That is all I ask of you. Give it time. Time is the only thing that heals this sort of scar. You have so much to live for. You're an intelligent, talented young man; you should go to college. Like you and your mother had always planned," she says in a yearning voice.

"My mother is a selfish, fucking bitch."

"Please don't say that, especially not today."

"Well, Doctor, I sure do appreciate you stopping by, as usual. But we have a big day ahead of us, don't we? And by the way, is your mother still alive?" he asks.

"Yes, Brendon, she is."

"Well, then you *don't* know what this is like, now do you?"

Chapter 17

The Wrong Team Wins

The three of them stood motionless while slowly exchanging quick and awkward glances. Three pairs of eyes darting in unison as the clock's ticking grew louder. The sheriff tried to speak first but was quickly interrupted by Deputy Lawrence Vintage.

"Did I ever you tell you two about the time?" he says, pausing to make sure he had everyone's attention. "I was at the border and got arrested for impersonating a police officer?" asks Lawrence in his patent slow Southern drawl.

Why on earth would he say something like this, thought the sheriff, *especially in front of the doctor? What a fucking asshole anyway.* "Lawrence, I hardly think this is the time for stories," says the sheriff but was interrupted by the doctor.

The doctor appeared surprised and peeked quizzically at Lawrence. "But, Lawrence, you are a police officer," she insists.

"But I *wasn't* when I got arrested," answers the deputy, wagging his finger.

"Thanks for the intro, Lawrence. Now, could you please give the doctor and I some time? And do me a favor. Check in on Billy Kudray and his mother," says the sheriff. *Just walk out of here before I break your fucking skull,* he thought. *Can you imagine what it would be like if Lawrence actually had a job that involved authority?* "See if they need help with anything," continued the sheriff. "It's the least you can do," he says, closing the door behind his deputy. *Just make yourself useful for once,* he thought, *just once.*

He turned around to face the doctor who wore a cross look as she had the last time he'd seen her. She'd been chewing on a ball of stress for quite some time by the looks of her. This wasn't going to be an easy day for anyone. "I'm afraid we have a rough day ahead of us, Doctor," he says. "Funerals are about bringing families together, but what do you do when the only person left"—he hesitates breaking eye contact and looking at the top of his desk—"has no family?"

"Well, I tell ya. One thing we do is rally. We need to help this young man. It's as simple as that!" she says, betraying her disheveled look.

"Did you see Brendon today?" asks the sheriff.

"Yes, of course. I've seen him every day since Maddie's death. Matter of fact, I just left his place."

Young Brendon has a friend in this doctor, thought the sheriff. *The woman's been by his side since the day of his mother's suicide. She probably feels responsible for Christ's sake after treating Maddie and all. Strong woman she is, or at least that's her reputation. But what odd behavior recently, writhing around the front yard of a suicide scene. But that's what happens in these fucked-up scenarios—everyone feels personally responsible for the person that is gone.*

"You know, there isn't a person alive who understands what he's going through. And if there is, I sure feel for them," says the doctor.

"We need to focus on what is best for Brendon, Sharon. That is, quite frankly, all we can do," says the sheriff. "How is he today? I mean how were his spirits?"

"If anything, a bit listless. He's in a very annoyed state; he snapped at me a few times, which is obviously a good thing," says the doctor.

There she goes with her psychology mumbo-jumbo bullshit of which I am not in the mood for. "Doctor, I don't mean to switch gears here, but would you mind telling me about your relationship with Maddie? Obviously, you told me that you treated her, but I mean—I don't want to violate any sort of doctor-to-patient stuff—but why do you think she killed herself?" he asks. *Jesus Christ Almighty, that came out well. You might as well put her in charge of the investigation.*

"Well, she had always suffered from deep depression. It's something she acknowledged and tried to beat. Unfortunately, sometimes the . . . the wrong team wins. She . . . she had the disease," says the doctor.

Yeah, but to take your own life and leave your only child with this, he thought, *what an incredible mess. No one deserves this, especially not Brendon. He's one of the finest young men around this town, just like his father that I grew up with. Just genuinely down-to-earth folks. Poor kid would absolutely light up any room he entered, and now he's teetering on the edge.*

"Sheriff," asks the doctor, "I don't mean to change the subject either, but I heard you found Billy at his home. How is he doing? I mean he had to be in shock after seeing Brendon and Maddie in that condition."

"Oh, I'm sure he was in shock there for a while, but he seems OK now. He's very worried about Brendon, the key word being *very*. When I spoke with him—I don't know—I think he feels guilty in some way. He bawled his eyes out when

I questioned him, told me that he'd recently offended Maddie in some way. Seems to think that Brendon knows about it somehow."

"What do you think Billy did to offend Maddie?" asks the doctor, moving her body forward toward the edge of her chair.

"He wouldn't tell me. My guess is that he flirted with her or something stupid like that. All those boys had a crush on her," says the sheriff. *Yeah, all those boys, including myself. I could always get lost in those beautifully sad eyes.*

"And what on earth makes you think that?" she asks, slanting her head slightly, straining to hear his response.

"Let's not get caught up in this gossipy rubbish, OK?" says the sheriff.

"Maybe you had a crush on her too, Trent," she says.

"Sharon, not now. Back to Billy, OK?" he says.

"Well, anyways, I hope no one saw him running around in his underwear. He's going to have enough to deal with. I do find it odd that I haven't seen him in my visits. I've been over there every day," she says.

"Well, Brendon's been staying in his bedroom. I think Billy is staying with his dad, you know. Billy Sr. moved out of the house recently?"

"Yes, I haven't seen *him* in my visits either. Trent, don't you think that it might be a good idea to speak with Billy today?" asks the doctor.

"In regard to?" asks the sheriff.

"Trent, Billy needs to be prepped on how to deal with Brendon's state of mind. He could be the only person that Brendon reaches out to. I hate to say it again, but the kid probably doesn't think he has much to live for right now. And God knows he's sick of my visits," she says with a forced smile.

The sheriff looked at the ceiling for a second before fingering the button on his PA. "Sadie, can you get Billy Kudray on the phone for me please?" *Actually, no,* he thought. "Sadie, Lawrence is on his way over there now. Get him on the line."

Sadie quickly answers as the sheriff began to massage his throbbing temples. *This is not going to be a day without an early drink. I do know that,* he thought.

"Sheriff, I am more worried about the next two to three months, ya know. What is he going to do from here? He just can't stay holed up at the Kudrays forever."

"You know, he and I talked about that when I was over there. I think he is going a little stir-crazy over there myself."

"Well, Trent, I'm sure he doesn't want to go home," she says.

"No, we talked about that as well. He mentioned going traveling, and who knows? Maybe that's the best thing for him right now," says the sheriff.

"Oh no, Sheriff," says the doctor, shaking her head. "How can you say that?" she says.

"Who's to say, Sharon? One of his best friends is backpacking around Europe. It might do the kid some good to get outta here for a while."

"He needs therapy, Trent. This is academic," the doctor says in a raised voice.

"Sharon, the kids gonna do what he wants," says the sheriff.

"Oh, Trent, you've been like this since we were kids, for Pete's sake!"

"Like what?"

"So nonconfrontational!"

"Don't speak to me this way, God damn it! Whose name is on the door?"

"Sheriff, speaking as a doctor and psychiatrist, leaving town and running away is the last thing he needs," she says, as the familiar tears began to flow.

"Sharon, don't get all emotional on me again. I'm serious this time. You are overinvolved," says the sheriff.

"I'm sorry, Trent. It's just . . . he . . . he has so much pain in his eyes."

"I know he does, Sharon. *He always did.* And so did his mother for that matter. *They* always did. It . . . it was just part of them."

"And what? Just put him on a flight to God knows where, and that's it? What on earth are you thinking?" she says.

"Sharon, you don't necessarily know what's best," says the sheriff.

"For your information, I have a medical degree," she says.

"Well, you wouldn't have fucking known that on Saturday when you were lying in their front fucking yard, Sharon. What a performance that was," says the sheriff.

"Performance! How dare you!" she gasps.

"Doctor, you are a deputy of the medical examiner. Either do your job or hand over the title to someone who has the game face for the job. Understood?" he says. *Damn it, this has gone too far. She can't handle this sort of criticism. At least make it constructive. Keep your eye on the ball. Now she's really crying.* "Doctor, now please listen. I have already looked into helping him get some money. Maddie's house was paid off. It was all she had. It should go to Brendon."

"Did she leave a will? Her sister's still alive, ya know," says the doctor, trying to regain her composure.

"No. No note and no will. It makes me feel like she wasn't really planning this," says Trent.

"You don't suspect foul play, do you? I mean I didn't call an autopsy, as you know. And as *you* recommended," she says.

"You know I couldn't answer that even if I did suspect foul play. And by the way, I don't," he says.

"What about Maddie's crazy sister, Mary?" asks the doctor.

"Believe it or not, Sadie tracked her down. She's living in a motel in Detroit," he says. *No surprise there,* he thought. "Fortunately for us, she has a record and a parole officer, and if it wasn't for that, we would probably have never found her," he says. *Poor girl, troubled as they come—left high school at the age of sixteen and moved to the big city. No one ever saw her again.*

"Is Mary coming to the funeral, I hope?" asks the doctor.

"No, said she couldn't make it. She's too ill to travel, apparently," says the sheriff.

"What has she done to have a record?" asks the doctor.

"Why is that your business?" says the sheriff.

"Well, it's a shame she can't make it to the funeral," says the doctor.

"Yes, it is. Looks like we're all Brendon's got right now, which means let's try and get along, OK?" the sheriff says, nodding his head with a forced smile.

"Does Brendon know about Mary?" asks the doctor.

"No," he answers, "not yet, but I'll tell him."

"Well," Dr. Jury says, touching the bottom of her now-elevated chin, "Maddie told me that Mary lived a dark life and was *always* asking for money. As a matter of fact, I think she actually borrowed money from Brendon and lied about it to Maddie. Never paid him back either."

"And your point is?" he says.

"Well, I was just sayin'," she says.

"Yeah, well, you're always just sayin'—"

"What's that supposed to mean?" she asks.

Calm down, Trent, just calm the fuck down. I need to get her out of my office so that I can actually get some work done before this funeral.

The PA starts to crackle again.

"Sheriff, Lawrence is at the Kudrays now," Sadie says. "Said Shirley hasn't seen Billy in two days. She hasn't seen him since *you* spoke with him actually. Lawrence said she is pretty rattled right now."

"What? How come no one told me?" he says. *This is it. Time for a drink. What else could possibly go wrong? At the rate this week has gone and the people I am dealing with, a lot could go wrong. I need to get Sharon out of here and kiss my bottle.*

"Oh, Sheriff, this is terrible news. Poor Billy. And if Billy's not around," says the doctor, "who is going to be taking Brendon to his mother's funeral? It starts in less than two hours."

"Sharon, I told Brendon that *I would* take him to the funeral. Someone has to, and I have known him for about the last twelve years," he says, quickly pressing the button on the PA. "Sadie, tell Lawrence to offer Mary Kudray a ride to the funeral," he says, staring at the ceiling. "Doctor, if possible, let's speak to Billy at the funeral. Let's just hope he makes the right decision and actually shows up."

The PA began to speak. "And by the way, Sheriff, Mary Castleman just called. Wanted to know how she could get a hold of Brendon," says Sadie.

"And?" answers the sheriff. *That's odd,* he thought. *What could she say that is going to make his day any easier?*

"I just gave her the Kudrays' phone number. I hope that was OK," she says. "I put her on hold just in case you wanted to speak with her, but she hung up."

"Well, I don't like the sound of that!" snaps the doctor.

"Sharon, you shouldn't even be here to be hearing this, quite frankly," says the sheriff.

"She can't even make it to her own sister's funeral, and she's calling him? On the day of? What good could possibly come out of that?" she says loudly.

"Sharon, God damn it, quiet down!" says the sheriff. *If anyone is going to keep their cool today, it is me,* he thought. *These God damn bleeding hearts are going to give me a coronary one of these days.*

"Sharon, listen to me. I'll try and talk to Brendon about his aunt Mary on the way to the funeral. You go home and get yourself gathered up and get ready for this funeral. Understood?"

"Yes, Sheriff, I understand, but—"

"No buts, Sharon. Get there early in case I need your help. Lawrence and I will be taking Brendon and Shirley," he says.

"Just one more thing, Sheriff," Sharon says, placing her hand on her chest.

"Sheriff," again the PA rang, "I have Joseph Deacon on the phone for you," says Sadie.

"Who?" asks the sheriff.

"The FBI officer that was here on Saturday," answers Sadie as Sharon's head again tilts in interest.

"Tell him I'll be right with him, Sadie," says the sheriff. "Doctor, what did you say? I have to take this call."

"Nothing, Sheriff, we'll talk about this later. I just think we should be on the same page as to what is best for the boy," she says, standing up to leave.

"Oh, we're going to be on the same page, Sharon. But let's just try and get through today, OK?".

Chapter 18

A Case—a Real Bonafide Case

There it goes, the damn cell phone ringing again. Wireless harness is what it really is. Wait a minute; this might be the man calling. We are getting close to game time.

"Hello, Joe Deacon here."

"Joe, it's Tom Hayward. How are ya?" asks the voice on the phone.

"I'm fine, sir, yes, um . . . what can I help you with?"

"Well, I gotta make this quick. Don't have much time. Hey, here's the deal. I'm in Chicago now; and I can honestly say that I think we're getting a little closer to wrapping up this case; and I want you to know why. I'm down here meeting with our street agents in regard to how they're buying the drugs. What I'm gettin' at is we're gonna round up a bunch of these local shithead drug dealers that are selling the heroin to the consumer and lean on them a little. Get my drift? Pinch 'em a little bit and try to go up the ladder. The piss-ons talk about where *they* bought it and so on."

"OK, sir, continue," he says.

"This helps in actually convicting the pieces of shit that are bringin' the drugs into this great country of ours," says Mr. Hayward. "Do you understand me?"

So the drug dealers testify in court where they bought the drugs. I see where this is headed.

"I said do you understand me?" repeats Hayward.

"Yes, sir, of course," he answers.

"Well then, fucking say something; I need you to acknowledge me when I speak," says Hayward. "You understand?"

"Yes, of course. I was just thinking about the case. Sorry, my mind drifted," he says.

"The wiretaps are going to be crucial, speaking of which, where are you?" asks Hayward.

"I'm pulling into the trailer in about twenty minutes."

"Cuttin' it a little close, aren't we?" he asks.

"Well, you said they speak every other Thursday at four o'clock," says Deacon. *Oh boy, here it comes. I can't disappoint this guy.*

"It's three fifteen. What if they happen to speak early this time?" asks Hayward.

"I'm sorry, sir."

"Don't fuck this up, kid, or it's back to Detroit. I told you once."

"I won't."

"I would have been on that wire since noon personally, but that's just me," he says.

The seconds of silence began to tick by. God damn it, he's right. I should have been on that wire all day for that matter. I best get with it.

"Joe, are you confident the wiretaps are hooked up correctly?" asks Hayward.

"Yes, I am," he says. *Of course, they are. Setting up a friggin' wiretap isn't exactly brain surgery.*

"Better be," says Hayward with a huff.

"Should I call you when I'm done listening to their conversation?" he asks.

"No, I won't be available until late tomorrow afternoon. I can't. Way too much going on down here. Anyway, I will call you then. Make sure you are available. Now listen. I know we've talked about this before, but it's important. Remember how I told you that the sheriff's the one who arrested Frank Pierson's brother Lance years ago?"

"Yes, absolutely."

"Well, it was huge mess. Leave it to Lance Pierson to wear a handcuff key around his neck. What I am getting at is the sheriff hates him; he hates them both for that matter. Lance took a carpet knife to the sheriff's lower back during the escape. The sheriff almost died due to loss of blood."

Jesus Christ, thought Deacon, *a carpet knife?*

"This is the reason," continued Hayward, "and the only rationale I have for trusting the sheriff on this one. Nothing against the guy, but you can't trust anyone on one of these. Now, you need to go in strong with this sheriff. Sounds like he already has a little chip on his shoulder concerning your presence in his county. You don't know this yet, but uncooperative local law enforcement fuck up more cases than everything else combined. You hear me?"

"Yes, sir."

"You'll learn that through time, so just keep this in mind. *He* doesn't know it, but the sheriff needs to be put in his place."

"But, sir, the only way the sheriff is going to warm up to me is if I give him something or at least tell him why I am up here or *something*," Deacon says, beads of perspiration begin to collect on his brow.

"Exactly. Now, how you gonna do it?" asks Hayward.

I can see him smiling now, thought Deacon. *The guy just loves to watch me squirm.* "Well, I can't tell him about the drugs," says Deacon.

"Correct. Not yet anyway," answers Hayward. "There will be a time when you let him in on the true nature of this case," he says. "Think about it, Deacon. You need to befriend this man. All he wants is to be 'in the know,' you follow? Tell him that Lance Pierson is out of prison, which he is, and that we, the FBI, are keeping an eye on things. Appease him, stroke his ego a little, do whatever it takes to manipulate him. Make him feel special."

"Gotcha," answers Deacon. *He's right. What a great way to stop all of the sheriff's God damn questions.*

"Are we clear?" asks Hayward.

"Yes, sir."

"I said are we clear?"

"Yes, sir, we are very clear."

"You call me *sir* one more time, and I'll reach through this phone and jap-slap you across the face, understand?" he says with a laugh.

"OK, Mr. Hayward," Deacon says, trying to keep the car on the road and the pedal to the floor.

"We need this one, Deacon; this is what promotions are made of, young man. This may sound strange to a greenhorn such as you, but if we don't have a success story like this hit the papers every once in a while, it means *we* aren't doing our jobs."

"You mean a drug bust?" he asks after hesitating.

"No, a member of law enforcement being caught on the wrong side of the law. I want this piece-of-shit Frank Pierson bent over and pinned in the corner of a shower in Jackson Federal Penitentiary. You understand what I'm sayin'?"

"Yep, got it."

"And I need an airtight case. You stay close to that sheriff too, boy. We're going to need his help at some point in time."

"Yes, I will. I promise. I'm going to call him right now," Deacon says, hearing dial tone on the other end of the line. *Oh great. Hung up on me just like that. God damn him. What a pretentious bastard, treating me like this. I can handle this. As a matter of fact, I can handle this case in my sleep. But damn it all, I only have a half an hour until Frank Pierson uses the pay phone. I'd better call the sheriff now, but what if he starts in with all those God damn questions again? What are you doing in my county, blah, blah, blah. I gotta be strong with this guy, just like Hayward said. Can't let him push me around like the last time. The sheriff's a bastard too, looking at me like I'm some eighteen-year-old kid or something. I'll call the sheriff, and I'll call him now. If the bastard starts ramblin' on, I'll just tell him I gotta go. That will work. After all, I do have to make this quick. I gotta get on that wire.*

Chapter 19

The Worst Things Happen to the Best People

"Sheriff," yells Sadie for the second time, "are you going to take this phone call from the federal boy?"

There she goes again, picking and choosing her choice of when to use the PA and when not to, thought the sheriff. He shook his head in dismay as he watched Dr. Jury walking down the stairs of the building. *Now I've got Sadie talking about this FBI officer in a derogatory manner. I need to clean up my act around here. How can I correct Sadie if she hears this kind of talk from me?* he thought. *I'm her boss, for Christ's sake.* "Yes," he says. "I'm just going to shut my door. Sadie, what's his name again?"

"Umm," she answers, "Special Agent Deacon."

"No, his first name," he says.

"Joseph, I think. I can ask him if you want me to," she says.

"No, that's OK," he says. *That's it. Joe. He looked like a Joe as a matter of fact. No, actually, he looked like a city boy. Maybe I'll call him Joey just to piss him off.*

"Hello, this is Sheriff Mayfair," he answers.

"Sheriff, this is Agent Deacon of the FBI. We met the other day. Last Saturday to be exact. How are you today?" he asks.

"Oh, I've been better, really busy. What can I help you with, Joe?"

"Sheriff, I was wondering if we could get together. I've got something that I want you to be aware of. And I'd rather not talk about it over the phone. I hope you understand," he says.

"Well, things, as I mentioned, are really busy around here. Is it important?" says the sheriff.

"Yes, it is, and quite frankly, I feel kinda bad I wasn't able to fill you in on things when we met at your office," says Deacon.

"Yeah, you wasted my time that day, didn't you?"

"As I said at the time, I was just being polite. I was instructed to let you know that I would be working in your county."

"Anyway," says the sheriff, hesitating, "when were you thinking?"

"When are you free?" asks Deacon.

"Why don't we meet out at Reedsburg Dam? Where you are staying," asks the sheriff. Where you are *supposedly* staying is more like it.

"No, not there," answers Deacon.

"And why not?" asks the sheriff.

"Because I am in plainclothes on this assignment, and I really don't want to alert anyone to my presence," he says.

"Oh yeah, the assignment," answers the sheriff sarcastically. "By the way, when you gonna tell me what you're doing in *my* county?" he continued.

"Today, when I see you," says Deacon.

"Well, it's not going to be today. I don't know what you have on *your* plate today, but I have to go and pick up a nineteen-year-old boy and take him to his mother's funeral."

"It's not the suicide," Deacon says, hesitating, "that was called in when I was at your office, is it?"

"Yes, Joe, it is," says the sheriff.

"Wow, I'm sorry to hear about that. It . . . it sounded like an awful tragedy," says Deacon.

"Yeah. Well I'll tell ya, sometimes the worst things happen to the best people," says the sheriff.

"Well, how about we get together tonight?" Deacon says, weighing his next sentence. "Can I buy you a drink?"

"You know, that's not a bad idea. I'm gonna need a drink after a day like this," the sheriff says. *How about you buy me about five drinks?* "Meet me in Merritt. Can't miss the place. There's only one bar in town. It's just west of where you're stayin', and I live out that way anyway."

"Sounds good to me," says Deacon.

Yeah, good to me as well, thought the sheriff. *Just outside of my county. Don't need anyone seeing me getting sloshed again in my county, that's for sure.*

"How's eight o'clock?" asks Deacon.

"Sounds good, and, Deacon, you best not waste a minute of my time with this," the sheriff says.

"I assure you, Sheriff, this will be worth your time," he says. "Why don't you take my mobile number just in case?"

"Oh, I'll be there, with or without you," answers the sheriff.

"OK. See you there," answers Deacon.

Well, looks like it is going to be a long one, thought the sheriff. *Might have to have a quick nip now. Why not? After all, I deserve it dealing with all this bullshit. Between my wife, Maddie killing herself, and this fucking J. Edgar prowling around my county, a man needs a drink.*

Sadie's voice quickly erupts through the PA, knowing that he was now off the phone. "Sheriff, I just got off the phone with your wife. She's called twice now. What should I tell her?"

I'll tell you what you can fucking tell her, he thought. "You tell her," he spouts, "you tell her that if she wants to see me today, she can come to this damn funeral," he says, clenching his teeth. "And I'm not kidding you, Sadie. You tell her exactly that if she calls again. I don't have time to talk to her right now," he says, fumbling through the bottom drawer of his desk. "I have to go and pick up this boy," he continues. *That poor boy. It's going to be a long rough day. This is unbelievable. She says she's leaving me unless I give up drinking and seek help. Yeah, that will look good. Hi, I'm Trent, the sheriff of your county, and I'm an alcoholic. Who the hell does she think she is? Who brings home the bacon and who pays the bills? She's got too God damn much time on her hands; that's the problem. She gives up her job; that was a great idea. She claims that "I have driven her away" and that she doesn't know me anymore. What the hell does that mean anyway? It means that she's sleeping with someone. That's what it means. And if she isn't already, she will be. I'm really not sure that I can deal with this anymore. And now I have to go and face this poor boy. This is unimaginable, not to mention that I'm going to have to keep an eye on Dr. Jury all afternoon as well. She's likely to have another fucking conniption at any point. Where is that fucking bottle anyway?*

Chapter 20

A Lot of Love

Today, I feel truly older than time. But far more importantly, I feel absolutely nothing. It's this newfound euphoria that helps me recognize that I can now get through this occurrence called today. After all, I didn't have any control over my mother's actions—or did I? She was incredibly alone that morning when she decided to lay the metallic-tasting barrel of my shotgun across her tongue, and I will never stop wondering if leaving me alone in this world ever even crossed her mind. Do you think it was a matter of worry? Don't you think it must have at least crossed her mind once, if only for a transitory second? She left her only son to deal with and fend off this rage, bitterness, and absolute loneliness on his own. But then again, and after all, it's just going to take a lot of love to get through these unforeseen circumstances, or at least that's what was whispered into my ear after her accident. The words were slowly and repeatedly whispered into my ear by one of Mom's few and true friends, Dr. Jury. The doctor needs to relax and embrace the facts that have been laid before her; some people just leave this world at different points in their lives. My mother only chose to pick her own date. Who am I to point the finger?

It's going to take a lot of love. That's all; it just takes a lot of love. Dr. Jury preaches faith as if it were just around the corner, and she had very recently experienced her first fleeting glimpse. It's there, Brendon. Be patient. Just give it time. It's right around this next corner, young man—just like the funeral the sheriff and I are now driving to and waiting to attend.

I cannot help but wonder what this day is going to yield as my heart skips a beat. How is this going to unfold? They are putting my mother's much-damaged body and soul into the ground. I mean what am I supposed to do, and how the hell am I supposed to behave? Am I a horrible person if I choose not to cry, or is that not a choice at all? I may just laugh hysterically at the top of my lungs, and why fucking not? Now that would really get a rise out of the watchers. Yeah, I'll give them something to chew on and talk about. Nothing but a horde of watchers in small-town America. Thanks,

Mom, I owe you one. Life has just been a bowl of cherries after your departure, never mind the pits or the burning in the pit of my stomach. There is really only one question to ask. Answer me this, my new found friend. Where did it all go wrong?

If I remember correctly, and I always do, last Saturday was the opening day of trout season in the state of Michigan, and we tried to fly-fish on an ice-riddled beaver pond. Billy and I. One of us fell through the ice, and one of us didn't. Upon arriving home, one of us discovered our mother with the back of her head sprayed across the crystalline white walls of our bathroom.

This is how I am beginning to look at the last four days of my life. The future seems obvious really. I am going to get the fuck out of Dodge and leave this town and never look back. Other than a lack of money, there is absolutely nothing stopping me. I am going to leave this piece-of-shit small town, and I am going to see Lilly if it kills me. She'll not know what has transpired over the last four days. She won't know that I've been ripped and torn apart. She'll have no idea; she doesn't live here, and England is a long way away from northern Michigan in my book. As a matter of accurate accountability, that girl has haunted my ever-waking moment since we met. I distinctly remember my mother noticing a new quickness in my step when Lilly arrived for the summer. My mother called it a force of nature, and I had no idea what was going on, but life did have a new purpose.

In hindsight, those were the days when I used to feel sharp and so definite. It was during this time, the era of optimism and clarity, when I worked on a crew that installed the docks at her family's house on Higgins Lake. I was in the process of surmising that the guesthouse of their home was at least four times the size of my own house when I entered their front porch after a cold spring morning's work for a warm drink. It was clearly the most influential and important cup of coffee in my life. I caught her out of the corner of my eye and the temple of my brain simultaneously. There was no taking my eyes away from the movement she created, and I'm sure it was painfully noticeable to anyone alive in the room. I'll never forget the brilliant sparkles in her blue eyes that morning. One couldn't help but notice the way she glides across a room while never once touching the floor. Fourth of July sparkles within bright blue eyes and long golden hair. It was as if she had exacted a method of pumping large amounts of oxygen into the air in some unknown and illegal manner. I do know my attention was eerily crisp in her presence. I touched her hair for hours that one summer night, and it was obvious that her hair was a shade of blond that the sun imitates. She slept in my arms until dawn, and when she awoke, I'd never felt so vulnerable in my life.

"Brendon, have you, by chance, spoken to Billy today?" asks the sheriff out of the corner of his mouth, trying to keep his eye on the road. "I . . . I'm sure he is going to be at the funeral today, but . . .," stammers the sheriff.

Look at him. Please look at the way he shakes and hesitates. Even the sheriff is a nervous harbinger of the events ahead of us today. It seems as though everyone is a bit apprehensive in my presence these days. This weakness in people will be a power that I will have to exploit in the very near future. "No," I say, "I haven't. Actually, I haven't spoken to him since the morning of my mom's accident." The sheriff scratches his head and continues to stare out the window of the cruiser. "Sheriff," I say, thinking that this might be an odd question to ask. "What exactly do I have to do to sell my mom's house?" I ask. "I have a feeling that I am going to need some money here soon. Just to get by and all."

"I can help with that," he answers, giving me a glance. "I mean I will do whatever I can. We may need a lawyer's advice for some of it, but we can make it happen," he says.

"Good, because I need to get out of here for a while. I'm sure you understand," I say.

"To go and travel like you talked about?" he asks.

"Yes," I say.

"Well, as I said, I will help with anything I can," he answers. "This travel thing," he says before hesitating, "is this something you really need? I mean have you definitely made up your mind?" he asks.

"Yes, it is, and yes, I have," I say, nodding. *You're God damn right it is,* I thought. *I'm not going to sit in this little shithole and grow old and die like the rest of you.*

"Brendon, I've known you since you were a kid, and I want you to listen to me," the sheriff says, taking in a deep breath. "You're going to make it through this. You understand me, boy? And I'm going to help," he says, trying to hide the tears in his eyes.

The emergence of a tear was the first time I noticed the alcohol on his breath. Some things never changed with Sheriff Trenton Mayfair. My mother had always hinted that he'd had a problem. In fairness, what she actually said was that he was a very darling man with a drinking problem.

"I sure appreciate your help, Sheriff," I say, trying to break the new silence.

"Call me Trent, Brendon. You always used to," he says. "Hey, I'm not sure if this is the right time, but I spoke with your aunt Mary today," he says, as we approached the now-open gate of the welcoming cemetery.

"Oh God," I say. *No, you're right, Sheriff. This isn't the right time. The bitch owes me money, and I still haven't heard from her.* "What is she up to? I mean what does she want?"

"Well, she really wants to speak with you," he answers, putting the car in park.

"Well, she's shit out of luck," I say, noticing the small group of huddled people gathering near the hole in the ground.

"I know you two never really saw eye to eye, but you may need her to sign off on the house. I don't know because your mother didn't leave a will. As I said, I don't know," he says.

"No will and no note—that seems to be Mother's style," I say.

"I'm just saying that if we do need her signature, I know where Mary is. She called the post yesterday," he says.

"I'm not dealing with her. I promise you that," I say.

"I'm sorry. I shouldn't even have brought it up," he says.

"She owes me over $800 right now," I say. "Not to mention she can't make it to her own sister's funeral."

"Brendon, I'm sorry. Hey, let's talk about this another time. Tomorrow or something. We have a funeral to attend," he says, with his head down and a hand to his eye.

"Fuck that. Let's talk about it now," I say, as he rubs his fingers on his temples.

"Well, I'm no lawyer, but without her written permission, we can't really sell the house. You two are the only surviving family members," he says, as I play with my unfortunately unlit cigarette. "You may have to pay her a visit. She told me that she doesn't own a car," he says.

"Are you kidding me? I don't want to go down there. Me? A drive to Detroit? I don't think so. Can't we just mail her something?" I say.

"Well, maybe you're right. But you should give her a call. She says she really needs to talk to you. She's been calling everyone. She called the post three times already, and I know she's been calling the Kudrays."

"Oh, I know," I say. "Doesn't mean I have to take the call. What exactly did she say when you spoke with her?"

"She said that she needs to talk to you and that she's under the weather right now and she doesn't have a car and she can't make it to the funeral," he answers.

"That's a bunch of fucking bullshit, and you know it!" I say. "You knew what Mary was like," I say, pointing at him. "You went to high school with her and my mother."

"You could be right, Brendon," he says. "I haven't seen Mary since we were sixteen, but she is your mother's sister, and I'm sure she hasn't taken your mother's death lightly."

"Well then, she should be here!" I say.

"I know, Brendon," he says.

"She borrows $800 from me, my *only* savings, over two years ago, and this is the first I hear from her? And she doesn't make it to the fucking funeral? She can piss up a rope for all I care."

"Well, let's try and make sure you get your money back then. That's the least she can do," he says. "You look a little pale, son. We're here now. Let's get some fresh air."

"I'm going to have a cigarette."

"You do that," says the sheriff, opening the door of the car. "Honestly, Brendon, I still think it is a good idea if you two speak. Please at least think about it," he says, pausing. "That way, we can sort all of this out and . . . and you can get on with your life," he says.

The sheriff seemed to gain his composure immediately as his hand wiped the area around his eye socket, and I soon found out why—it was the ever-present Dr. Sharon Jury, and she was on patrol. She had a look in her eye as if she may very well have had an eye on everyone. And I think we all know who she was looking for.

I inhaled the beautiful smoke and also caught the pungent aroma of freshly dug dirt. I watched the sheriff sheepishly approach Dr. Jury and could already predict what was going on in his head. She was a nervous one who didn't miss a beat. She meant well and made a man's man very nervous. I'd always had the feeling that she could take control over any situation that she wished; it was just a matter of doing so. And it was here, at my mother's funeral, that she would indeed take charge. This sentiment was only more solidified as I saw Billy gingerly approach the doctor and sheriff in midconversation and, after following the quick head movement of Sharon, began to approach me. Tears began to flow steadily down his face as he placed both of his hands into his front pockets. Poor guy obviously had his tail between his legs having not seen me until now. It was time for Billy and I to talk about what had happened that fateful day only four days prior. It was also time for another cigarette.

"Hey, buddy," he says, through a red face full of tears. His hug hits me like a ton of bricks and nearly takes me to the ground. There would be no turning back now.

"Hey, Bill, you'd better watch it. I don't want to burn you with this thing," I say.

"You shouldn't be smoking those things anyway," he says.

"Yeah, well, trust me, this isn't the day to quit," I say.

"You're probably right. How you been, man?" he says, wincing and looking down at his feet. "I mean we do need to get this over with, don't we? I mean the funeral."

"Yeah, I guess we do," I say.

"Hey, I don't know if you've heard, but your aunt Mary has been calling all over the place," he says.

"I know, I know."

"Have you talked to her yet? I . . . I heard she's not coming," he says.

"No, she's not coming, and no, I haven't talked to her and have no fucking desire to either."

"You know I'll deal with her if you want."

"I know you would," I say. "But no, I'll deal with her."

"How's Dr. Jury? My mom said she's been to the house every frickin' day."

"She's fucking nuts," I say. "Speaking of your mom, how is she doing?"

"She's been pretty down since my dad moved out, but I guess that's expected. Yep," he says. "But they're both here; it's nice to see them together to be honest."

I felt a bubble rise from my stomach to my chest. I'd really missed this kid. This was it; I wasn't controlling my composure anymore. "I don't want to be here, man!" I sob, leaning into him, as he once again hugged me.

"We're going to get through this one, my friend. Together. We're gonna just take it day by day, OK?" he whispers. I soon realized that his crying began to become much stronger than my own as he began to sob uncontrollably.

"It's gonna be all right," I whisper. *God, who is this day going to be harder on? Certainly not my mother.*

"I made a huge mistake, man. I am so sorry," he says in between helpless sobs.

"It's OK. It's gonna be OK," I say.

"No, you don't understand. I made a huge mistake," he says.

"It's gonna be all right," I say.

"I came over one day to see if you wanted to drink, and I . . . I was drunk," he says, rubbing his eyes with his hands. "I kissed her. It was my fault. It was just a mistake," he says, again staring at the ground.

"You kissed her? Why?"

"I don't know . . . I . . ."

"What kind of a kiss was it?"

"Just a kiss."

"Well, that can't be the reason that she killed herself," I say, not knowing what else to say. "Calm down. People are starting to stare at us."

"I'm so sorry. I've been in love with her for a long time, more than you know," he sobs. "She was so nice to me; she was so good to me," he says. "And I fucked it all up, and now she's gone."

"What? In love with her? Is that why you kissed her?"

"I don't know. I was drunk," he says, sobbing as he slammed his hands against his face. "I didn't mean it. I swear to God. She got upset; she pushed me away. It was the last time I saw her alive."

"I can't believe you kissed her that way. You don't even belong here!" I say. "Just get away from me, seriously. Is this why you came here today? To tell me this? They're putting her in the ground today," I say, turning and walking neatly into an almost-worse-looking situation. There, the sheriff and the doctor stood. She was trying to force a sympathetic smile, and he still had tears in his eyes. No, actually, he was still crying. I looked back at Billy; he had fallen to his knees and was visibly distraught and crying.

"Brendon, please come here," the doctor says, as I stomp by her and the sheriff.

"Not today, Doctor. Today isn't about you," I say, fingering another cigarette. "Come on now, Sharon," I say. "We do have a funeral to attend." This just wasn't my day, but then again, it never was. I take a quick step away from the sheriff and doctor and toward the fresh-smelling hole in the ground. *Fuck them all today. To hell with them all. To hell with them and the selfish bitch that guided me to this very special date on the calendar. And after all, maybe I'm not really here, and this isn't really happening. It can't be. To hell with them all, and if these people are really here to see me, I know how I'll end this day. If they want a show, then I'll give them a show. I'll put an end to this day precisely as my mom did last Saturday. Yes, that's it—the last thing before I go. I'll end all of this nonsense forever.*

Chapter 21

The Wire

The silver Airstream travel trailer parked discreetly next to the smooth water known as the Deadstream flooding, appeared to be very similar to the model owned by the fisherman parked a mere 150 yards away.

Special Agent Joseph Deacon worked fervently with the surveillance equipment inside the highly specialized mobile unit. *Jesus, it's almost four o'clock. The time is now. I have to get something solid out of this; Hayward has a lot riding on this wire. Damn it, I hope this works.* The overly large headphones slipped on his head and over his ears, his mind racing. "This had better go well. Yep, better go well," he says out loud as his fingers tapped. *There, I have a signal. Three forty-seven is the time. Damn! That was cutting it a bit close.* He began to slowly dial down the volume of the never-ending hum of a dial tone, hearing a faint metallic click in the background. *Was that him? It can't be; they're early if it is. God damn it! I hope it's not someone else using the pay phone. Shit! I knew I should have installed a camera. I just didn't want to alter the surroundings and tip them off. The guy's a cop, for Christ's sake, and I think I know how cops think.* He cranked the dial, hearing the coins being dropped through the small metallic slot. *Whether it's them or not, this is show time. What am I missing? What am I forgetting? Jesus Christ, I'm not even recording. God damn it! Is the reel even on yet? Yes, thank God, it is.* Click went the record button.

"Hello, Frank?" asks the slight French Canadian accent.

"Yeah, it's me," says the other voice. *That's them, son of a bitch.*

"How are you?" asks Lance. *Lance seems to have a stronger accent than his brother,* thought Deacon.

"Not so fucking well, Lance, as a matter of fact."

"Why, what's the—" Lance asks.

"What's this I hear about you drunk at Sugar Springs Country Club with that fucking idiot Cliff Stoink?" Frank says.

"Relax, let me explain."

"Don't tell me to relax. I tell you to lay low, and I tell you not to bring any attention to yourself, and you're here! In Roscommon County? The county where *I* work?"

"As a matter of fact, I was working."

"Working?" Frank asks.

"Yeah. Cliff's gotta good connection for us in Chicago," Lance says.

Connection in Chicago, thought Deacon. *I like the sound of this.*

"We already have a connection in Chicago?" Frank says.

"Yeah, but I looked into it. Cliff's guy is in Gary, Indiana, ya see? There's a shitload of people down there, ya know. Help us expand our network a little."

"I wouldn't trust Cliff to take out the fucking garbage."

"Frank, relax and listen to me, and listen to reason," he says.

"And you told him what we're doing?" interrupts Frank.

"I didn't tell him much of anything. You know Cliff. He's a dealer," Lance says.

"I'll kill Cliff if need be. You know that," Frank says.

"He's not tellin' anyone shit. The guy sells drugs as it is, weed and stuff. He's just looking to make some extra cash," Lance says.

"There are only two people who know about this, Lance—you and me."

"And that remains the same, brother," says Lance. "Now listen, we can only sell half of each shipment to Detroit and Chitown because we are getting so much per shipment, which means we're losing money with the other half just sittin' around."

"I don't mind half sitting around. What if one of these shipments doesn't arrive? Huh, did you ever think of that?"

"Yer bein' a worry wart, as usual."

This is great. Keep on talking, boys. Keep it relevant. C'mon, let's talk business here, Deacon thought.

"For someone who just did a ten-year sentence, you're awfully fucking thick sometimes," says Frank. "You listen to me, Lance. We're only doin' this until October like we planned. After that, we'll have more money than God. And after that, I'm taking an early retirement from the state and gettin' the fuck out of here."

"Just listen to me," Lance says.

"Shut the fuck up! You stay away from here. You stay up at Drummond like we planned."

"There ain't nothin' goin' on up at Drummond. It's so God damn boring, Frank. I've been in the friggin' pen for ten years. I wanna have some fun, chase some pussy, ya know."

"One summer, Lance, and that's it. You can afford to be bored with the money we're making. Go fishin', get some sun, do whatever. Just remember, greed is the only thing that can hurt us. I've said that from the beginning. One year of work, get in, and get out. Now, I'm going to do the pickup tonight and then meet you."

"Ok."

"Now, I want the stuff taken south tomorrow at the latest."

They want the stuff taken south. Where south? C'mon, you gotta give me more than that, Deacon thought.

"Of course, it's payday, baby," says Lance. "When do you want to sell the stuff I'm sitting on?"

"When you see our people tomorrow, tell 'em we got extra if they got the cash. And no bulk-discount bullshit either. We'll sit on it if it makes us more money."

"Yeah, more like I'll sit on it. There's risk in sittin' on this stuff, ya know," he says.

"Shut the fuck up, Lance, and one more thing. I hear about you drunk around town again, and I'll be the one who puts you away. That was dumb, Lance. Real fucking dumb, and it can't happen again. You are on probation. Remember that. My little brother won't be the one to take me down with him, you understand?"

"Understood. I'll stay low."

"Just stay in the islands or in Canada unless you're delivering. Stick to the plan, OK? We'll be in the Caribbean in December. Just think about that. I'm heading north in about an hour or so. I want to get to the boat a little early."

"I still don't think it's a good idea with you using the law's boat."

"Are you kidding me? *I* am the law. *No one* can touch me. It's a safer bet than you running around out there after dark like we've been doing. We already decided we should both be able to do the pickup, just in case. It just makes sense. By the way, how's the weather?"

"Fine. Nice and calm."

"Good."

"The big boat should pull through just as the sun is setting. They pulled past Detroit yesterday, right on time. And remember, they used a green light last time," says Lance.

"I know."

"That bag is damn heavy, especially when it gets wet, I'm tellin' ya."

"I know, I know. See you after the pick up."

"Ok."

"If anyone is on to us, they'll be watching the marinas that we're using."

"Don't be paranoid," says his brother.

"Take it from someone who has never done jail time. Be careful."

"I know, Frank. I think I have it down by now."

"I gotta go."

"Why so quick?"

"I don't know," he says. The silence began to lengthen as Deacon waits with a tilted head in the trailer. "Sometimes this phone makes me nervous," continues Frank.

"Don't be ridiculous. We don't even get to see each other, and this is the only time we speak."

"I know. I just want this to work, to continue working."

"It will. Trust me. It will."

"Just a few more of these, little brother, and we are retiring for good."

"I hear ya, brother."

"See you after dark. Good luck," says the stronger of the French Canadian accents as the dial tone returns to the bugged pay phone.

How are they doing this? The whole conversation seemed cryptic. They can't know I have the phone bugged, thought Deacon. *No, they can't know. Heading north tonight? Heading north where? That doesn't make any sense if they are taking the drugs to Detroit and Chitown. But Frank did say that he wanted the stuff taken south tomorrow. And they are using a boat, and that's a solid lead. No doubt about it. Frank Pierson, you crazy fucker. He's using the boat of the Department of Natural Resources? That's either really ballsy or just plain stupid. But it could be a brilliant idea if you're in his shoes. He's using the law's boat so that no one will mess with him. Who would pull him over? He is the law. The slimy cocksucker works for the local drug task force SANE, or whatever it was called. Hayward's right. This guy needs to go down and go down hard. And where is Drummond? I'll have to ask the sheriff tonight when I see him. I'll just pose the question as if I'd heard they have good fishing or something. There is a lot I need to ask the sheriff. Hopefully, he'll be nice and lubed up and ready to run his mouth. This is all too cryptic, though. Hayward's not going to be happy with my report. All I have for him is that they use a boat, and they're only doing this for the rest of the summer. And Frank sounded nervous. No, Hayward's not going to like this at all. He'll want more. I can feel it already. He'll want something with some more meat on it. Something to break the case. I better get some of these questions answered and get ready for his telephone interrogation tomorrow. Well, you wanted a real case—a real bonafide case. Here ya go, kid. You got it. I'm swimmin' up to my ears on this one, and it's like what Hayward said, "Fuck this one up, boy, and yer back to Detroit." Time to go meet up with the sheriff. Yep. Time to go.*

Chapter 22

Dry Eyes

Dr. Sharon Jury and Sheriff Trent Mayfair carefully approached their respective cars, each pretending that nothing had just taken place. The sheriff's crying had at long last subsided as he finally glanced in the same direction as the doctor with a car key in his hand. The final and last of the other cars attending the funeral crunched at length in the gravel as it left.

"I'll talk," he says, "uh, to you later, Sharon."

"Talk to you later? How can you just say that?" she screeched. "Trent, listen to me! You showed up visibly drunk to Maddie's funeral. Do you understand this? How do you think that makes Brendon feel?"

"Sharon, shut your mouth," the sheriff says, shaking his head.

"I can smell alcohol on you—you . . . you were out of line!" she says through a shaking finger. "I can always smell it on you. You are losing control, Trent. You need to listen to me. You will drink yourself into an early grave at this rate."

"Don't you point your finger at me, woman!"

"Don't speak to me that way, Trent. You know I care, you just can't drink every day," she says. "We're not in high school anymore."

"Stop preaching to me, just once," he says.

"You should consider AA, Trent."

"Are you fucking kidding me?" he gasps. "That will look good! Me, the sheriff showing up at an AA meeting. Yeah, I'll make sure I wear my uniform, Sharon."

"Trent," she says.

"What the hell are you thinking?" he says.

"I know that Nancy left you, and I would like to help."

"You want to help, that's your problem. Look around you, Sharon . . . all you try and do is help people. Help yourself," he says. "My wife is none of your business. Today's not about you or me. It's about Brendon, and Brendon's gonna be OK."

"He's not OK, Trent. Be realistic."

"Give that poor kid a break. You *hardly* knew him, and now you want to be attached to his hip."

"He is going to go to the brink. I can feel it," she says.

"What?" he says, snapping his glance back toward her direction.

"I'm sincerely worried about him," says the doctor.

"Well, there's a fucking surprise."

"I am surprised he has made it this far," she says.

"You and your cryptic shit," the sheriff says.

"Brendon is technically suicidal right now. Do you understand that?" she says.

"What are you talking about, for Christ's sake?" says the sheriff. "You don't understand that boy," he says, shaking his head.

"Oh yes, I do," she says.

"As a matter of fact, I don't think you understand men at all."

"Oh, I understand men very well," she says. "Very well, indeed." *I understand your kind decidedly well, Trent. Very well,* she thought. *You're all the same, noticeably weak, that is. You all hide behind your wall like it isn't even there. Fragile and helpless human being is what you are.*

"Sharon, we can't keep doing this, seriously," he says. "I can't take this . . . this way we keep interacting. This is exhausting," the sheriff says, propping himself onto his car.

"I'm sorry. It's just . . . I mean . . .," she says, "I agree. As you said before, this isn't about us," says the doctor. *Or is it?* she thought. *I hope this isn't about us.* "I can't believe Brendon left with Billy," she says, trying to change the subject. "They looked like they almost got into a fight before the funeral."

"Yeah, well, think about it. Billy was probably a better option than you or me."

"Yeah, you're probably right," she says.

"Poor kid," says Trent. "Didn't ask for any of this and here we all are."

"Trent, I think this may be the worst week of my life from an emotional standpoint."

"I get the point, Sharon."

"How was the ride over with him?" she asks.

"Kind of rough. It's almost like the kid's in denial or something."

"Trent, I have to ask you this. You . . . you had a crush on Maddie, didn't you?"

"And you have to ask me this? Why?" he says.

"Because of your behavior today, for one thing," she replies. "Did you or didn't you?"

"Well, no," he says.

"You did back then?"

"Well, yeah, in high school. Everyone did," he stammers.

"Did you notice that Brendon didn't shed a single tear here today?" she asks. "Can you believe that?"

"Yes, I can. People deal with these things differently, you know," says the sheriff. "You should know. You're a doctor."

"He looked absolutely numb to me," says the doctor. "It's just that the boy has *so much* pain in his eyes."

"He always has. Admit it. And so did Maddie," he says. "It's just part of who they are."

"Do you really?" She winces. "Do you truly believe that, Trent?" She asks.

"Yes, Sharon, I do," the sheriff says. His chin rose slightly as if his ego were balanced upon it. "Sharon, I'm gonna be honest. I don't want to see you for a while," he says. "No offense, but this week has been too much for all of us. You need to leave Brendon alone for a while. Just let him be."

"But where is he going to live?" she asks.

"Trust me, Sharon. Leave him alone. We've all been a bit over involved. He can stay with the Kudrays if necessary. Hell, he can stay with me if necessary," he says. "We all need this funeral to be over with. You follow me, Sharon?" he asks with his arms outstretched as she forced a nod of her head. "Let's just get life back to normal around here for a week or two," he continues. "I'll keep you in the loop regarding Brendon. I'll be keeping an eye on him. At least *I* know him. Billy will tell me everything. You know that. And another thing. I talked to a lawyer. The house goes to Brendon, and Mary isn't going to get her hands on it. She's not entitled to it."

"If Brendon gets a bunch of money and goes traveling, he will end up drunk in some ditch somewhere. You know that as well as I do," she says.

"Go home, Sharon. You look worse than I do," says the sheriff.

"I'm warning you now, Trent. Money won't help his situation," she says. "It's not the answer."

"I'll see you later, Doctor," the sheriff says, as he starts his cruiser.

Look at him go. Run away, run away Trent, away from all of this. He'll have another drink in him within an hour, she thought. *His wife left him, and she won't take him back unless he dries up. Maybe he likes the booze because it keeps her away. Could be true. Nancy never treated him well in my book. He's a good man beyond the drinking. Yep, when it comes down to it, he's a good-hearted man. I could use a man like him, minus the booze.*

Imagine having dry eyes as you watch your mother being lowered into a hole in the ground. There were barely a dozen people who showed for Maddie's funeral, and her son was the only one with a dry face. Maybe he hates her now. That's it. He blames her for all of this. How could I not realize this until now? Of course, he blames her. She pulled the trigger of his gun. I watched your halo slip off, Maddie. You just couldn't maintain the charade any longer. Oh, Madeline, today, we officially say goodbye. I will always miss you. You know that. You know I tried. You have to know that I tried. After all, I tried to help you so much. It just wasn't meant to be. Dear sweet Jesus, take her under your wing. Help her, my Lord. Oh, Lord, please help her.

Yes, God, you've helped her, helped her do what? You helped her exit this world, how is that helping? Who am I to say this and more importantly, what kind of God would let her stick a gun barrel down her throat? How could you! What kind of so-called Lord would let her do this? Where is the good in that? Where is the love, the Godforsaken love? Where is the love? You tell me! God damn you! God damn you!

Chapter 23

They Grow Gray

If I were you and I were so inclined to offer advice, I honestly don't think I would read the words that have been placed so tidily before you. But if you really must know how it all began to sink and go under, read on. This is precisely how my mother's suicide note would have begun. I know this in my heart as we are of the same mind, especially now. What I have seen this past week is unimaginable, and I keep planning on leaving this confusion behind, but the confusion never stops. I now own this constant edge of uncertainty that keeps my mind sharp and my heart numb. I have come to the conclusion that I no longer want to feel this world swirling around me, and fortunately, I no longer have to. I must focus on slicing away at the ties that surround me including the ties that bound me. More importantly, I must begin my quest to leave. None of any of this will be relevant to the people of this town, if only a year from now. I can see them now nodding their pointed heads over a cup of tea. "Oh yes, I remember Maddie Castleman. She blew her head off, didn't she? What a shame that was. And whatever happened to that boy of hers?"

They grow gray speaking of such things. I can't expect too much from these people. Look at them all in their weakened state. I am stronger than all of them put together, and it will be this key element they will always overlook no matter how apparent it may be. For I have been through more than most—certainly more than anyone my age. As the funeral finally begins to end, the nervous shuffle is now set in motion. Most have walked past cautiously staring at their shoes while giving their most sincere condolences, and fortunately, they are almost gone. Thank fucking God for that.

Oh, but here he is, my best friend, back again for another try. What now, poor Billy? You feel like filling me in on a few more little tidbits of information? Let me guess. Not only did you kiss my mother and tell me that you were also in love with her, but you fucked her as well. He approaches gingerly as it became obvious that he was one of the only people left.

"Hey, buddy, I'm sorry about earlier. I really am. Please, I will take you home. Just let me explain," Billy says.

"I don't want to go home, Billy," I say.

"Oh sure. I'm sorry. What was I thinking?" he says, rubbing his forehead. "Let's just take a drive or something," he pleads.

"Let's go," I say. "I'm going to need your help, anyway."

"OK. Anything," says Billy. "I am so sorry for earlier, seriously," he says. "It's been a really emotional day."

"Quit blaming yourself for fuck's sake! Just quit fucking blaming yourself!" I say at the top of my lungs, slamming the door of the truck. "*She* pulled the trigger, not you. Don't forget that. Fucking bitch, anyways."

"OK, uh . . .," he stammers. "I'm sorry."

"I know that you're sorry, Billy—everyone is. Now, turn the keys and let's get out of here," I say, noticing the sheriff and doctor approaching the parking lot. "I'm going to need your help with getting out of your house, if ya know what I mean."

"Yeah, sure."

"Just treat me like you used to, for Christ's sake. I'm really sick of the way everyone has been looking at me over the past week. I didn't do anything. Do you understand me?" I say. "Believe it or not, I don't need much right now. I just need to get out of your house and out on my own. That is the first thing I need to do. Then I need to get that money back from my aunt Mary and get the hell out of here. It's really quite simple," I say.

"No problem, man," Billy says, smacking the steering wheel of his pickup truck. "Seriously," he says, "we can do that."

"You're God damn right we can," I say.

"You really," he says, "really going to go to Europe and hook up with Scotty?"

"Absolutely. Soon as possible."

"You going to the see Lilly while you're there, right?" he asks.

"I sure hope so, Billy. She's the one I think about when I want to get away from . . . from . . .," I say, "this past fucking week, man. How the hell did we end up here?" I say as the tears began to flow. "You tell me."

"I don't know," Billy says. "I just don't know."

"I should have knocked you on your ass last Saturday out there on that ice. That was a dumb move on your part."

"I know. Yer right. Sorry about that," he says as we each tried to wipe the tears away. "So, what ya want to do today?" he asks.

"Find some solace. How is that for a plan?"

"Do you want to go have a drink?"

"That depends on where."

"I told Pascal we might stop by. His boss," he says, "the owner of the bar, is out of town."

"You look like you've been doing some drinking this past week. Jesus, you look awful, man," I say as he nods. "Where you been staying, by the way?" I ask.

"With my dad. He's at a motel right now, but I'm moving back in with Mom when we get you moved out. Hopefully, he will be too," says Billy. "You sure this is OK going to a bar? I mean I realize we just left the funeral and all."

"Where the hell else are we gonna go? Unless you want to go fishing."

"Let's go drinking first. We can always fish afterward." Billy's truck turns onto the dirt road that led us north toward the ancient lumber town of Michelson.

"You know, it's not exactly a good idea for us to be sittin' up at the bar drinking, whether or not the owner is there," I say. "You know that, you're the one who worked for him?"

"Pascal will just put the whiskey in a Coke can. No one will even know we're drinking."

"Whatever," I say, hoping to end the conversation as I gaze out the window watching the never-ending trees go by. *What on earth am I still doing here? For Christ's sake, this is it. This is my chance to get out of here and see the world—and to see her. Fortunately, she's there every time I close my eyes, simply hovering. I always notice her hair before all else when my eyes close. There is no doubt I wasn't the first boy that had carefully devised a technique to somehow find a way to swim in the silk of her hair. She was simply a creature that proved the fact that there is nothing more important in this world than a beautiful woman. She is the only seamless grace left in my life. And she'll not know of this past week. She'll not know of any of this Godforsaken hell that my mother has cast around. If I could only hold her for a moment—if only. If I could even speak to her—that's it! I must call her. I need to step up to the plate and call her. I need to hear her voice and that accent. The soothing joy of—*

"Hey, buddy," interrupts Billy, "you're smiling? That's great. You need to."

"To be honest, I'm just glad this day is over," I say. *No one will ever know what an immense step forward this is,* I thought. "Because after today, it's not about her."

"You mean after today it's not about your mother?" he asks, with his head down.

"That is exactly what I mean."

"Yeah, I feel a little better too, now that you mention it. I always do after a good cry."

"Well, isn't that special?" I say. "Are we in touch with our feelings now? Thank God for that."

"Hah! Even your sense of humor is back," he says. "This is a good sign. Only two cars in the parking lot—that's another good sign. And one of them is Pascal's."

"Good. I don't feel like dealing with anyone's shit," I say, opening the door of Billy's truck. I could already smell the place from twenty feet away as I hopped in between the moist potholes of the parking lot.

"Tim, how ya doin'?" Billy says as the screen door slammed behind us.

"Good, Billy," answers the shiny bald head.

"What are you doin' out in these parts?" asks Billy.

"My brother Cliff lives out this way. I just dropped off his kids. Brendon," he says with an outstretched hand, "I'm awfully sorry to hear about your mother. I wished I could have been there today, but I was at the furniture store all day."

"No problem and thanks," I say.

"I was very fond of your mother. I really was," he says.

"Thanks, Tim," I say, noticing his clipboard lying on the bar next to a cup of coffee. Tim had always literally smelled of organization, being the exact polar opposite of his brother, Cliff.

"Time heals, young man. Remember that," he says as Billy takes a seat at the opposite end of the bar.

"Tim, I haven't seen your brother Cliff in ages," says Billy. "How's he doing?"

"Not well to be honest. Phyllis just bailed him outta jail recently."

"Really," I say as Billy and I both nod our heads.

"Yeah, I met with his probation officer this morning. She said he's in a reentry program. She's also acting as his counselor."

What the hell is a reentry program?

"And it's official," Tim says. "He's lost all of his driving privileges."

"Is that why he's driving around on that moped?" asks Billy, with a laugh.

"He's not even supposed to be driving that. But he and I aren't exactly speaking much these days. His counselor seems optimistic though, but I'm sure he'll be up to his old ways soon."

"I'll take a Coke, Pascal," Billy says, with a winking eye.

"Pascal, I think Brendon is ready for one too," adds Billy.

"No thanks, Pasc. I'll pass."

"Why?" he whispers.

"My stomach feels a little off, that's why," I say.

"You look pale, man," he says.

"Thanks. You look a little ugly today yourself," I answer as Pascal hands me the Coke can anyway. I take a drink out of the foul-smelling aluminum. "Jesus, this is terrible," I say, shivering. "It isn't even cold."

"That's why you just gotta pound it," whispers Billy. My stomach creaks at the now-warm whisky in the Coke can. A car pulls up outside followed by a car door slamming. Pascal immediately begins to look agitated. From the look on Tim's face as he glances through the screen door, we had just been speaking of the devil. His brother Cliff lumbers through the door with the agility of a hungover ape as the air grows tight. Timmy's hands tremble on the coffee saucer like he is going to explode. The room takes on a foul odor, and it looks as if Cliff has never left the place.

"Well, if it isn't my little brother Timmy, the scurrying cue ball," Cliff gasps with a chiclet, yellow-toothed smile. "What the hell you doin' in a dumpy little bar like this?" he asks. "And how's the little woman? Woman's gotta ass like a tractor!" He cackles. "I know who wears the pants around that house. Shit, pants . . . more like overalls."

"I told you *never* to refer to Beatrice in such a vile manner," Timmy says, as their eyes met.

"Yeah, well, you tell ole' swamp puss I said hello," howls Cliff, chuckling at his own laughter. Tim stands up as his jaw muscles begin to tighten. "I'll see you boys later. Pascal, you call me if you need to."

"Yeah, Pascal," says Cliff, "cuz my brother here is in charge," he crows again as he takes over Tim's former seat at the opposite end of the bar.

"Hey, Cliff," Billy says, as Tim made his way out the door, "we were just talkin' about you. Haven't seen you since that day out at Sugar Springs. You remember eatin' all them tropical fish outta the aquarium?"

"Nope," he answers. "Don't remember a God damn thing. Sure have heard about it, though. My wife sure managed to hear about it quickly."

"Well, yeah, she works there, Cliff," Billy says in astonishment.

"Ah, whatever. Them golfin' folks ain't for me anyway. Where's Roy at today?"

"He's out," says Billy. "Pascal's watchin' the place."

"Oh, ain't you big shot now, Pascually," mocks Cliff. "No wonder Timmy's in here. He makin' sure the beaner don't run off with the cash. Did Roy ever tell you guys about how he ended up ownin' Pascal here? Damnedest story, but you know how these Mexicans are. Anyway, so Roy is up in Green Bay, Wisconsin, ice fishin', and some guy pulls up in a pickup truck full of Mexicans. No shit. Roy said they were stacked like cordwood in the bed of the pickup, see? Roy says, 'I'll take that one there,' pointin' at Pascually here. Turns out Pascal here was the only one that didn't have bloodshot eyes. Hah, I can still hear him. 'Last thing I need hangin' around is a doped-up Mexican.' Ain't that right there, Pascually?" Cliff laughs, slamming his hand into the bar.

It's times like these that I could start throwing punches and never ever stop. You're time will come, Cliff . . .

"Get me a beer, you wiggly little wetback," barks Cliff in his usual tone, "and some smokes too."

"You have . . . uh . . . money today?" asks Pascual.

"Of course, I do, bean boy, and make sure they're filterless. Almost had to punch the fuckin' Arab at the corner store in Prudenville," he huffed. "Stupid son of a bitch doesn't even speak regular English. Ahknob, or whatever his name is."

"His name is Archie," I say evenly, trying to establish eye contact.

"Archie my ass. Ahknob Licknob is what I call him," Cliff says with another roar of laughter.

It is easy to envision Cliff's yellow teeth popping out ever so easily.

"We got everything up here these days, what's next, niggers?" he says. "I moved up from the city to get away from that shit; now I'm gonna have to move to the U.P." He says, as a piece of yellow foam begins to collect at the corner of his hairy mouth. Pascal busies himself cleaning the mirror behind the bar.

I can't decipher what exactly he is trying to clean—the mirror or the reflection of the fat-assed redneck in it. "I can't believe that asshole is here," I say to Billy a bit too loud, hoping Cliff would notice.

"Keep your voice down," Billy says.

"Relax, Jesus. This guy couldn't fight his way out of a wet paper sack," I say, eyeing the miserable piece of human waste. "You know he's just a piece of shit anyway," I continue. It was always fun watching poor Billy squirm. Squirm Billy, squirm.

"C'mon, man, another time," he whispers. "Not now," he says, holding up his now-illegal Coke can.

"Hey, you know he beats his wife?" I say, looking Billy in the eye. "You know he does. There should be a special place in hell for people like him," I say, staring down the bar at the fat fuck. Billy's hands start to shake a little, just as Timmy's had. "Look at him. I'd like to take the small end of a baseball bat to his forehead for a while. Imagine what that thing would look like all swollen and bruised."

"Why the small end?" asks Billy in a whisper.

"Because the other end would kill him, and he doesn't deserve to go that quickly. Let people like him suffer for a while. Know what I mean?" I say, nodding my head. Pascal systematically begins to wash every glass in the place, even several that were not dirty. He was clearly listening to me and dearly hoping that Cliff wasn't able to. He made an assortment of strange facial movements while conducting an arsenal of activity, and he bounced around the inside of the small bar as if he were sliding on ice.

"Hey, Cliff, you ever think about renting out that forehead of yours?" I yell. "You could show a fucking film on that thing," I say with a smile.

"You talkin' to me, punk?" he grunts. "You best not, you skinny little fuck."

"You should treat your brother with some respect," I say. "He's a good man. Not that you would know anything about that."

"He's a bald little money-grubbin' prick is what he is," Cliff says, in a raised voice.

"Well, at least he's not a moped-riding, wife-beating son of a bitch," I say, as I took a long drag out of my Coke cola.

"I'm not fucking kiddin', kid. I'll take yer head off," he says.

"Cliff, can you do me a favor?" I ask.

"What's that?" he says.

"Shut the fuck up," I say.

"I'll knock you into the middle of next week you keep shootin' your mouth off," he says, gaining his feet below the barstool.

"And what exactly are you going to do about it?" I say. Cliff stood there with a cocky, slimy grimace on his face. It was obvious. I was in the midst of a trauma. My time was now, and this was obviously my window. I'll kill this piece of shit if they let me.

"Brendon," Billy says, as I began to move and feel his hand grab my arm, "he obviously hasn't heard about your mom yet," he says. "Just let it go," he pleads. I removed his hand from my arm.

"You come over here, boy, and I—" he says, as I close the distance.

"Das eeet," screeches Pascal jumping onto the top of the bar. "You no break anythin'!"

"Why don't we do Pascal a favor and take this outside?" I ask, within three inches of his eyes and the foul odor from his mouth.

"I'm not fuckin' around, kid. You walk away, or I'll kick yer ass in front of yer friends here."

"I'd love to see you try, Cliff. See, because unlike your wife, I'll put up a fight," I say, glancing back at Billy's horrified face and pretending to scratch the back of my head as I punched Cliff in the nose as hard as I could. Blood sprayed evenly on each side of his face. He went down like a ton of bricks. I instinctively jumped on him, pinning each of his arms under my knees and began punching as hard and as fast as I could. One more punch and one tooth gone. Two punches and another tooth missing. Oddly, the organization of the punches and the missing teeth reminded me of a video game. I lifted my fist again and heard the faint whimpers below me. It wasn't until then that I realized that I had also thrown Billy halfway across the room. Pascal danced on top of the bar as if he were going to wet his pants.

"Please stop," mouths Cliff, as I try to make out the words and watch blood bubbles rise and fall from his nose. His hands lay next to his face as if he were begging for his life. *What a fucking pussy. But by the looks of this, maybe, just maybe, I've gone too far.*

"Brendon, you gotta relax, man!" Billy yells, as he walks toward us with outstretched arms. "Just take it easy. Get off him," he says, grabbing me by the shoulders and leading me out of the bar and into the harsh sunlight of the day.

"You just got us into a lot of trouble. Seriously, you knocked his teeth out, man. That was gross," he says, grabbing my arm. "You looked deranged in there," he says, with a gasp. "Cliff Stoink doesn't have anything to do with this . . . all of this anger you've been feeling."

"He beats his wife," I say.

"We'll never be let back in here now. You know Roy will find out. I could lose my job in the fall. Pascal not only could lose his job, shit, but they'll also ship him back to Mexico!"

"He still beats his wife."

"He could even find out we were drinking."

"Don't be ridiculous," I say.

"Listen to me. You looked like you could have killed someone in there," he says. "You just lost your mother. Just try and settle down. It's like what you said to me earlier. It's not your fault; she pulled the trigger. It's not *your* fault, it's not my fault, and it certainly isn't Cliffy's."

"Just get me the fuck out of here."

CHAPTER 24

What Bridge?

Wow, talk about a one-horse town, thought Deacon, peering through the dust his vehicle had made in the barren parking lot. *There isn't anything out here. Kind of spooky really. I wonder how many people there are up here per square mile. Two cars. I guess that's a good sign. The fewer the people that see me in the company of this sheriff, the better. Shouldn't even be seeing him in public really, but I do need to get some of these questions answered. Hayward was right. I am going to need the sheriff's help on this one. The problem remains that he isn't exactly thrilled at the fact that I am working in his county. Our first meeting went horribly wrong. God, I would like to go back in time and change that one. This case and my friggin' career could hinge on a drunken sheriff. That's just great. Well, Mr. Sheriff, do I have some news for you.*

The pungent smell of ancient cigarette smoke greets Special Agent Deacon as he enters the small bar. There is only one person on each side of the bar, but the sheriff did show, as promised.

"Sheriff, how are you, sir?" he asks.

"I've been better. How about you?"

"Ya know what," asks Deacon, "I think I'm actually startin' to like it up here."

"Why's that? Cuz it isn't Detroit?"

"Yeah. Kind of."

"What were you doin' down there, anyway?"

"Working, Trent, working," Deacon says, motioning to the transfixed bartender. "No traffic up here, the air is fresh, and everyone, and I mean everyone, says hello. It's amazing really. So, Sheriff, someone told me there is a bridge up here I should see," says Special Agent Deacon. *C'mon, Sheriff, spill the beans. Speak to me.*

"What bridge? Oh, they must have been talking about the Mackinac Bridge," he says, with authority. "Sight to be seen. Big bridge, much larger than the

Golden Gate as a matter of fact. But of course, it doesn't have a bunch of queers swinging and hanging all over it," he says, waving his hands wildly. "So on account of that, I guess it doesn't quite get the same attention."

"Really," Deacon says, nodding his head. *Boy, he's had a few by the looks of it. Must of been here awhile.*

"Yeah, we kind of like it that way," replies the sheriff with a slight smile.

"I can see why," answers Deacon. *Gonna have to play the redneck card with this guy. Either that, or he's playing it with me,* he thought, *although something gives me the feeling that the sheriff's not afraid to act dumb if necessary.* "Bartender, can we get another round here?" Deacon says. "Sheriff, can I buy you a drink?"

"You can buy me about five if you'd like."

"Whattya drinkin'?"

"Wild Turkey, on the rocks, and make it a double."

"I'll take the same," Deacon says, realizing the shriveled and yellow bartender had managed to smoke an entire cigarette without once taking it out of her mouth. "Sheriff," says Deacon, nodding his head at a distant corner, "why don't we grab a table?"

"Whatever," the sheriff says, rising from his barstool. "You're buying, right?"

"Yes, I'm buying," he says, as they both made their way to the dimly lit booth. "So you mentioned on the phone that you had that funeral today."

"Oh Jesus, yeah. What a mess. Poor fucking kid I'll tell ya, not to mention a local, gossipy, psychiatrist of ours had another one of her meltdowns. She's a retired physician who's found God and likes to give out his phone number, so to speak. So I had to take care of her and the boy. She's driving me nuts."

"At least you're not in Detroit, right?" Deacon says, with a laugh as the sheriff forces a smile and looks into his drink. "What an experience that was, working down there," continues Deacon. "There's just no place like it."

"Oh, believe me, I know. I grew up down there. So what exactly were you working on down there?"

"I was assigned to a drug task force. Essentially, we were on a lot of stakeouts and a lot of interviewing," he says. "To be honest, I really liked it."

"Honest, huh?" says the sheriff. "Did you actually work in the city?"

"Oh yeah. Downtown the whole time. There was only one rule, and that was to have at least two agents per car if we were technically in the city. That was the rule."

"That's no place for a white man," says the sheriff.

"You got that right. We stuck out like sore thumbs, no question. Hey, it's the nation's murder capital, and now I know why."

"After the '67 riots," says the sheriff, "things have never been the same. I grew up in Livonia, became a cop, and took a transfer north as soon as I could. I suppose that was my version of white flight."

"Sheriff, did you know that it's common knowledge that local Detroit businesses pay the police force to only release approximately 25 percent of the crime that actually occurs in the city to the media?"

"What?" says the sheriff.

"True story," answers Deacon.

"Are you shittin' me?"

"No, seriously. We worked with state and local boys all the time. It's just how the city works, part of the ecosystem, so to speak. No one, and I mean no one, would go into that city if they knew what really went on down there."

"Well, that's fucking insane," the sheriff says, with a sideways glance, "if it's true."

"Oh, it's true," Deacon says, taking a deep swig of his drink. "It was insane. We'd have two to three armed bank robberies *every* single Friday in the city. It was just nuts."

"Why Friday?" asks the sheriff.

"Because Friday is payday. The banks would stock up on cash for people's paychecks. The robberies literally happened like clockwork," says Deacon, as the sheriff finally eyed him with the beginning of respect. "They were some brash fuckers too. They'd even hit the same bank two weeks in a row just to fuck with us."

"Well, that seems like it would make it easier to catch them," says the sheriff.

"Are you kidding me?" Deacon says. "Would you look forward to a gunfight every Friday afternoon with a bunch of thugs that had absolutely nothing to lose?" says Deacon. "They were better armed than us sometimes. But that's where they send a lot of us fresh out of the academy. I guess they figure if you can cut your teeth in downtown Detroit, you could actually survive in this business. Fucking combat zone is what it was."

"So," says the sheriff, "here's the obligatory question. Did you have to shoot anyone?"

"Yes, unfortunately, I did. Twice, actually," Deacon says. "Bartender, another round please," Deacon says. *Gotchya, Sheriff. Gotchya right where I want ya.* "So, Trent, how about you? Ever shoot anyone?"

"Nope. Never had to shoot anyone."

"Good for you. It's a very overrated experience. The problem is it's not like Hollywood. They don't die immediately. They never do. I don't care where they take lead—in the head, the chest, or the guts—they squirm and wiggle and holler and make a big old mess."

"Deacon, how old are you?"

"Twenty-nine."

"Jesus Christ, you are a young fucker. You look it too," the sheriff says. "Drug task force huh? So is that why you're here? Working in my county?"

"What do you mean?" Deacon says.

"Because of drugs," the sheriff says.

"Why, no, actually, it's not."

"Well then, Special Agent Deacon, I am going to ask you one final time. Why the fuck are you in my county?" he says, as the next round of drinks appears from the now-mobilized bartender.

"Trent, mind if I bum one of your smokes? Whisky does it to me every time," he says as the sheriff nods. "Sheriff," he says, watching the bartender make her way to the other end of the room. "Just for the record," he says, whispering as he leans across the table, "we are very aware of your history with Lance Pierson. Trent, he is one of several that we, the feds, are keeping an eye on. What I'm trying to say, Sheriff, is that his being released from Jackson Federal Penitentiary didn't go unnoticed."

"Really," the sheriff gasps, amid a cloud of smoke. "Well, how . . . why the hell didn't you just tell me that up front? How much do you know about Lance Pierson and me?"

"I know he took a carpet knife to your lower back when he escaped from your custody. I know it took over a hundred stitches to put you back together."

"Do you know that he had a handcuff key on his necklace?" the sheriff asks.

"Yeah, I think I heard about that too. Career criminal, they know they're not going to change their ways, and it's just a matter of time before they deal with the law again. Lance Pierson was *ready* to get caught. He knew he'd cross paths with the law. He sounds like a first-class scumbag."

"I would rather eat cat shit with knittin' needles than see that man free of prison. He . . . he . . .," stammers the sheriff, "threatened my family is what he did after we caught him again. I had a brick thrown through my bedroom window after we caught him the second time. How do you think my wife and kids took that?"

"Trent, he's on our radar screen. People like Lance don't exactly come out of prison reformed. All they do is expand their network while they're on the inside."

"He was in town recently," the sheriff says, his cigarette shaking in his hand. "I couldn't believe it. I didn't get a notice of his release or anything. I just can't believe ten years has gone by already."

"Do you know why he was in town? The guy's from Canada, right?" Deacon asks.

"Yeah. He and his brother are originally from Canada. His brother's a DNR officer, believe it or not. He's one of us, works for the law. Based outta Roscommon, he was probably seein' him," the sheriff says.

"No shit?" Deacon says. *Just keep runnin' your mouth, Sheriff. Just keep it coming.*

"Oh yeah, true story. Never liked him either. Arrogant bastard. You know how those fucking French Canadians are."

"How did you know he was here?"

"Well, here's the deal. Lance was in town apparently getting drunk with one of our local assholes Cliff Stoink. They ate all of the tropical fish out of the aquarium at a country club between here and Gladwin, speakin' a which, I am supposed to talk to Cliff about that one. Anyway, the manager of the country club hates Cliff. They go way back. Cliff's on probation for about a dozen things right now."

"He *and* Lance are on probation," Deacon says, correcting the sheriff.

"True."

"Why don't you bring in Cliff to the station for some questioning?"

"You mean about the fish?"

"No," answers Deacon. "When are you planning on bringing him in?"

"I don't know. Why?"

"Because I'd like to be there," Deacon says.

The sheriff stared at him with a confused look on his face.

"Sheriff, tell me this. What is Lance Pierson doing right now that would violate his parole and send him back to prison?" Deacon asks.

"I don't know," the sheriff says.

"I'll bet ya another round of drinks that Cliff Stoink knows."

"I got ya," the sheriff says, nodding. "When do you want me to bring him in?"

"Soon. Sooner the better," Deacon says. "Here is my card again, the real card, that is. This one has my mobile phone number on it."

"Thanks. Yeah, I appreciate it," the sheriff says. "I'm glad, ah, I'm really glad that you guys are watching Lance, seriously. Him being back out kind of rattled me to be honest. When I heard he was here . . . in Roscommon County."

"Well, let's bring in this Cliff Stoink character and see what he knows. Lean on him a little," Deacon says.

"Hopefully, it won't take long. Trust me. You can smell him coming. He may very well be the largest asshole in Roscommon County, and considering the competition, that's sayin' something," the sheriff says.

"Stoink—kind of an odd name, isn't it?"

"Oh, he's just another fucking Polack from Bay City is all he is. Name used to be Stoinkowski or something like that."

"Sheriff, why don't we," he says, offering a toast, "let's put Lance Pierson back in prison for a very long time?"

"Make my day, kid. Make my fuckin' year, I'll tell ya. You don't want me to bring in Lance for questioning too, do you?"

"No, not yet. No good reason yet. Let's see where Cliff takes us first," Deacon says. "Trent, I don't mean to change gears on ya here, but I heard the fishing is pretty good up near Drummond," Deacon says. *Answer this question for me, Sheriff, and I am out of here. According to Frank, Lance should be staying "up at Drummond" during the wire.*

"Drummond Island? Yeah, smallmouth fishing is really good," the sheriff says.

"Where exactly is Drummond Island?" he asks.

"Up north, between the U.P. and Canada. Nothin' much up there except bears and fish. Why's that?"

"I was thinking of getting away for a while after this, you know."

"After what? This case?"

"Yeah, something like that," he says, with a smile. *Thank you, Sheriff. Thank you very much. You are going to be of great help on this one.*

Chapter 25

And This Is Why I Love the Doctor

Sharon Jury paced methodically in her office. *I wonder what that boy is up to. I've been out there in that Godforsaken swamp a half dozen times to visit him in that cramped little shack and haven't even laid an eye on him once. I can't believe that everyone seems to think it's just fine that he's holed up there. It's thoroughly unacceptable. He has absolutely no one and lives in a cabin without power in the middle of nowhere. Yeah, that's just what he needs. But he has to have gotten the notes that I've left him. He must know that at least someone cares. He probably hides when he sees my car coming. Just not in the mood to see anyone. I'll bet that's what he's doing. Maybe Trent is right for once. Maybe I should just leave him alone for a while. It's been almost a month now. He should be past the most critical stage of his recovery by now. But who's seen him? I sure haven't, and what in God's name is he doing every day? He's not around town. I've asked, and Billy's not returning my calls either. I need to get to the bottom of this. I think it's about time to visit Billy and the sheriff and find out exactly what is going on. Yep, that's what I'll do as soon as I get through some of this work. Darn it. Have things stacked up lately. Oh, God, help me. I need to focus, and that just hasn't been easy lately.*

A soft knock on the door brings her to attention as she says, "Come in."

"Hi, Sharon, do you have a moment?" Dr. Jonathon Ray says.

Oh no, what does he want? He's back from his extended vacation or whatever he calls it. Things have been so pleasant around here with him gone, but by the look on his face, those days may be over.

"Not really, Jon," she answers, "to be honest, but come right in. I was just catching up on some work."

"Good. Things been busy?" he asks, sitting down.

"Yes, I'm afraid they have been," she says, "in more ways than one. So how was your vacation?" Dr. Sharon Jury asks, fiddling with the end of her chewed-up pen. "Feels like you have been gone for a while."

"Good, and yes, it was awhile," he says with a huff, "but I'm afraid that's not what I want to talk about."

"Well, OK, shoot," she says. *Oh boy, here it comes.*

"I was looking at our scheduling since I've been gone. You haven't seen many patients at all. Is there something I should know about?"

"Well, no, but things were crazy, Jon. I'm sorry," she says, with a sigh as her hands cover her face and gradually move through her hair. "The week you left was the same week that Maddie Castleman committed suicide. I'm sure you've heard. It was awful. That week was a write-off for me. I canceled all of my patients. I should have told you or offered an explanation or something."

"I know. I heard," he says. "Have you ever lost a patient to suicide before Sharon?" he asks dryly.

"No, I haven't, and I hope I never do again."

"It's not fun, but it is part of the job. We treat people with issues, Sharon, serious issues. That is what we do. That is part of our livelihood."

"I know that, Jon, and you know that I know that. It still doesn't make it any easier."

"I'm not saying it's easy, but it is part of the job."

"Jon, I've known Maddie since school. We grew up together. This *was* a little different."

"OK, relax," he says, with his hands up.

"What's your point?" she asks sharply.

"Don't get defensive, Sharon. I own this office, and you work for me. And I have bills to pay. You have seen an average of one patient per week since I left."

"Jon, I said I'm sorry, and it won't happen again, OK?"

"OK, help me out on that front, will ya?" he says. "But that's not all I need to talk to you about."

"Go ahead," she says, with a quick nod.

"Sharon, you are aware that the back door of the clinic was left open one night while I was gone."

"Well, yes, I am aware," she says. *I was positive I locked up that night. But now, I wonder if I forgot to lock the door when I left. But that is always the last thing I check.* "And yes, I was working that night. So you can blame that one on me if you want to."

"Sharon, I'm not blaming anything on you. Quite frankly, you are acting really odd right now. Are you sure everything is OK?"

"Yes, Jon, everything is OK."

"Sharon, I had Jerry take an inventory yesterday, just in case. I mean after all, someone could have broken in here that night and forgot to lock the door when they left. The locks in this building are antiquated at best, who knows?"

"OK," she says, with a lowered chin. "And?"

"Are you aware of what is missing?" he asks.

What the hell is he getting at? Oh, not now, Jon, not today. Art school—I knew it. I should have given it a try. I even had my mother's support on that one. I wouldn't be dealing with a micromanaging annoyance like Jonny Ray right now. "No, Jon, you lost me there."

"The bottle of morphine is missing from the lab. Our only bottle. Are you trying to tell me that you aren't aware of this?"

What? What on earth is he talking about?

"Sharon, did you hear what I said?" asks Dr. Ray.

"Yes, of course. I just don't know how . . . I just don't know how this can be. I mean are you saying that someone broke into the office?" she says. "I just thought that one of us forgot to lock the back door."

"Sharon, we've known each other for a long time. I want you to level with me."

"What are you insinuating?"

"I don't know anymore, Sharon," interrupts Dr. Ray.

"Jon, I admit that I had been giving shots to Jeffrey Stoink—rest his soul—but he passed a week later. That was two weeks ago. He was eighty-two. Meredith just didn't want him in any pain at the end."

"You're the only person on staff who has signed out any morphine usage this year," says the doctor. He stands up. "What do you want me to think? That you know nothing of this?"

"I can't believe you think I'm responsible for this!"

"I'm just dealing with the facts, Sharon. And the fact of the matter is that you have been rather disengaged from your job and now this."

"Well," she says.

"No *well*, Sharon. Are you using morphine? Answer the question and look me in the eyes when you do it," he says, crossing his hands.

"No, absolutely not. And I'll take a test to prove it," she says, through teary eyes. *Take that, you stupid jerk.*

"OK, that's all I needed to hear," he says. "I don't know then. Maybe one of Jeff's family members heard you had been over and broke into the office or something. I don't know," he says, again throwing his arms into the air.

"I don't even remember using the word *morphine* with her," Sharon says.

What if . . . no, oh no—not Brendon. What? That can't be. That's impossible. Who would? Oh, God, no, this can't be true. Oh no, oh no. Oh, God, no. I think I'm going to be sick. Not Brendon. Not him. Not again. He told me that he was awake the whole time, and I didn't believe him. He'll shoot himself into oblivion with that much morphine. What if he ODs? What if that's what he wants? It has to be him. That's enough to kill a horse. You could open the back door if you really wanted to. That door has never shut correctly. Oh, this can't be true. If he was awake, then he heard us talk to the paramedics. I am responsible for this, not to mention I could lose my license over a situation like this. This can't be. This absolutely cannot be.

"Sharon, just try and relax. I have been dreading this conversation all day, OK? You understand that, don't you?" he says, sitting back down. "These things happen. Pharmacies get robbed all the time. People will do whatever it takes to get their fix. I was more worried about you than anything. I knew how heavily involved you were in Maddie's treatment. When I heard what she'd done, to be honest, I wasn't surprised," he says.

"OK. It's just upsetting, you know. I have always taken my job seriously and then Maddie. It has been awful. So where do we go from here?"

"I don't know. I'll file a police report, we'll order another bottle of morphine, and that's it, I guess."

"Do you have to call the police?" she says, fiddling with the same wrinkled pen. "I mean that's all we need is them poking their nose into this," she says.

"Well, yes, of course, we do. That stuff's not cheap, you know, not to mention it is a controlled and illegal substance. Plus I want our insurance to cover this."

"Well, let the state cops know that they can call me if they need to. I mean if they have any questions or anything," she says. *God, let him please call the state police and not the sheriff. Trent will kill me. Please help me on this one, please. Just this one. This can't be . . . this cannot . . . oh no! Be careful. Be careful with him. I have to lie about this. I'll lose my job if I don't. I could easily lose my job for this mess. I hate this. I hate doing this. But I cannot pin this on Brendon. No. Not him. This is my fault. I can't turn him in for this. And what if Trent hears of this? I have to get this stuff out of Brendon's hands. I've got to do this on my own. I own this one. I cannot believe that I am responsible for this. I've got to do this today.*

"Thanks, I will. By the way, I'm going to get all the locks changed too. Should have done years ago, you know."

"Yes, Doctor, I know."

"I'll get you the new keys."

"Yes, please do."

Chapter 26

Bring 'Em In

The slippery and lovely nozzle of the bottle left the sheriff's mouth after a long hard pull. *Um, that's it, much better. First one of the day is always the best. Much better indeed, thank you. Yes. Thank you for making this day bearable, and maybe, just maybe, I won't have to wring someone's freakin' neck today. Yep, time for a quick smoke and a breath mint, and no one will be the wiser. Gotta keep an eye on that fucking Southern deputy of mine. My gut tells me that he wouldn't mind sitting at this very desk someday. And this desk—this desk is mine.*

The shrill bark of the PA began, "Sheriff, Joe Deacon is still here, and Lawrence just brought in Cliffy Stoink."

"Good. Sadie, send Deacon in. Send him in immediately," the sheriff says, stamping out his cigarette.

"Sheriff," asks Sadie, "Cliffy looks just awful. Is it true that Brendon Castleman beat him up?"

"Sadie, where did you hear that?" asks the sheriff.

"Ah," she answers, "at the library."

"At the library," he says. "Sadie, that is none of your business." *Jesus Christ, the rumor mill is already churning—that's the last thing I need. Can't anything go smoothly in this town?*

Joe Deacon's sleek figure opened his door and entered the room after a quick knock. *Look at him. The kid looks like an FBI agent, even in plainclothes.*

"Hey, Deacon, you're here, and Lawrence just brought Cliff in. Let's get this thing started," the sheriff says.

"Yeah, OK," Deacon says. "No offense, Sheriff, but I didn't think it would take you four weeks to bring him in."

"Listen to you," the sheriff says. *Back off, Deacon. I am not in the mood.* "It's only been three weeks, by the way. Now listen. The guy pretty much disappeared. Even his wife claimed to not know where he was. But then again, poor woman is probably used to that," the sheriff says.

"Sounds a little fishy, don't ya think?" Deacon asks.

"Yeah, it does, especially considering the guy's on probation."

"Trent, I saw Lawrence bring him in out in the lobby. Awfully rough-lookin' character. Looked like he'd just had the shit kicked out of him or something."

"Oh, he did. I should probably be looking into that, but I'm sure he deserved it," the sheriff says, with a sigh as he folds his arms. "He apparently started givin' poor Brendon an earful of shit at a local bar, and Brendon beat the hell out of him," he says. "You remember that boy who lost his mother to suicide? Those two got into a fight, same day as the damn funeral. Poor kid. What a day he had. But Cliff shouldn't have been runnin' his mouth."

"The kids a little prone to violence?"

"No, not at all," the sheriff says.

"Cliff's a little rough around the edges huh?"

"That, Deacon, would be an understatement," the sheriff says.

"His walk seemed to be a little off too?" Deacon asks.

"Oh yeah. His walk is a little off, all right. And that's not all that's a little off. That man's lucky to be alive right now. He was riding a three-wheeler around midnight, drunk as usual, and hit a cow doing over fifty miles per hour," the sheriff says, with a pointed finger.

"What?" Deacon asked, with a sideway's glance.

"No shit," the sheriff says. "One of those three-wheeled ATVs. Anyway, Lawrence found him lyin' in the ditch the next morning, still breathing. He tore the cow right in half, one of the damnedest things I've ever seen. Hasn't had a driver's license since, and the judge banned him from operating any motor vehicle for the rest of his life. Still hasn't paid the farmer for that cow now that I think about it."

"That is unbelievable," Deacon says.

"Yeah, it is," the sheriff says. "Deacon, let me tell you something about our boy Cliffy Stoink out there, and I mean this as the truth. I was at a local bar years ago and watched Cliff bet a flatlander from Detroit twenty bucks that he could shit his pants. Well, to make the long story short, he did just that—at the bar! He took the guy's money, ordered another beer, drank it, and got up and left. It was one of the most disgusting things I have ever witnessed."

"Jesus Christ, you got some real wackos up here or what."

"Oh, he's just a good, old-fashioned welfare redneck," the sheriff says. "Most of his family now live in St. Helen or St. Felon, as I call it. These types are dime a dozen over there."

"And why's that?"

"It's the closest exit north of Flint and Detroit where they feel like they're up north. All of them are the same, runnin' from the law, so we get to deal with them up here."

"Now, Sheriff," Deacon says, "back to the task at hand. Remember, Cliff's gonna lie for at least forty-five minutes. Trust me. They always do."

"And how exactly do you know that?" the sheriff asks.

"Trust me. We did a lot of these over the past two years in Detroit, mostly drug-related stuff," Deacon says. "What I'm getting at is we might be here for a while."

"OK," the sheriff says, with a smile. *This kid thinks he knows it all already. Look at him. I saw this coming a mile away. I've got a Master's degree from U of M and he thinks he's got everything all figured out.*

"Now, remember," Deacon says, "if at any point, he uses the term *swear to God* or he swears on someone's life, you look at me, we gain eye contact, and immediately leave the room."

"What?" the sheriff asks. "Why?"

"Seriously, as soon as these guys swear on a Bible or use the word *honestly*, you know they're hiding something. It means they're lying."

"Wow, that's quite a formula ya got there," the sheriff says.

"I'm not kidding," Deacon says.

"Keep this in mind, Deacon. I know this fucking idiot."

"Take it easy, Sheriff. We're here for the same reason, aren't we?" Deacon asks. "I did say that I had done some interviewing of this kind, didn't I?"

"Oh yeah," the sheriff says. "You seemed real proud too."

"Well, I'm just tellin' ya."

"Now you listen to me, Deacon. I've done some interviewing myself and let's not forget whose name is on that office over there," the sheriff says.

"Seriously, Sheriff, give it a try," Deacon says. "If I'm wrong on this, I won't ever bug you with my advice again."

"Let's go, for Christ's sake," the sheriff says, standing up as Deputy Lawrence knocks on the partially open door.

"Come in," the sheriff says, rolling his eyes at Deacon.

"Sheriff, how can I help?" Lawrence asks, with a finger on his chin. "I kind of interviewed him myself on the way over here, and I think I have a pretty good idea of—"

"Lawrence," interrupts the sheriff. *The son of a bitch was listening to our conversation. I could fire him for that.* "You just watch the phones. Sadie's on lunch and will be back by one."

"I'm sick of bein' a secretary around here," Lawrence says.

"C'mon, Joe, let's do this thing before we waste any more time already," he says, stomping out of his office and past the deputy and into the hall. He glances over his shoulder to make sure Deacon is following him. The sheriff opens the door as Deacon quickly walks into the room toward the far corner of the little used interrogation room. There, Cliffy sat with a cocky grin on his face as if he were proud of his newly missing teeth. The blackness around his eyes had altered to a faint green line around each eye.

That boy gave you a good, old-fashioned ass kickin', didn't he? Damn, he smells of beer already, and its 10:00 a.m., for Christ's sake. He may be the only person in Roscommon County that beats me to the first nip of the day.

"Cliff," Deacon says, breaking the silence with an icy stare, "why don't we get down to business?"

"Sheriff," Cliffy says, turning his head away from Deacon and to the sheriff, "this ain't about eatin' all those tropical fish at Sugar Springs, is it? I'll pay Mel for those, I promise. I'm real sorry about that. We was awfully drunk that day. I mean," stumbles Cliff, "I knew we shouldn't have been in there and done that. It did seem like a mistake the next day, if that means anything."

"Gee, Sheriff," Deacon says, in a high-pitched voice, "sounds like Cliffy knows the difference between right and wrong. Now, cut the shit and get down to business, Mr. Stoink," Deacon says.

"What business is that, sir?" Cliffy asks, raising his handcuffed hands. "I'm sorry, do I know you?"

"Cliff, the business of today is your life," Deacon replies, approaching the table. "How about it? What would you give for it?"

"What?" Cliff asks sharply.

"Don't act stupid, Cliff. We already know about that part," Deacon says, slamming his fist down into the table. "How about I knock out what few teeth you have left and treat you like the little bitch that you are?" Deacon says. "How does that sound?"

Jesus Christ, what is he up to? thought the sheriff. *This is no way to start an interview.*

"Oh, oh," Cliff says, under his breath as the chains of the handcuffs begin to jingle and shake.

"Sheriff, do me a favor. Take his handcuffs off. I don't want Cliff to consider himself defenseless."

"OH!" Cliffy screams, at the top of his lungs as Deacon approaches him and brings his face next to Cliff's.

"That's what they do to people in prison, Cliff," Deacon whispers, into his ear, "especially Jackson. Ever know anyone who's done time in Jackson, Cliff?"

"Probably," Cliff mutters.

"Probably?" Deacon shouts, again slamming his fist into the table. "*Probably* isn't an answer. Why don't you just spill the beans as to what is going on?"

"About what?" Cliff asks.

"It's your turn to talk, Cliff. I'd take advantage of the gift you've been given," Deacon whispers.

Just what the hell is this J. Edgar up to? Screaming and then whispering. Look at him, passive aggressive. He's really in his element right now. I knew he was keeping me in the dark about something in that first meeting. Cocksucker anyways. But what the hell is he really up to?

"Well, this just ain't fair," cries Cliffy.

"Why should it be?" answers Deacon.

"Oh fuck," sobs Cliff, snapping his head in the sheriff's direction. "C'mon, Trent, I've known ya for a long time. What the hell is this about?" Cliff says. "You gotta tell me. I ain't been driven nothin' but that moped a little since my license's bein' takin' away. Damn straight."

"Hey, Cliff," Deacon says, roughly grabbing Cliff's hairy chin, "if you haven't noticed yet, I'm the one speaking to you," Deacon says, smiling. "And if I need to remind you of that, I will."

"OK, OK, stop. What do you want to know?"

"How are they doin' it, Cliff? That's it. Simple fucking question. How the hell are they doing it?" Deacon asks, within three inches of Cliffy's foul-smelling face.

How are they doing what? thought the sheriff. *Nothing worse than being stroked, especially by a Fed.*

"Doing what? I don't know what yer talkin' about," Cliff says.

"You little piece of white trash, you fucking listen to me. How are they getting it into the country? That's it. You give me that little tidbit of information; and you walk out of here; and this never happened," Deacon says, glancing at the sheriff and giving him a wink. "Let's face it, Cliff. You are nothing. But if you answer my question, you could be something."

Kids got some balls. I'll give him that. But he does need to remember that he isn't in Motown anymore. And what in the world does Cliff have himself involved in?

"Sheriff, can you leave the two of us alone for a few minutes?"

"They get it," Cliff stutters, "up north somewhere. I don't know everything. All I know is that I would have to meet Lance in Grand Rapids if we were gonna do a deal."

Jesus Christ, what do you know? I cannot believe he brought up Lance's name before we did. That's damn near brilliant. Unbelievable. Maybe this federal boy does know his stuff.

"What are they dealing, Cliff?"

"Well, I thought you knew that part," Cliff says, shifting his weight in the chair.

"Answer the fucking question, Cliff."

"H—, ya know," Cliff whispers, staring down at the table.

"No, I don't know. Spell it out for us, Cliff," Deacon says.

"Heroin," he replies, exchanging glances with them both.

Heroin? What the hell is going on here? In Roscommon County, heroin? You got to be kidding me. Bingo! So that's what Deacon was hiding by coming into my county. But why?

"How do they get it into the country, Cliff?"

"I don't know, seriously. I don't know *that.*"

"Use that big fucking melon of yours," Deacon says. "How would you get it in?"

"They could be drivin' it across the border from the Soo for all I know," Cliff gasps, as tears start to roll down his face. "Jesus Christ, Trent," he says, sobbing, looking at the sheriff, "can I at least have a fucking cigarette or something?"

Trent nods his head, gaining eye contact with Deacon. "Why don't you go and get Cliff a cigarette from Lawrence?" he says, to Deacon. *I need to get Deacon outta the room for a second,* he thought. *Cool him off a bit. He knows damn well I have a pack on me as I nod my head again at the door. Good. He's going.* The sheriff approaches the startled man, smelling the strong aroma of ammonia. *Dear sweet Jesus, look at the floor. Jesus Christ, I'm standing on it. He's pissed his freakin' pants, for Christ's sake. I ain't cleanin' that up. Lawrence is going to be real happy with that job, let me tell ya. Ha-ha. I gotta fire that guy, and I gotta do it soon. Well, after he cleans up the piss, that is. Maybe having to clean up Cliffy's urine will be the straw that breaks the camel's back. Wouldn't that be nice? Rather have him quit than have to deal with firing him. No love lost there.*

"Cliff," the sheriff says, as Deacon finally shuts the door and leaves the room, "I want ya to relax a bit now; and I want you to tell this man and me everything you know; and that's it. From here, you'll be let go, and none of this ever happened. I mean that. You do that, and I'll call Mel out at Sugar Springs and let him know you and I had a word and that he shouldn't press charges, speaking of which, you are never to step on that property again. Understood?"

"Yes, sir," Cliff says.

"Even if your wife does work there."

"Yes, sir."

Deacon quickly walks back in with a cigarette and lighter.

"If anyone asks about you speaking to the cops, you tell them it was about the incident at Sugar Springs. Got it?" the sheriff says.

"Yes, sir," Cliff whimpers.

"Here's that smoke, Cliffy," Deacon says, ramming the white cylinder into Cliff's mouth. "Now, Sheriff, where were we?"

"I think we were talking about how they get the stuff into the country," the sheriff says, glaring at Deacon.

"See, they—" Cliff says, blowing out smoke.

"Define *they*, Cliff," interrupts Deacon. "Let's talk about this on a third-grade type of level. Make things a little easier for you."

"Lance and someone. I honestly don't know who. But he did mention he had a partner a couple of times."

"Who do you think his partner is?"

"I honestly don't know."

"Who would be your guess?" Deacon says, giving the sheriff a quick glance.

"I don't know. Probably someone he met in prison. That would be my guess."

"Sheriff, whatta ya think? I feel like I'm being lied to," Deacon says.

"Well, Cliff, what else is there we should know?" the sheriff asks. "Maybe Mel should press charges. What would that mean to you? And how would that affect your probation? Actually, I think that could send you away for quite a while."

"Sheriff, I swear on my mother's life, I don't know," Cliff pleads.

Deacon and Mayfair's eyes met simultaneously as they quickly head for the door.

"Seriously, guys, I swear to God, honestly," Cliff pleads, as the door slammed behind him. The sheriff and Deacon looked at each other and stared at Cliff through the two-way mirror.

"Good Lord, look at him, Trent. He's crying again," Deacon says.

"Yeah, he knows we're watching him, he's pretending. Anyway, exactly where are you taking this, Joe? Level with me."

"Who do you think is Lance's partner? That's the magic question."

"You tell me, kid. Could be his brother for all I know. But he's a member of the law. Never could stand that guy."

"Really." Deacon nods. "Well, if it is him, this changes a few things, don't you think?"

"Well, yeah," the sheriff says. *Jesus Christ, bringing down a member of law enforcement in my county. Wow! Now that would make the paper.*

"That would make this an internal investigation," Deacon says, "speaking of which, what county does Frank work in?"

"Frank, huh?" the sheriff says. "You already know his first name, hah, Deacon? Or are you going to tell me that you *happen* to remember his name from the last time we talked?"

"Well, I'll tell you this. I do know that his ex-con brother is smuggling the purest form of heroin known to man into the interior of the United States."

"You knew that before today, didn't you?"

"Yes, Trent. Quite frankly, I did."

"You and I are going to need to have a talk after this. I don't appreciate being left in the dark with these things. I've been doing this for fifteen years, young man, and you're on my watch right now."

"Understood, Sheriff, and I do appreciate your time. Please remember that. Now, what I was getting at earlier, Frank Pierson is based out of the DNR headquarters in Roscommon, correct?"

"Yep, he's been out there for almost twelve years I'd say."

"Now, Sheriff, that's your county. I mean this is *your* county, which means I can use you on this, understand?" Deacon says. "Trent, I'm gonna need your help on this one."

"Yeah, well, I don't even know what the fuck is going on."

"OK, OK, just roll with me on this one. Now, what about Cliff? I think he's already told us what he knows. He sure as hell doesn't want to implicate a member of law into this. He isn't that dumb. Guy can already picture himself in a courtroom over that one. I say we play it cool now and loosen the strain. Let him leave here with some dignity, make him feel important, and that way, we can use him again. We need his set of eyes and ears out there. We need to get him some new pants, by the way. I'll cool him off now, and then you talk him down. He needs to think of us as his friends now, got it?" Deacon says, with a wink.

"Sounds good. *Now* we're on the same page," the sheriff says, opening the door of the small smoke-filled interviewing room.

"Cliff," Deacon says, pulling a chair next to Cliff, "I just want you to know that I appreciate your time here today only because you held up your end of the bargain. You keep your eyes and ears peeled out there for us, and we'll try to remember that this little conversation we just had never happened. Cliff, do you understand what I'm saying?"

"Not really."

"What I'm saying is that you never talked to us, period. This visit was about the fish. Considering all the scumbags you hang out with, do you think they'd be happy that you were talking to a couple of cops?"

"No."

"Now do you get my point?"

"Yes, sir."

"So we're going to make sure they know why you were here. What do you say we slap a fake fine on you, or you pay Mel for his losses? That would give you something to grumble about at the bar," the sheriff says.

"Sheriff, I'm going to go and see if Lawrence and I can get Mr. Stoink here a new pair of drawers," he says, as the sheriff nods his head.

"Cliff, you smell like a brewery, and it's 11:00 a.m.," the sheriff says.

"Yeah, I had a few last night."

You're making me thirsty, the sheriff thought. *Guy drinks beer in the morning. Never thought of that. Too time-consuming. It would take me an hour just to get where I need to be.* "You had a few last night or a few this morning?"

"I only had two this morning."

"Cliff, just keep your nose clean. I don't want you in my jail again, but I do have a job for you to do."

"Yes, sir."

"Cliff, you do remember what Lance did to my life, don't you?"

"Yes, Trent, I do," Cliff says.

"You and I have known each other longer than you've known that piece of shit. Remember that. Don't be afraid to call me if you think you need to, but we shouldn't really see each other, ya know what I mean?"

"Yep, I do. That's fine with me."

"Now, follow me, and you can use the showers here and be on your way."

"Thank you, sir," Cliff says, as the sheriff leaves the room.

"Lawrence, come here for a second," the sheriff says, closing the door behind him. Lawrence ambles around the corner with his usual sheepish grin. Lawrence had always maintained an uncanny ability to look as if he were in midyawn and had just been woken from a very deep sleep. *He could use a good smack across the face,* the sheriff thought. "Now, Lawrence, take off Cliffy's cuffs and show him to the showers and then take him home. Use your car when you take him home, not the squad car, got it?" the sheriff says. "By the way, I also need ya to clean up the mess that he made in there."

"What?" Lawrence asks. "What mess?"

"You'll see it when you go in there," the sheriff says.

"Hey," spouts Lawrence, "I ain't no God damn janitor, ya know."

"That's an order, Larry. Now get the job done, or I'll find someone to do it for ya."

"What? Hey, don't ever call me Larry," Lawrence says in disgust. "I told you to never call me that right from the beginning!" he says. "I never asked for anything 'round here, just that ya'll never call me that."

"You know what, Larry," the sheriff says, sticking out his chin as Deacon appears at the opposite end of the hallway, holding a pair of sweatpants, "you don't seem to be very into your job lately."

"Oh yeah, well, at least I'm sober," Lawrence says loudly, making sure Deacon heard him.

"What did you just say?" the sheriff says.

"You heard me."

"Fuck you, Larry," the sheriff says, grabbing Lawrence by the throat and lifting him off the floor. The two men became an instant tangled mass of arms and legs as Deacon ran down the narrow hallway and closed the distance.

"Guys, guys!" he barks. "Hey, break it up! Stop it now!" Deacon says, finding himself in the middle of the mess. "Lawrence," Deacon screams, holding him with one hand, "you tend to Cliffy! Sheriff, you come with me God damn it," he says, trying to catch his breath. "We'll have that chat we were talking about." They glared at each other as Deacon held a hand on each of their pounding chests. He grabbed Trent by the shoulders and led him down the hallway as Lawrence put his hands on his hips.

"What the hell was all that about?" Deacon asks.

"Why the hell don't you tell me?" the sheriff says, turning around. "Yer not in fucking Detroit anymore, ya know, with yer interviewing style in there."

"Yeah, well, starting a fistfight with your only deputy isn't exactly a good way to end an interview."

"The door's right over there, Deacon. Don't let it hit you in the ass when you leave."

Chapter 27

A Visitor

There was a point during the spring and early summer when absolutely nothing occurred. I saw no one for weeks on end and hiked and fished as if it were my job. I've never felt so little for so long—I remember these as being wonderfully painless times.

Just me and the green buds forcing their way through slivers of bark toward the light, the northern air beginning to finally smell of life again. Today is just another gorgeous morning within the confines of the Deadstream Swamp, and, more importantly, another beautiful day of being left alone.

My renewed existence now allows me to basically remain solo and focus on what is truly important. What is clearly evident is my newfound sanity and this new light that has now been placed directly in front of me. There will never be a day that passes when I won't find myself visiting the thought of her very still body that silent morning. It has been over a month since this hell arrived, and now, finally, I am free of what you have brought upon us. You, Mother, cast this hell around as if you were at a wedding, dispersing rice. And now you are gone, having lost complete control over this world of mine.

I recognized from a very early age that we had all been dealt a certain deck of cards in this life. I never once questioned this conundrum or the fact that my legs were uncomfortably skinny to look at. I just dealt with it. My gym teacher once told me that he'd seen better legs on a table, and he'd meant it. It was precisely then that I knew I must face this small hurdle and somehow find a remedy to this situation. It took me only a week of wearing sweatpants instead of shorts to overcome this small hurdle. But what I do know is that this past month has not been fair, and I am now starting to feel that it wasn't meant to be.

I distinctly remember the smell of entering our bathroom that morning. There she lay oh so still, the smell of immediate death and decay utterly taking my breath away. Everything made sense up to this point, and then the crumble began that continues to this day. I need to quit asking questions and thoroughly stop acknowledging the hangover of it all. Don't just be another fatality. Don't be a victim—anything but that. There are different angles that can help take away the pain, even if only for the transient moment.

I've had plenty of time to think. My mother may very well have wanted to see my father's face again, and this could be the reason that she pulled the trigger. She could have just wanted to see him again. After all, I would surely love to see him too, even if it was for the first time for me and my memory. So maybe I'll join them.

My life now slowly revolves around the simple fact that I must and will leave this place. I will find a way, and I will never set foot in this town again. Furthermore, I will see the blond of Lilly's hair once again, and on this occasion, it won't be in my dreams. Her golden arm in my hand just once more. Doesn't one need to dream? Isn't this state of mind what saves us from the horror of reality? I'll follow that girl 'til the end of time no matter if I am in actual fact chasing a dust trail created by her very own blue eyes. Other than a few miles and the Atlantic Ocean, what is the real obstacle? And why can I not achieve life at her social level? Why? You tell me why. So what if it kills me? And if it did, would anyone really notice?

The now-familiar sound of tires in the gravel brings my attention to my most recent visitor who is probably under the false pretense that checking up on me is a necessity. No one ever drives down this small dead-end dirt road, and if they do, they are looking for me. It's probably Dr. Jury. God damn it, here we go again. I take my position in the usual shuffle about the cabin that takes place when certain objects lying about need to be put away. This doesn't take but a second as I glide out the back door of my hallowed cabin and down along the bank to the water and into the thick surrounding brush. When are people going to get it? I think as I attempt to pry apart two large tag alders. They aren't welcome here.

Ah, the mosquitoes are starting to show. This is miserable—this is absolute crap is what it is. Here I am out here on my hands and knees for what seems to feel like an eternity. Oh boy, look who has finally arrived. He's made his first visit to see how I am faring. This isn't good. No, this may be far more difficult considering my new pursuant is Billy, and he knows me and the ways about me. Just leave already, young man. Go home to your now-perfect home with your mother and father. They miss you. Oh Jesus, he's outside of the cabin already. Look at him, craning his neck. Damn it. Stubborn bastard will probably be here for hours.

"Come out and come out now!" he yells, across the woods and water surrounding us. "I know you're here!" he screams again.

Jesus, Billy, quiet down already. I can hear you just fine. I'm less than twenty yards away. "You can avoid that doctor, and you can avoid the sheriff, but you can't avoid me. I'm not fucking kidding. I'll spend the night out here if I have to," he says, into the silence of the marsh. "I've got the next two days off, even brought my fly rod. Yep, think I'll stay out here for the next—"

"God damn it, Billy," I say, standing up and brushing off the dirt and leaves and swatting at the now-hovering cloud of mosquitoes around my head, "what the hell are you doing out here?"

"Look at you," he says with a chuckle, "lyin' in the brush, and I knew you would be. What's wrong with you?"

"Go to hell."

"Hey, I was just making sure yer OK. Seriously, no one's seen you lately."

"Give me a break," I say.

"What have you been doin'?"

"Just give me a fucking cigarette already," I say, trying to hide a smile. It was good to see Billy. I've missed him.

"Good to see ya, kid," he says, with a slap on the shoulder. "Hasn't been the same kind of summer without you around."

"Yeah, whatever," I mumble, as he lights my cigarette.

"Seriously, the marina has been rockin' since Memorial Day bein' here."

"Yeah, I'm sure it has."

"All those suburban girls from Detroit are here, and they ain't gotten any uglier, let me tell you."

"I'm sure you're right about that."

"Couple of 'em even asked about you."

"No surprises there, I guess."

"C'mon, there's got to be something ya need. Ya got groceries, for Christ's sake?"

"Yes, I do."

"What can I help ya with?"

"You want to help me, Billy? Why don't you drive down to Detroit and get that money from my aunt? Do that for me, will ya?"

"Well, OK," he says, playing with his cigarette. "But I don't know where she lives and—"

"Of course, you don't. Listen, I may need to borrow your car."

"For what?"

"I need that money. Trent said we haven't even had one interested buyer in the house yet."

"I'll go with you to see your aunt."

"No, you don't need to go with me. See? This is why I don't need your help. You don't ever listen to me."

"Why can't I go with? It's my car after all."

"Screw it. I'll just take the Jeep."

"No, no, you don't need to take that rickety old thing. You can use my car. It's just—"

"It's just what?"

"Why can't I go with you?" he asks, with his head tilted back.

"Because I'm going to have to speak to her, right? And I don't want you around for that. She fucked up by missing the funeral; and she's out of line; and I'm going to tell her exactly that."

"Well, I'll just sit in the car the whole time. Promise."

"Quit being so damn insistent."

"Listen, you need contact with people. You need people around you right now."

"Oh, do I now? You're startin' to sound like the doctor. So I see you two have spent some time together recently."

"Trent agrees too."

"Oh, does he? Well, isn't that nice to know. Is that the plan, Billy?"

"It's not a plan. It's just that—"

"Fuck all of you! You don't understand a thing about—"

"People care about you, Brendon. Get over it!" he says, with an intense stare.

"So that's why the doctor has been stopping by the cabin every other day leaving her stupid little notes. She even left a Bible the last time."

"Listen, this is just the way that it is, and just because your mother's gone now doesn't mean that we no longer exist. Get that through your head!"

"Fuck you too."

"Brendon, look around you. This place doesn't even have power. You're in the middle of nowhere. You just can't—"

"Yes, it does. It has propane."

"That's not my point. We care about you, and you aren't going to stay out here all summer all by yourself."

"I just don't want . . .," I say, as my eyes began to water, "I just don't want to have to deal with anyone's shit right now. Understand?"

"Yes, Brendon, I do. And that's to be expected. But life goes on, brother. And those of us who love you aren't going to just up and disappear, OK?"

"OK."

"Let's take a spin. C'mon," he says, pointing his head toward his car, "hop in. We'll go to my house. You can use our phone to call your aunt," he says. "Hey, and while we're at it, when is the last time you spoke to Lilly?"

"It's been over three months now."

"Well, don't let this past month fuck that up too. You need to call her."

"Yeah, maybe."

"She doesn't deserve that. You two had big plans. You need to chase that one, man," he says, pulling out a cigarette. "A man without dreams is no man at all. You know who told me that?"

"Yeah."

"You did, don't underestimate things with her because of your mom's actions. You care about that girl. You need to call her, and you need to immediately," he says, gazing across the marsh in front of us.

"You're probably right."

"There ain't no probably about it," he says, turning his attention to me. "And if you don't call her, I will. I always thought she had a thing for me."

"Sure, she did, yeah. You calling her?" I say, with a laugh. "Let me grab a few things from inside, and we'll go."

"All right. Hey, you need to get some sun, man," he says, wincing. "You looked pale as a ghost these days."

"Thanks, man. It's good to see you too."

"No, seriously, you're as pale as a sheet."

Chapter 28

Rolling the Dice

"Hey, Deacon, sit down. Ya hungry?" asks the tan face and white teeth, with an overly firm handshake for a man in his fifties. "Welcome back to Traverse. How ya been?"

"Good. Busy."

"I listened to the taps. What did ya think?" Hayward says, with a wink.

"I thought it was excellent, very exciting. I mean to be involved with," I say, realizing for the first time that I was again nervous in his presence. "It was the first tap that I had to set up, outside of class, that is," I say. *Good work. Why don't you just remind him some more that you're basically fresh out of the academy?*

"Sorry, I haven't been here to help or at least to strategize," he says, shaking his head. "I didn't mean to just dump this on your lap. Well, that's a lie," he says, with a laugh. "We have a lot on our plate right now. I have a few too many irons in the fire, so to speak. I've been in Chicago since we last met."

"Hey, no problem," I say. "I've been all over this case every day. Obviously, this is all I do. I just—"

"Chicago is an absolute mess right now in regard to heroin, and these Pierson boys aren't helping the cause," interrupts Hayward, under his breath. "Get this. We actually think that the Colombian's entire operation is being run inside the water department of the city. That should be a fun one to bring down. It's kind of scary, but we've tracked it. Looks like their entire Midwestern branch is being hidden behind an office of the government. I wonder how high the money goes up the food chain in that city. Trust me. We'll find out, and we'll get them when the timing is right. All signs point to the same man in the Windy City. And that's the part that makes me nervous. I'd call it the most corrupt city in the nation, but you've worked in Detroit!" he says, with a laugh and a slap of his hand to the table. *Hayward seems awfully comfortable with information around me. Good. I don't need him keeping me in the dark about anything involving this case.*

"Anyway, back to our case," he says. "Talk to me, what is your gut feeling right now?"

"Well, my gut feeling is that you were 100 percent correct," I answer. "Both brothers are obviously involved, and—"

"Yeah, it's like we thought it was," he says, again lowering his voice. "I just met with one of our guys in Chicago. He's a mole for us in the largest Mexican cartel in the heroin trade, and it's exactly as we thought."

"Which is?" I ask, scratching my head. *Guy interrupts me one more time, and we're going to have to have a word.*

"They don't even know who it is, son. That's the beauty of it. Like I told you before, they'd just kill 'em if they knew. It's a pretty competitive business, you know, the kind of biz where laws don't apply, if you know what I mean."

"Yeah, I think I do."

"But *they* don't know, and *we* do, correct?" he says, giddily.

"Yes, sir. Correct."

"I've been doin' this for a while, kid, and this is the first one that I've ever seen when the cartels don't know who their competition is. It's fucking brilliant really. Usually, it's us trying to arrest these assholes while the Colombians are trying to put a bullet in their heads."

"Really?"

"The Colombians are usually more effective, by the way."

"Seriously?"

"Yep, seriously. I admire these two fucking idiots to be honest."

"Why?"

"Because—don't you get it?—they figured out a glitch in the system, in *our* system. And for that, I owe them for the education. The Colombians and all the South American cartels," he says, waving his hands and laughing, "not to mention all of the shit that pours out of Afghanistan—that's expected and very easy to track. But this—this is different. Remember, the drug's genetic content is Asian, and we still don't know how they are getting it into Michigan unless, of course, you know something I don't."

"Well, I do have—"

"Now listen, if they would have been bringing those drugs into Detroit and Chicago directly, we would have pinched 'em by now, but I don't think they are."

"Hayward," I say, in a raised voice, "as I was saying, I have my suspicions. How about the marina comment in the tap? What do you think?" *The guys had a few too many cups of coffee this morning or something.*

"Ya know, I've been thinking about that," he says, taking another bite of food, "as you know from my faxes. But something isn't making sense here. This isn't exactly Miami, ya know. How on earth are they getting it into the country? I mean if they are indeed using a boat? Maybe they have it flown into Canada and boat it in from there. Maybe they're speaking in code over the pay phone," he says, cocking his head to one side.

"Well, I don't—"

"One of my early hunches is that they were using a float plane, and it meets a boat," he says, excitedly, "not to mention that they referenced Drummond on the tap. You know where that's at, right?"

"Yes, I do, but—"

"God knows it's no man's land up there around the Upper Peninsula and Canada. It could easily be done. Talk about a porous border. Give me a break."

"You know, they make coffee in decaffeinated form these days."

"What?" he says, again tilting his head.

"Nothing, Hayward. Listen, I need your attention. What if they're getting it from the freighters that come through the St. Lawrence Seaway every day? There are tankers in the Great Lakes from all over the world—literally every day—that come through the locks and down to Chicago. Chicago is the westernmost port of the Great Lakes, not to mention the tanker traffic that goes up to Duluth."

"No, no, I've had men working those docks 24/7 for six months now—nothing. Duluth, Detroit, and Chicago. Absolutely nothing. We figured it was the docks right from the beginning."

"What makes you think they are unloading it at the docks? That's not how I'd do it. That's far too obvious. And more importantly, that's not new."

"What are you suggesting? That they—"

"That they are somehow getting the drugs into the country without using the ports; that is what I am suggesting."

"But—," he says, with a mouthful.

"We're talking originality here, right?"

"Well then, how?"

"They could have someone throwing the goods over the side of one of these tankers for all we know."

"Well, I don't know, kid. We never thought of that. These boats are over seven hundred feet long. But I suppose it is feasible. How would you get the drugs from there?"

"Pick it up with a smaller boat."

"Gotchya," he says, nodding his head. "Well, look into it, at the very least."

"Oh, I already am. I've got a schedule of every tanker that comes through and where they are coming from and where their destination is, not to mention every marina in northern Michigan. Did you know that Michigan has more registered boats than any state in the nation?"

"No."

"Well, this isn't going to be easy is what I'm sayin'. This entire state is surrounded by nothing but water."

"I might be able to get you some backup, but it's not looking good."

"Any help would be good. Get me some of the people I was working with D-town. Good people."

"OK, I'll look into it. Had to shit a golden brick just to get you up here and not some green fuckhead straight outta Quantico."

"But hey, get this. Apparently, the DNR stores a boat at a marina in Mackinaw City."

"And where is that?"

"Tip of the mit," I say, raising my hand, "right next to the Mackinac Bridge. Remember, Lance mentioned a bridge in the tap. I just found out about the DNR having a marina there today."

"Excellent. Check that out. That could be big."

"I agree. Wouldn't it be nice if we could use SANE on this one?"

"But we can't. I told you."

"I know, I know," I say, with a smile.

"Hey, more importantly, when is the next wire?"

"Tomorrow. Hopefully, they will show on time. I check the recordings every evening just in case they use a different day, but they haven't used the pay phone once."

"That tap will be our trump card. Keep me in the loop."

"Believe me, I'll be on it."

"You get something big out of that, we go in. We go in immediately. We just need a smoking gun, drugs in hand in this case. The more the better."

"Tell me, Hayward, how do two brothers like this fly under the radar for so long?"

"They don't," Hayward says, in a huff.

"Well, how long have they been doing this then?"

"Not long, not long at all. Probably just under a year now, actually. The drug started hitting the streets not long after Lance got released from Jackson, and once we put two and two together, we started keeping an eye on Frank ever since. We couldn't track Lance. He's a slimy bastard, he's a lifer, and nothin's gonna change with Lance. He hangs with prison scum, and they all protect each other, bikers and people like that. But we essentially think Frank kept his nose clean for a very long time, and this was just too much of an opportunity for him to pass up."

"Gotchya."

"That's just my hunch, though. Something kicked in with him, and it's typically greed. Imagine making about fifty mil in six months. This is America. It can be done," he says, bringing a napkin to his face. "Hey," he says, "I haven't said this yet, but good work on that wire. God damn it. I was relieved when we got that recording. I knew that was going to be the key," he says, slapping the table. "I knew the wire was going to hit pay dirt!"

"Thanks. God damn it, that was exciting. Makes my hair stand on end just thinking about it."

"You're damn right it's exciting. But we need to put this one to bed, kid. If this works out, I could use your help for a while. I never have enough people around me that I can rely on. Be good for your career, ya know."

"Trust me. I'm in this game to win."

"We're getting off track here. Tell me what you've learned about the Pierson brothers."

"Well, quite a bit actually. Put it this way. I'm glad you're here. Our boy sheriff Mayfair would like to see Lance die a very slow death, that's for sure, which, as you know, will work very much to our advantage."

"By the way," Hayward says, "who is this Cliff Stoink guy they were arguing about in the tap? This is a new name?"

God damn it, here we go. I knew he would ask about this. "He's just a local redneck. The sheriff said he's a serious asshole."

"Wait a minute," Hayward says. "You talked to the sheriff about this Stoink guy?"

"Ah . . . the sheriff . . . already . . . kind of knows more . . . more than you think he does," I say, stuttering.

"What? What are you talking about?"

"Hold on for a second, Hayward. You told me to use the sheriff when need be. Well, I did."

"Talk to me, Deacon," Hayward says, tapping his finger on his now-empty coffee cup.

"Listen, I hooked up with the sheriff for a drink to let him know that we were aware that Lance was out of prison. Befriend him, ya know, like you mentioned. Anyway, the sheriff mentioned Cliff's name and said that he needed to bring him in, something about Cliff violating his probation and getting drunk at a country club and eating fish out of an aquarium. Anyway, I asked the sheriff if I could sit in on the interview."

"Go on."

"Well, during the sheriff's questioning, Cliff just let it all out. No shit. He spilled the beans. He mentioned Lance's name without us even bringing it up. It was amazing."

"So the sheriff knows about the drugs and the Pierson brothers?"

"He does now. It's not a bad thing, seriously. Well, he assumes Frank is involved, but I didn't really clarify that we already knew that."

"This is very worrisome—very. I wouldn't have given you the go on that one, just for the record."

"You don't understand," I say.

"I understand everything. You could have already blown the lid off this entire fucking case."

"But—"

"Shut the fuck up and listen to me, Deacon," he says. "If this Cliff guy mentions any of this to Lance or Frank, then they know that we are on to them. Not good. Not fucking good. They will change their pattern for sure. They will probably drop the whole operation," he says, with his hand on his forehead, covering his eyes. "God knows they've made enough money already."

"What pattern?" I say. "All we know is that they use a pay phone. That's it. We need more than that."

"Listen to me," he says.

"And more than that," I interrupt. "Cliff is in all kinds of trouble. The sheriff could throw the book at him right now and lock him up if he needs to. I knew that going in, Cliff doesn't want to go back to jail. Cliff is our eyes and ears out there right now."

"Jesus Christ, Deacon—you're out of bounds with this move. You fuck this case up—"

"I promise you this will turn out to be a very good move on our part. Right now, we have nothing."

"Well, listen, now that *you've* decided to go ahead and do this, I think you and the sheriff need to become very close friends," he says, with a glare.

"I don't think my liver can handle it."

"Young man, you do whatever is necessary. This case is your life; your life doesn't change until this is wrapped up. Do you follow me?"

"Yes, I do."

"You're sure?"

"Yes, very. You've got to give me some room to move on this one."

"OK."

"You picked me for a reason, right?"

"Yes, I did."

"All right then," I say, with a nod.

"Just give me your all, kid. This case is your life. That's it."

"That's academic."

"This is how we exist in this business, and that's the reason I now have three ex-wives," he says, laughing. "But on a serious note, just remember, blend in up here. Your job is to not attract attention. Don't forget that. Fucking small town up here. We wrap this one up, and you can take a week or two off before your next assignment. I'll see to that."

"I'm not too worried about vacation time right now, sir."

"Believe me, you will be. Call me if you need to, and I will do the same. Be careful with this Cliff guy. I don't like the sound of him at all. My gut tells me that he's a loose cannon. This one's personal for me. This scumbag Frank Pierson is on the inside. He's one of us," he says, covering his eyes again. "And just play the sheriff however necessary."

"I hear ya, loud and clear."

"Anyway," he says, standing up, "you get the tab. I'm still pissed you rolled the dice on that interview without calling me first. It's shit like that that can ruin a case like this."

Chapter 29

A Drive to Detroit

I am going to make this phone call if it kills me, and if I don't, I am not the man I wish to be. What is the worst that can happen? "No, Brendon, she isn't home. Can I take a message? Yes, your name and phone number please. Are . . . are you . . . the American boy? It sounds as though you are."

"C'mon, man, just call her," says Billy's annoying voice.

"Shut up," I say. "I will. I'm trying to concentrate on . . . on what I am going to say."

"Just pick up the phone and—," Billy says.

"Do you, um, have a pen and paper?" I ask.

"What?"

"Well, I was going to—," I say.

"You're going to make notes or what? Just dial the number before I smack you one," Billy says.

"I will, I will. And don't worry. I'll leave your mother some money for the long-distance."

"I don't think anyone is too worried about that. Just dial the number," he says. "I'm going outside for a smoke."

I cannot break the stare at this wonderful portal placed before me. A device called a phone with a transatlantic door that causes my voice to quiver and will allow me to once again hear her lovely voice. Lilly knows none of this. She'll only remember the wonderful but brief summer we spent together. No, you're right. She'll not know a thing as my fingers begin to move and tremble. Deh deh . . . deh deh . . . deh deh . . . *goes the strange dial tone for an eternity.*

"Ah, hailo," the English woman's voice answers on the other end of the line. *Oh God, no, no, don't do this to me. I can always hang up.*

"Ah, hello, ma'am, this is Brendon Castleman from Michigan," I say, as the words stumble out and I begin to feel numb. "May I speak to Lilly please?" I say, as an echo of my voice rings down the line and back into my ear.

"No, Brendon, she's traveling now. She left less than a week ago. She's been trying to reach you."

No? What? What do you mean no?

"It's good to hear your voice. I know she desperately tried to reach you, and she said you weren't able to speak. Oh, Brendon, how have you been?"

"Oh, she's . . . she's traveling," I say, as my manners begin to stumble. "Oh, I'm fine, thank you." *I knew it. I gave it too long. I could pay for the mistake for the rest of my life.* "Fine, Mrs. Baker. How have you been?"

"Well, I would be better if I were on the lake. This summer just hasn't been the same. And of course, I miss my daughter," she says.

You are not the only one, Mrs. Baker. You have no idea.

"Ma'am, I don't mean to be abrupt, but how do you recommend that I speak to Lilly?"

"I have her mailing address, but she unfortunately has to call us."

"Where exactly is she?"

"I'm afraid she's teaching English in Thailand. I shouldn't say it like this, what a wonderful adventure? Why, I wish I would have done something so bold when I was younger."

Thailand. What the hell has happened? This can't be true.

"It's just that I worry for her sometimes. I hope she hasn't bitten off more than she can chew this time. These islands off the east coast of Thailand—some of them don't even have electricity, you see?"

"Oh," I say. *Asia, Thailand—what the hell is she doing there? Of all the places for her to go. That must literally be on the other side of the globe from here. I could fly to London but not Asia.*

"Have you ever been, Brendon, to Thailand?"

"No, God, no, no. I haven't had the chance to travel like you and Lilly. I do plan to travel someday, though. How long is she gone?"

"She assured us she would be home for Christmas this year. I'm afraid that is all that she would commit to."

"Oh," I say. *Christmas. Jesus, it's June.*

"She did promise me a Christmas together, though, and I am holding her to that," she answers sternly.

"Where exactly is she?"

"She's on a chain of islands, there are three of them, she's on Kho Samui."

"Ok, I'll remember that."

Your daughter can be rather stubborn, can't she, Mrs. Baker? What a pleasant way of saying that your daughter has a very willful mind of her own. This is not what I needed to hear today. Not at all. How can I speak to her? The fact now is I cannot.

This is a shit pill to swallow. Not today, God damn it. Just as everything was starting to somehow look a little brighter.

"It's been nice speaking to you, Mrs. Baker. It really has. Do you think you will make it over this summer?"

"Probably not. We haven't missed a single summer for ten years now. What a shame. But John is busy with work, and now both girls are gone. That house is sitting empty," she says, as the echo finally arrived, "but—"

"Mrs. Baker, I have to go now. Please tell Lilly hello and that I will mail her a letter soon. Will you forward it on to her please?"

"Why, yes, of course. Thanks for calling, Brendon. Have a nice summer."

"Please tell her I called when you speak next. Nice speaking to you," I say.

"You too. Bye now," she says, as I set the receiver down.

"How did it go?" asks Billy, popping around the corner. "Wasn't she home?"

"What? Are you listening?" I say. "Give me a break."

"Did you talk to her?"

"No."

"Not home?"

"No, not exactly. Why?"

"Relax. Of course, I am going to ask," he says, with a slight laugh. "Hey, at least you tried. Now, don't lose your momentum. Call your aunt. Find out when we can go down there. Shit, we can go today if you want. I sure as hell don't have anything better to do. We'll get you that money for ya and make this day a success. The number's right there. She's called every week or so since the funeral."

"I'm not really in the mood now, to be honest."

"Please do," he says, glancing down. "I think she's gettin' on my mom's nerves, to be honest."

Well, in that case, you asshole, thanks for the guilt trip. "I'll call her. Leave me alone for a while, for Christ's sake," I say. *Oh, here we go. Just get this done with. Make it quick. Pick a date and a time Mary and I will be there. You skip the funeral, and you're demanding that I call you. God damn it.*

"Hello," Mary says, answering the line.

Oh God, here we go.

"Mary, it's me, Brendon," I say. "I hear you . . . you've been calling?"

"Oh," she says. "Thanks so much for calling me back. I . . . I didn't think you were going to."

You got that right. I can hear the surprise in her voice. I wasn't going to.

"Well, yeah, you weren't at the funeral, and I wasn't exactly interested in calling you," I say.

"Oh, Brendon, you never gave me a chance to explain. You wouldn't return my calls."

"Mary, don't start, OK? I'm calling for a reason; and the reason is that I need my money; and I need it soon," I say. "You've had it long enough, I'd say."

"Well, yes," she says. "Of course, I can give you the money I owe you. One thing, though. Can you please visit me and pick it up? Just this once, it would give us a chance to speak. I really need that."

"Mary, I don't really care what you need, not to mention Detroit is almost three hours from here, you know," I say, as she interrupts.

"I know, I know," she says, pleading. "But please make the trip. I'll never ask anything of you again for as long as I live. I promise. Just this once."

"OK," I say. *All bullshit aside, huh? OK, Mary.* "Well, how about today then?"

"Oh, today," she says. "Well, I am . . . I . . . I can be home until eight o'clock. But after that, I have to work."

Sure, you do, sure, you do. You're half the reason my mom worried herself to death. And now you have a job? I wonder what Aunt Mary considers work these days.

"Mary, I can be there before eight if we leave soon. You better be there, and I won't be staying long. Just long enough to get my money and be on my way back here. Understood?"

"Yes, of course, of course. OK, now, take down directions from I-75. Do you have a pen?"

"Yes, I do. Shoot," I say. Her voice sounds tinny and weak as I hear her exhale a long drag off of a cigarette. *I cannot believe it's finally time to face Mary. God help me. I've got to get this over with. Billy's right; this is one of the many things that I must move past.*

"I got it. Sounds pretty simple. Two blocks from Tiger's Stadium, just follow the signs. You said third floor, right?"

"Yes. Now remember, the elevator doesn't work. You'll have to take the stairs."

"OK, got it."

"Are you coming alone?" she asks.

"Yep, yes, I am."

"Good. Can't wait to see you," she says, weakly.

"Yeah, see you then," I say, hanging up the phone and begin digging for a cigarette.

"How did it go, buddy?" Billy asks, popping back into the room with a slap on the back.

"Fine. It looks like it's time to take a drive to Detroit," I say, feeling slightly relieved.

"Cool. You feel better or what, man? You should."

"A little bit. Jesus, do I need a cigarette, though. Wow," I say. *My God, have I been dreading this call.*

"OK. Me too. When are we going down?"

"Today. We should leave soon too. She said she has to work tonight."

"All right. I'll tell my mom. What do we need?"

"A lot of cigarettes. Just a lot of smokes."

"Great. Just bought a carton. Let's do it."

"I . . . I have to use the bathroom before we leave," I say, looking out the window and into the bright sunlight.

"You want to eat something before we hit it?" Billy asks.

"Nope. I'm not hungry."

"You look it."

"Well, I'm not."

"OK," Billy says. "I'll start the car. Might as well get the show on the road."

After my visit to the bathroom, I climb gingerly into Billy's car, quickly light a cigarette and stare out the passenger window. Now was not the time for conversation. *This could be the day that I would take a step forward. A means to an end. That is what this trip is. Hell, I can be in and out of her apartment in less than two minutes if I want to. I'm not going to let her talk me into a God damn thing. Miss the funeral? What the hell is she thinking anyway? I don't even have to speak to Billy if I don't feel like it. This will be the day that I do things my way.*

The trees soon begin to turn to farm fields and then into buildings as the traffic gets much heavier.

"So Roy is letting you use the bunkhouse all summer?" Billy says, finally breaking the silence.

"Yep, rent free," I say. "I just have to guide some pike fisherman in August and some duck hunters in October. Good deal really."

"Yeah, it is. Great deal. Probably a good place for you right now. So you still haven't told me what you've been doin' with your time." he asks again. "You've been out there almost a month now."

"I've fished every day. It's been great. Things are really startin' to warm up out there."

"Yeah, a little different from the morning I fell through the ice," he says, laughingly.

"Yeah, in more ways than one," I answer.

"You know, anywhere south of about West Branch, and I start to feel like an opossum squashed on the road or something. You know what I mean?" he asks.

"You mean all these people and cities? Yep, I do," I say. *Yes, I do.* "Sorry for not being much for conversation. I kind of have a lot on my mind right now," I say, looking at Billy.

"No problem, my friend. I'm just here to help."

Billy and I had gone through the token list of questions for each other as we began to enter the city of Detroit. I think it was obvious to us both that we weren't back in the same saddle as we had been only a month and a half before. Things would really never be the same, and it only took one quick moment to change it all.

"What is my exit again?" Billy says.

"You've got a ways to go. She lives right down by Tiger's Stadium."

"Really? That's great. I've never been . . . always wanted to go to a Tiger's game. Are they playing?"

"I have no idea."

"Maybe we can get tickets if they are. Well, it must be a nice part of downtown then," he asks.

"I don't know. Never been either. I've only been to Detroit twice that I can remember. Those field trips in the fifth grade or whatever. Hey, that's it," I say pointing. "Take the next exit."

"OK, got it," he says, quickly changing lanes, the car slowing on the off-ramp. "You sure this is it, man?" he says, taking a left and onto the street. "Looks kind of run-down around here, doesn't it?"

"Yeah, I guess. It's a city. Now, just head east. She said we can't miss it. It's a ten-story high rise on the left, the north side of the road."

"Dude, check this out," he says, in amazement, pointing to all the people milling around. "Are you sure that your aunt lives around here because there ain't any white people on these streets. As a matter of fact, I think we might be the only white people around here. Do you realize that?" he says, excitedly.

"Hey, I get it. Just keep your eyes on the road and," I say, taking in the surroundings, "don't stop at the red light. Seriously, not here. Roll through it."

"Oh my God, this is unbelievable. This is a full-on ghetto," says Billy, nervously.

"And how would you know that?" I say.

"Because, man, this is what it looks like on TV, right?"

"Yeah, I guess. There's a sign for the stadium. There's the building. This must be it."

"I can't believe they'd put the fucking baseball stadium here. Who's idea was that?" huffs Billy.

"C'mon, do you know anything about the history of this city?"

"What? The murder capital and all that?"

"Just park over there, behind that van. It's out in the open and all. I'll just run in and make this quick."

"Dude, I'm not sure about this. This looks like a good place to get shot. Can we call her or something?"

"You want to stand around and use a pay phone?" I ask.

"No."

"OK then," I say.

"I hate to do this, but do you mind if I come in?"

"Yes," I say. "I mind."

"C'mon, man," Billy pleads.

"We're here. Slow down," I say. "Just park right here. Keep the windows up and the doors locked and the car running if it makes you feel better."

"I'm not sitting here, man, not like a sitting duck. Look at these guys," he says, nodding his head.

"Would you just relax?" I say. "I won't be ten minutes. Up the stairs, get the money, and we are out of here."

"Well, you just hurry the fuck up. I don't like it down here, and if I'm not parked here when you come out, it's because I am doin' laps around the block."

"OK, you're being a little dramatic, buddy. Just relax."

"Bullshit. They'll fuckin' shoot ya down here for a decent car like this. I don't know what your aunt is doin' down here cuz last I checked she's white, right?"

"Ten minutes. That's all I need. Got it?"

"Yep," he answers, as I step into the hot, foul-smelling city air.

What a different world this is. Billy was right. This was no place for two white boys from Houghton Lake, and what the hell is Mary doing down here? Gotta work at eight, huh? Yeah, as soon as the sun goes down, you gotta go to work, all right.

I approach the tall and run-down building looking back at the car and Billy. His head wasn't even visible. The freak must be lying down and acting like no one is in the car. What the hell good was that going to do? The pitiful sound of a coughing baby brought my attention back to the building as I entered the cement stairwell that smelled of urine. Good Lord, this is no way to live. What a hellhole. These people don't even have a chance growing up in a place like this. Thank God, she only lives on the third floor. Room 320 was all I needed as I was greeted by a small black man asleep in the stairwell. What a dreadful place this is. No wonder my mom worried so over Mary. I need to get this over as soon as possible. I need to face her and just get this done with. I peeked over the ledge before knocking. *Yep, Billy's car was still there. OK, Mary, you wanted it? You got it.*

The knock immediately seemed like a mistake. Is this really worth $800? Hell no, it isn't, but Jesus, we did drive all the way down here—and I am at the door. I reach up to knock a second time when I hear shuffling, the dirty red door begins to open. *It was her, or at least what was left of her. My God, she looks half dead.*

"Oh, Brendon, it is you. You look so good; you look so—," she says, giving me half of a hug and starting to cry.

Just what we need, Mary. Yes, just add tears, and everything will be fine.

"You're so tall now," she says, with outstretched arms. "I cannot believe how tall you've gotten already."

"Yeah, what's it been?" I say, sarcastically. "Three years now? And about ten before that?" I say, to the frail woman standing before me. "So, Aunt Mary, how have you been?" I ask.

"Oh, I've been better," she says.

When, Mary? When have you ever been better? I'll bet it's been a long time since you've really been better. A very long time.

"Well, I sure do appreciate your coming down here to see me. We . . . you and I," she says, staring at the shag carpeting, "we don't have much anymore, do we?" she says, looking up at me through a face full of tears.

"Well, I guess that depends on what you consider much now, doesn't it?" I say, shutting the door. "Now, Mary, do you have my money?"

"Well, kind of. I have six hundred dollars for you," she says.

Unbelievable. You couldn't have told me that over the phone. Drive all the way down here, and you don't even have all of the money.

"Please take this," she says, trembling, stuffing the wad of dirty bills into my hand. "I know I should have it all, and I will get you the other two hundred as soon as possible. I just knew," she says, sobbing, "I just knew if I would have told you . . . you . . . you might not have come."

I take the money from her small hand as she put her head in her hands and sat down on the bed in the tiny room. *Fresh air. I need some fresh air.* I take a step toward the slightly open window across the room. The pathetic sound of the baby crying made its way through the thin walls and open window. I glanced out the window thinking of Billy's situation and turned on my heels. "You know what, Aunt Mary?" I ask, staring at the sight of her sitting on the edge of the bed. *This is more like a hotel room than an apartment. I wonder how long she has lived here. Look at her. She couldn't look weaker right now. Maybe her excuse for missing the funeral was legitimate after all. She doesn't even resemble my mother anymore. Thank God for that. I don't think I could handle the resemblance right now.*

"So this is it. I should be going. Billy's out in the car," I say, pointing my head toward the door. "Not exactly the nicest neighborhood around here."

"No, it isn't," she replies. "This is temporary, though. I am sorry you had to come all the way down here," she says. "I—"

"What's that?" I ask, to break the silence.

"I just want you to know that," she says, breaking eye contact and fumbling with a cigarette, "I was having such a hard time."

"Yeah, well, so was I," I reply.

"Well, I called your friends, and they told me that you were having such an awful time of things. I'm so sorry, Brendon," she says, crying again. "I really am."

"Oh really?" I ask. "Tell me, Mary, when was the last time you saw her? When was the last time you saw your own sister?"

"Please don't get mad at me, Brendon," she says.

"Don't tell me what to do," I say, lowering my voice.

"It wasn't my fault, Brendon. It wasn't our fault. You don't—"

"I know that."

"Just don't blame yourself. She—"

"And what if I do blame myself?" I say. "I blame myself every day. Don't you? You should—"

"You shouldn't. You just don't understand."

"I don't understand what?"

"What she was going through before she—"

"Before she what? Blew her head off with one of my guns? Why the hell did you make me come down here? Why?" I ask. "Do you feel better now?"

"You don't know," she says again. "Just remember, it wasn't your fault."

"I know it wasn't my fault, OK? I know that!" I scream.

"No, you don't understand. Maddie . . . Maddie was expecting . . ."

"What?" I say. "Expecting what?"

"She was . . . she was pregnant, Brendon. Oh God, I know you didn't know. I'm sorry."

"Expecting a child?" I say. *This can't be. She's off her rocker.*

"I'm so sorry, I didn't want you blaming yourself the rest of your life. You're young, you have so much to live for."

"What?" I ask. "What are you talking about?"

"I may regret this for as long as I live, but you deserve to know—she'd been raped, I'm sorry to tell you this. You deserve to know that it wasn't your fault. She was going through an awful time. She hid it all from you. She loved you so."

"Hid what? She—" I say, trying to catch my breath.

"She just didn't—"

"Raped? What? By who?" I say, interrupting as I approach her, she begins to sob harder.

"I don't know," she says. "She just couldn't go on anymore, Brendon. She called me that morning. I knew something was very wrong."

"You knew something was wrong?" I ask, as the floor tilts and begins to spin below my feet. *Uh, here it comes again. Oh no.* I taste the salt of my tears as Mary stands up quickly and looks at me through a sideways glance.

"I think she called to say goodbye. I am so sorry," she says. "Brendon, sit down. You look pale. Are you OK?"

"I'm fine. Who raped her, Mary?" I ask, placing a hand on the wall. "Who? Answer the fucking question," I say.

"I don't know. She's gone. It won't solve anything."

"Answer the fucking question, Mary," I say, grabbing her by the shoulders.

"She didn't. She never used his name. But . . . he . . . he was a cop. That's why she was so afraid of him. She knew no one would believe her. That fucking asshole."

"A cop? What? Are you sure?"

"Not a real cop, but a . . . ya know. They only have them up north. What do they call them? A fish cop, ya know. A wildlife-officer type of cop," she says, sobbing as I let go of her and she again sits down on the bed.

My lungs aren't . . . my breath . . . it's just not there.

"She said they'd been dating and she broke things off, but he came over one night and took things too far," she says, as I stumble toward the only other room in the apartment. "Do you need to use the bathroom?"

I can see myself in the discolored mirror, grabbing the sink. *It will be OK. The coolness of the floor feels wonderful. Just lay down, my body is very heavy again. I've been here before.*

Vomit and the salt of my tears greet me as Mary lightly dabbs a cold washcloth on my face. "I'm fine. No, that's it. Let me up."

"Brendon, you passed out cold. Please lay down on the bed."

"Nope, I'm out of here."

"No, you shouldn't leave. You shouldn't go anywhere. You've been sick. I—"

"Mary, how long have I been here?"

"What?"

"In your apartment?"

"About a half an hour."

"Oh Jesus! Billy's out in the—"

"Bring him up here. I'll fix him a drink or something," she says. "I'm so sorry. I hope you . . . you understand that I felt it was the right thing to do by telling you, I mean."

"You did the right thing, Mary."

"I just didn't want you walking around blaming yourself for the rest of your life. It's just not fair. Don't do anything stupid."

"I'm leaving now, Mary. Billy's been waiting."

"Don't leave now. Please don't. It doesn't seem right. Stay for a little while at least."

"Goodbye, Mary, goodbye," I say, closing the thin door.

Chapter 30

Every Fourth Thursday

I'll be Hayward's right-hand man; that's what I'll be. The guy is a legend at the bureau, an absolute living legend. Not like those upper-level administrative types, this guy actually gets his hands dirty with real cases. He'll bring me in on the big cases, only the cases that he truly needs a steady hand on. I guarantee he admires me for what I did with that interview, but he can't acknowledge that to me. Obviously not. He can't have some cowboy flying off the handle on these cases. This case will bring a promotion. I guarantee it. What will my graduating class at the Bureau think of that, hah!

Deacon buzzed around the specialized surveillance trailer on the wheels of his chair with a nervous smile.

Three fifty-four and counting. Here we go. This is it. This is show time. C'mon, guys, be consistent. I'm ready for ya. Just throw me a bone. How ya doin' this? I don't need much, just enough. I'll break this case wide open, gotta catch you two red-handed just like Hayward said. Damn, that means we're gonna have to catch them with the gear on them. That could be intense. Especially with Lance being involved, I could see that guy having no problems going out in a blaze of glory. We'll probably have to catch them during the actual drop itself. That will involve some firepower.

Deacon peered out of the only window of the trailer he called home as his rotund neighbor started a small campfire. The man claimed to be an ornithologist researching the Kirtland Warbler which he was a local rare species of bird.

God, I hope that guy doesn't come over here again, always knockin' on the damn door. Not now, for Christ's sake, not now. Everyone is so damn friendly up here, always sayin' hello as if it were rude not to. I could probably learn something from that.

Deacon put his hands on the oversized headphones attached to his head hearing the now-familiar and crisp sound of coins being dropped into the metal of the pay phone. *This is it. Record button is on. Yep, here we go. Here we go. Bring it on boys, bring it on.*

"Hello," Lance says, picking up the phone.

"It's me," Frank answers.

"How ya doin?" Lance asks.

"Fine, how are things looking on your end?"

"Excellent, I'm ready as usual."

They sound happy this time, elated. Last time they sounded hurried and rushed, they think they've got this thing licked.

"Good, we're doin' the usual. They will be through the day after tomorrow, after dark."

"That's a day late, isn't it?" Lance asks.

"Yeah, they got tied up a while back in some weather before they hit Anticosti."

"What? Where the hell is that?"

"It's an island right off the mouth of the St. Lawrence Seaway. Trust me. It's like clockwork once they get into the Great Lakes."

"Oh."

"We'll meet up after I get the drop, same spot," Frank says.

"Got it. I'll be there," Lance says, sounding as if he's out of breath due to excitement. "You're addicted, aren't you, brother?"

"What are you talkin' about?" Frank says.

"You like doing the pickup now, don't you?"

"I'm doing this because it makes sense for me to be doing it."

"Yeah, but now that you've done a pickup, you like it."

"Hey, ain't nobody gonna fuck with the DNR out there. You know that, including the law in Canada. Now you, on the other hand, out there, bobbing around in a fucking fishing boat. They'll see your lights and pull you over to ask you what the hell you're doing out there after dark."

"You're paranoid as usual, and admit it, you enjoy this."

"Hey, I'm not gonna kid ya. Watchin' that green light drop out of the sky was pretty amazing."

Out of the sky? What the hell does that mean? Green light drops out of the sky? But then again, it is dark out, and a freighter's gotta be awfully high out of the water.

"That's what I'm talking about," Lance says, with a laugh.

"Yeah, it was perfect. I watched the whole thing through my binos. What a rush."

"Oh, by the way," Lance says, "considering we never get to talk, this new connection of Cliff is great."

Suddenly, there was a knock at the door of the trailer.

Oh shit, I knew it. Just ignore it. Just keep listening.

"The one in Gary, Indiana?"

"Yep."

"And why is that?"

"Because he took everything I'd been sitting on, and I mean everything. The guy was happy as hell. Had a suitcase full of cash, no bullshit, no negotiating, no nothing. On time and everything. Some Mexican-looking guy, the whole thing didn't take but ten minutes."

"You got rid of it all?"

There was again a knock at the small metal door of the trailer.

Go away, old man, not now. Not now.

"Everything, brother, and I mean everything."

"Great, I'm glad you got rid of it."

"Yeah, me too. That whole thing sittin' on the stuff—that made me more nervous than any of this."

Cliff's connection is working, that means Cliff's on the payroll.

"Enjoy this while it lasts. I told you I'm out of this forever come September. I ain't no career criminal like my loser little brother."

"C'mon now."

"I'm serious too, time for an early retirement. I deserve it. I'm using all my vacation time come September, and I'm gonna hunt every day this fall. And then it's time to leave the state for a while. A very long while."

"I can't wait, can't fucking wait," Lance says.

Jesus, we only have a month or two. One, maybe two, or three more drops to get them. That means we are going to have to go in for the drop the day after tomorrow. Wonderful.

"That is the one thing I will miss about Michigan, though, the hunting, the outdoors, and everything."

"Don't be gettin' all sentimental on me. Trust me, you won't miss a thing," Lance says. "With the kind of money we're makin', I'll send your ass to Africa on safari or something."

"Sounds good."

"See you the day after tomorrow."

"Yep. And nice talkin' to ya, by the way. I kind of miss talkin' to you, ya know. We talked more when I was in the pen."

"There will be plenty of time for talkin' this winter, Lance."

"Yep, sounds good," Lance says, as both phones hung up simultaneously, and the dial tone sounds again in Joe Deacon's ear.

Oh my God, this is it. This is huge. I have to call Hayward. I'll call him now. No, make some notes, be organized if you finally call him on his mobile. I have to make sense if I'm calling the man. Prioritize, get with it. What is most important? They are using a freighter that is huge. The next drop is the day after tomorrow. It's time to go in for the sting. Jesus, I am going to need backup. Going to need plenty of guns on this one. The connection in Gary, Indiana—that's important. We'll have to get Cliff's help on that one, shouldn't be a problem there. Dropping out of the sky, yep, it's a freighter, all right. God damn it, I was right on that one. Where is his number? Here it is. C'mon, Hayward, ya better pick up.

"Hayward, it's Deacon. We should talk."

"OK, OK, give me a second. I need to get—one moment."

C'mon, Hayward, just give me a couple of minutes. This is big.

"Deacon, shoot, what is going on?"

"We just had a very good wire; that is what is going on."

"OK, talk to me."

"I need you to look at a map. I'm serious."

"Slow down, young man. I don't exactly have a map on me. What's going on?"

"They *are* using a freighter. I guarantee it. My hunch was correct; it has to be. Wait till you hear the wire. They talked about the St. Lawrence Seaway and everything. Frank even tracks the boats once they enter the seaway. I'm serious. This is it, biggest lead we've had yet."

"Are you sure?"

"Absolutely positive."

"Good, good. Your hunch was right, kid. Don't forget that."

"You ever heard of Anticosti Island?"

"Ah, maybe. Why?"

"Frank referenced that too; that's why I need you looking at a map right now. It's right at the mouth of the St. Lawrence; that's where Frank starts tracking the boats."

"What do you mean?"

"Frank starts tracking the boats when they leave the ocean, once they hit freshwater he knows exactly when they'll pull past the Mackinac Bridge."

"Oh, when do the drugs arrive?"

"Day after tomorrow, around dark or so."

"Oh Jesus."

"What?"

"Shit, damn it all. That's too soon."

"What? I'll go in, no sweat."

"Hell, fucking no, kid! You listen to me. Here's how we do this. You stake out the marina where Frank keeps the DNR boat. All night. Until you see what you need to."

"What? Why? We have them. I know we—"

"I said listen, Joe, seriously. Now, I want you to put everything together before we spring, OK? I want you to take pictures of Frank using the boat—everything. Obviously, make sure the date and time is on that film. When he arrives and when he gets back, etc."

"Hayward, are you nuts? We got them. This is it. This is our time."

"No, it's not. Not yet."

"Why?"

"Because we don't really know where exactly they're doin' it, that's why."

"Yes, we do."

"No, we don't. Now listen, I can't have fucking helicopters flying around out there after dark, or they will abort, understand?"

"Well, what good is that going to do us? I mean, this is it, Hayward. We can crack this thing, the whole case. I just need some people."

"I don't have anyone for you that soon, that's the problem. Not one person, not a soul. Listen, I am maxed out down here right now."

"Hayward, you gotta do better than that."

"Joe, remember, we still work for the government, and I am short staffed in Detroit and Chicago right now. I'll get you people soon, but we do need to position ourselves on this one."

"Whatever."

"Listen, I know you're disappointed, but that is how we do these things, and more importantly, this is how we get these things to stand up in court. Now, don't get anymore bright, fucking ideas like you did with that Stoink character. If you so much as step on a boat during the stakeout, I will personally shoot you."

"What do you mean?"

"What do I mean?" Hayward says. "I'm dead serious. Don't step foot on a boat. You try and go out there and catch them in the act on your own and you're out of job, not to mention the Pierson boys will show you just how deep Lake Huron really is."

"Well, I don't know about that."

"You don't think those two scumbags are armed to the hilt when they do this? Frank carries a piece with his job, and Lance's sure as hell ain't got nothin' to lose. Remember what he did to the sheriff with the carpet knife? The guy had a handcuff key on his necklace, didn't he?"

"I get the point."

"Now, your surveillance is crucial, just as important as this wire has become. This is it, Joe. It's time to shine. The job you do the day after tomorrow is as crucial to us as landing the whole thing. We get everything lined up, and we will go in for the sting on the next drop. This is the last step, got it?"

"OK."

"You have set this up really well. And remember, right now, the stakeout is everything. Get what photos we'll need. Did they say anything about the rendezvous after they get the drop? I mean who is doing the pickup?"

"Frank is, just like last time, and yes, they said they are hooking up after the drop."

"Excellent. Do they transfer the drugs on the water or on land?"

"I don't know."

"Exactly, you will soon enough, last piece of the puzzle."

"Got it."

"Remember, I'd be there if I could."

"I know."

"Now, just because I don't have anyone for you now doesn't mean it will always be this way. When we do the sting on this one, I'll have you a small fucking army up there, but Jesus, I can't even be there within two days."

"I know. I will be at the marina."

"Hey, this is your case. You've handled it well up to this point, and I will personally make sure that those in power will know about this. I feel very good about where we are headed with this one, especially with your news today."

"OK, OK. Hayward, I'm going to meet with the sheriff ASAP. I just haven't had the time lately with all of this marina business I've had to deal with."

"Good. Yeah, the time is now for him to be on our side. Big time. I'm talking best fucking friends here."

"I'm calling him right after we finish this call."

"Well, call him then. We'll talk soon. You comfortable with this?"

"Yes, very. No one will even know I'm there."

"Exactly. Don't do anything stupid. If they catch wind of us now, this case is done, dead in the water. No pun intended."

"I know, Hayward, I know."

"OK, call the sheriff. Good work, kid. I gotta go."

What the hell can he be working on that is more important than this? Must be something big to be bringing me in on a case with this much responsibility. I mean, this is mine. I'm flying solo up here. Oh, well, screw it. Time to call the sheriff. C'mon, buddy, you better be in. It's after five; he's probably sloshed by now. But that's OK. He likes to run his mouth when he's about half loaded. C'mon, pick up already.

"Sadie, Special Agent Joe Deacon here. I need to speak with the sheriff immediately."

"He kind of has someone in his office right now," she says. "Is it anything I can help you with?"

Of course, it isn't, for Christ's sake. "Listen, Sadie, I need to speak to him now. Right now, tell him it's urgent."

"OK, I will, but he really doesn't like to be bothered when he's busy."

"Now Sadie." *Hurry up, come on, let's go. Get him on the horn, for God's sake.*

"Special Agent Deacon, I will patch you through now," says the high-pitched voice.

"Deacon, how are ya? I've got someone in my office, but go ahead."

"Hey, we need to get together—soon. When's a good time for you?"

"Ah, kind of busy, but yes, we can get together. When ya thinking?"

"Tonight's good for me."

"You a little lonely out there or what?"

"No, just excited. I think it's getting time to move in."

"OK, on what?"

"The Pierson boys. Put it this way. I just learned something."

"OK."

"I need an education on Frank Pierson. I . . . I need to know everything. Can you help me with that?"

"Oh, him. Sure, he's kind of a loner, but I think I know about as much as anyone."

"Good. Then we're on for tonight?"

"Well, I have plans to meet up with my wife, but I guess we could get together after that."

"Good, good, thanks for this. How's 9:00 p.m.?"

"OK, I might be a little late, but I'll be there."

"Good. Please make it, Trent. It's imperative."

"See you at nine, same place. Oh, and by the way, you're buyin'."

"You got that right. See you then."

CHAPTER 31

Seen a Ghost

Oh boy, sounds like the young J. Edgar is all fired up again, the sheriff thought as he delicately hung up the phone. *Need to run that kid next to the car for about twenty miles before a day on the job, just like ya would a young bird dog. Gotta meet tonight. It's urgent. But then again, it does involve that asshole Frank Pierson and his brother that should be about six feet under right now. If ever I'm lucky enough to be involved in a situation with Lance Pierson again, I'll put a bullet hole in him big enough to stick your hand through. That's a promise. No, actually, I'll put two holes in him. I'll find a way to legitimize it, and if I don't, I don't think anyone will mind.*

"Anyway, Billy," the sheriff says, "where were we?"

"I was gonna tell ya about me and Brendon going to Detroit."

"Oh yeah, to see Mary, his aunt Mary."

"Yep."

"So when did you guys head south?"

"Less than a week ago, and I'll tell ya, I'll never visit Detroit for as long as I live."

"It's not that bad."

"Oh really?" Billy says. "Do you know where they put Tiger's Stadium?"

"Yes, of course, Billy. I grew up down there. A lot has changed since they built that stadium, ya know. Now—"

"Pardon my French, Sheriff, but those fuckers took the hubcaps off my car while I was sitting in it!"

"Yeah, well, that's too bad, but can you imagine growing up in a place like that? You kids up here have it easy. Anyway, we're here to help Brendon," the sheriff says. "How was he?"

"He was all right until he saw that aunt of his anyway. He looked like he'd seen a ghost or something."

"What do you mean?"

"He looked like a zombie when he got back in the car. I'm not kidding ya. I felt bad he wouldn't let me go up and see her, wanted to go alone. And believe me, after checking out the people hanging around the streets, my car was the last place I wanted to be. Damn near laid on the floor of the car the whole time."

"So what happened?" the sheriff asks.

"I don't know," Billy says, shaking his head. "Something though. He never said a word for the next three hours. It was a real fun ride home, let me tell ya."

"So he obviously talked to Mary before you drove down there, right?"

"Oh yeah, he called her from my place."

"Were you there when he talked to her?"

"No, well, kind of, I mean I spoke to him before and after the phone call, if that's what you mean."

"How was he about calling her?"

"Oh, believe me, he didn't want to. I had to tell him that my mom was getting a little annoyed that she had been calling so much, which is the truth."

"So that's it?"

"Yeah, I guess, the kid's moody as hell. He had no interest in talking after he got back to the car. He was supposed to be at Mary's about ten minutes. Well, half an hour later, he shows and tells me to take him home and won't say another word."

"That's too bad, but I couldn't imagine anything good comin' out of a visit with her."

"Yeah, I guess, never met her," Billy says.

"Yeah, well, I have."

"You grew up together?"

"Yep," the sheriff says, "you keep an eye on him. I'm sure he's still in a pretty awful state of mind right now."

"Oh, I will, but it ain't exactly easy. He was hiding in the brush when I went out to see him at the cabin he's staying in. He knew I wouldn't leave, it's the only reason he came out," Billy says.

"That's too bad, poor fucking kid."

"Yeah, what a mess. My best friend's mom commits suicide, and I lose my best friend."

I wonder what the hell is going on with Mary. Sharon seemed to think that she'd borrowed some money from Brendon. What the hell could that have to do with all of this? Nothing, I am sure.

"Billy, give me a second, will ya?" the sheriff says. "Sadie, did Mary Castleman leave a number when she called," he says, "in regard to Brendon?"

"Yes, Sheriff, she did. I have it somewhere."

"Find it, will you?"

"Yes, Sheriff, I will. Lawrence just called. He said he needs to have a quick word."

"Not now, Sadie. Tell him I'm busy," the sheriff says.

Not now, Lawrence, good Lord. That guy has been about as useful as a limp dick lately. Maybe he's calling to say he's quitting. Wouldn't that be a delight. "Now, Billy, make sure you tell Brendon, the next time you see him, that I need to talk to him."

"OK, but I'm not exactly sure when that will be."

"I told him I would help out with selling the house. I just talked to the realtor. Not one person has even looked at it, no interest. I'm sure everyone within five counties knows what happened inside that house."

"That's too bad," Billy says, looking at the floor.

"Yeah, I know he needs the money."

The PA rang again and the sheriff brings his hands to the side of his face.

"Sheriff," Sadie says, "I hate to bother you again. I really do."

"Go ahead, Sadie. What's it this time?" the sheriff says, rolling his eyes at Billy.

"Dr. Jury's on the line again. She says it's important."

God damn it all. This has to stop. I can't take this. No, not anymore. "Sadie, put her through," the sheriff says. "Billy, this time, pardon my French."

"Trent," the doctor says, "it's Sharon."

"Sharon, I know who it is. Why are you calling me?"

"Don't take that tone with me."

"Sharon, you call here constantly. I'm busy, have someone in my office. What is it?"

"Have you seen or heard from Brendon?"

"Yes, I have. He is doing really well, by the way."

"That's not true. You know it, and I know it."

"What the hell do you want me to say? For Christ's fucking sake, Sharon, I have Billy in my office right now, and we are trying to talk about Brendon. Leave the kid alone!" the sheriff says, slamming the phone down, cracking the receiver.

I gotta get Billy out of here. This isn't working, I can't do this anymore. Oh, this isn't a job anymore; this is hell. I gotta go, time to leave. I'll finish the entire fifth in this state, and I can't wait. "Billy, I'm sorry you had to hear that," he says, with his head in his hands. "I just . . . I just . . . I'm having a hard time dealing with her right now."

"Understood, Sheriff. You don't need to say anything more."

"She calls here almost every day. I can't take it anymore."

"Hey, we're here for Brendon, right? I know that."

"Yes, young Billy," he says, with a sigh, "yes, we are."

"Can I call you Trent? Brendon always used to."

"Yes, of course, you can. Did you know Brendon guided my father, bless his soul, on duck hunts until the year before he died?"

"I know that. I was on one of them."

"Yep, my father loved watching the sun come up over the Deadstream flats, out there by Reedsburg Dam."

"It's awfully pretty out there," Billy says.

"Yep, nothin' like it."

"And that's where Brendon is now. That's where he's staying."

"Yep, probably a good place for him."

"I will call you," Billy says. "Just like you asked when I see him next."

"A lot of," the sheriff says, covering his watery eyes, "some of this will pass with time, Billy. Remember that. Don't give up on him."

"Oh, I won't, but . . ." Billy says, shifting his weight in the chair.

"But what?"

"The kid looks sickly right now. Have you seen him?"

"No, I haven't. No one has other than you. But obviously, the doctor is hunting him down."

"Yeah. He said she's been stopping by. She even left a Bible apparently."

"Oh boy, I would imagine he's sick of that."

"Yeah, but I'm serious. The kid looks like he hasn't seen the sun in a year and hasn't eaten in the same time. That's the part that worries me."

"He was always awfully skinny, though."

"Yeah, but this is different. His hands were shaking; he's a walking toothpick. I'm not kidding."

"Well, what do you think is wrong?"

"I don't know, it's just—"

"What are you getting at?"

"I don't know, it's just," Billy sighs, "something is wrong, something seems very wrong."

Chapter 32

Lies Like a Rug

Well, back to the local watering hole, Deacon thought as he put his vehicle into park. *Just two cars again. How the hell does this place stay in business? I just don't get things up here. And who the hell ever heard of Merritt, Michigan?* he thought as he enters the smell of stale cigarette smoke.

"Hey, Trent," he says, to the body propped up on the barstool.

"Well, young Joseph, where do we begin?" the sheriff says. "Judy, can we get two more of these? Both doubles."

"I'm not sure I need a double."

"I don't remember asking you if you did. Now let's talk," the sheriff says, motioning to the same corner booth they sat in last time.

"Well, like I said to you on the phone," Deacon says, sitting down, "what can you tell me about Mr. Frank Pierson? I need to start patterning him. I need to understand him, how he thinks. I think we are getting closer to figuring this one out."

"Well, what are they doing? You need to give me some info here as well," the sheriff says. "I think it's referred to as quid pro quo."

"They're using the Great Lakes to get the heroin into the country, and they are distributing the drugs through Michigan. He and his brother are working together, which you already know."

"Yep, I figured. Didn't know they were using the Great Lakes, though. Now, tell me something I don't know."

"They're selling it. Well, it sounds like Lance is selling it to his people in Detroit and Chicago. They are also now unloading product in Gary, Indiana. Cliff Stoink's connection, by the way."

"No shit?"

"These are no average amounts, mind you. These are huge shipments. My worry is that they are only going to do this for a while, cash in and get out. The clock is a tickin' if you know what I mean."

"Well, what can I do?"

"Help me track him. Let me know when you see him and what time of day it is. Think about him. Who does he hang out with? Nothing is irrelevant in regard to Frank; keep that in mind. I wouldn't be surprised if we go in for the sting very soon. I may need your help with that as well."

"Frank is a total loner, always has been," the sheriff says. "What about Lance?"

"We can't pin down exactly where he is or where he stays. So far, all we have is that he's drifting around the Sugar Island and Drummond Island areas of the Upper Peninsula, and he probably spends some time in Canada as well."

"Hence, you asking me about Drummond Island at this bar the last time we met."

"You got me on that one, Sheriff."

"What else do you have for me?" the sheriff asks, starting on his new drink.

"I think he, Frank, is using the DNR boat to do the pickup. He's using this boat out of a marina in Mackinaw City."

"Really? A boat owned by the state—that's a little brazen, isn't it?" the sheriff says.

"Brazen is exactly the kind of people we're dealing with right now. Two of them, brothers, they don't exactly lack balls," Deacon says.

"Yeah, brothers that need to be put away forever," the sheriff says.

"Yep."

"I remember you asking me about a bridge too, remember that? You obliquely asked me about a bridge."

Jesus, the guy must have had a pint of whisky in him that night, and he remembers everything. I guess that's what happens when you're a professional drinker.

"Yes, Sheriff, that is correct."

"And I mentioned the Mackinac Bridge. We would be a lot more effective if we acted like a team. I could have been keeping an eye on Frank since the day you arrived, ya know. Roscommon County isn't that big. I probably pass him on the roads at least a couple of times a week."

"Sorry, I was told to keep everyone, including you, on a need-to-know basis up to this point."

"I know. You're just doing your job; and this is my county; and I'm doing mine. I just saw Frank yesterday, actually. He was at the local donut shop. His truck is pretty easy to identify."

"Does he hang out there often or—?"

"Yeah, kind of. He was probably there picking up the old donuts. That is what bear hunters use for bait, ya know."

"What do you mean?"

"Bear hunters use donuts, among other things, for bait. It's probably not even legal to bait right now, but he's probably doing it. He's the DNR, you know. He probably just tells the people at the shop that he's freezing them or something. I've always heard the guy lies like a rug."

Hayward's file said that Frank was a serious outdoorsman. OK, I'm starting to get a better feel for our boy Frank Pierson. Keep it coming, Trent. Keep that mouth running.

"That's interesting. So bear hunting? I've never heard of such a thing. I mean this isn't exactly Alaska."

"Oh, but it kind of is. We have the healthiest population of black bears east of the Mississippi; people come from all over the nation at the chance to hunt bears in the Deadstream Swamp, especially Southerners. Kind of a right of passage for some of these macho types. I shouldn't say that; some of them are very serious woodsmen."

"Sounds kind of crazy to me."

"Yeah, especially the way Frank does it. He uses a bow and arrow."

"What? Hunting bears with a bow and arrow? That has to be one of the dumbest things I've ever heard of."

"Yep, archery, it's very popular up here. I hunt with a gun, personally. Never wanted to hunt bear, remind me of humans a bit too much personally."

"What else should I know?"

"Well, bear season opens a lot earlier than most of our hunting seasons. It's in September, I think. Not too far off, really. I can look it up if you want. That is one time of the year when he would be very easy to track," the sheriff says with a laugh.

"What do you mean?"

"The guy hunts almost every day during bear season unless he fills his tag. I've talked to Frank enough times over the last twelve years to know that, always small talk, though, usually about hunting or fishing. As I said, never liked the guy—and after we put his brother away, flat out, I just avoided him."

"OK, what else comes to mind?"

"Well, that's it really. The guy's passion in life is hunting, and when he's not hunting, he's fishing. Just like every other fucking redneck that moves up here."

"So this bear hunting, how do they do it?"

"They use a tree stand or just build a platform in a tree. They're up in a tree, and if they're lucky, the bear comes in before it gets dark. Most of the time, they don't."

"Really?"

"Yep, makes for an awfully interesting walk back to the truck in the dark, let me tell you."

"Do people ever get attacked?"

"Occasionally, not too often, though. You always hear of a few attacks in Michigan every year. You know Lawrence, that stupid, fucking deputy of mine?"

"Well, obviously," Deacon says. *You mean the deputy that you almost throttled at the police station? Yeah, I know him.*

"Well, a few years back, he was bow hunting bear and had two cubs get spooked and come up the same tree that he was in."

"Jesus Christ."

"Yeah, the sow was real happy, snapping her jaws at him at the base of the tree and all. Put it this way. Larry doesn't hunt bears anymore."

"That is unbelievable. That would be one helluva way to go."

"Yeah, we lost a bear hunter to the Deadstream last year. He had a heart attack, though. Fortunately, his buddies knew where his stand was, so we got him out of the woods the next day before the animals got to him. The birds got to his eyes already, but that was it."

"Jesus Christ," Deacon huffed. "Bear hunting, huh? Learn something new every day. Lawrence doesn't appreciate being called Larry, does he?"

"Nope, it's the only thing he asked of me when I hired him."

"And you enjoy annoying him?"

"He's probably fucking my wife right now, Joe. I figure I can call him about anything I want to."

"Oh," Deacon says. *Ouch, I wondered what was really going on with these two.*

"It's good eating, though."

"What?"

"Bear."

"You can eat bear?"

"Oh yeah. I love the back straps, great on the grill. We usually have a few hit by cars around the county every year. As a matter of fact, they used to serve bear in the cafeteria at the local schools back in the day when they had a roadkill."

"Wow, things are a little different up here, Trent?"

"Yeah, I guess. I'd rather be up here than anywhere."

"It's kind of starting to grow on me. People sure are friendly. Hey, I gotta go. Got an early morning ahead of me."

"You haven't even touched yer drink," the sheriff says.

"You mind taking care of that one for me, Trent?"

"Nope."

"Good. I'll pay the lady."

"OK."

"Call me if anything comes up regarding Frank. And I mean anything."

"You're dealing—we're dealing with some very dangerous people, ya know."

Lance used a carpet knife on you, didn't he, Sheriff? Why did he have to use a carpet knife? "Yes, Sheriff, we are."

Chapter 33

Surveillance

This should be just fine, yes, Deacon thought as he slid into the underbrush. *No one knows I'm here, and I've already watched that scumbag Frank Pierson park his truck and leave with the boat. And I have the pictures to prove it. He was obviously in a hurry, and he couldn't have noticed me from that distance. He has no idea that I'm here.*

I've got plenty of food, water, binoculars, and, more importantly, a 9-mm that will do the job. I can stay here all night if necessary. I hope I have to face Frank with a bag full of heroin on him. Bring it on, bitch. A cop who smuggles drugs into the country, yeah, there's a place for you in this world. If you're lucky, it's a hospital. If you're not, you're gone.

Yes, this is it. Just me and the smell of freshwater off the Great Lakes, tucked away nicely in a patch of trees and brush. I can see everything, or at least everything I need to. I can see every boat, the parking lot, and Frank's approach when he arrives.

But what if Lance Pierson is also watching this marina? What if he is doing exactly as I am? Jesus, wouldn't that be something? Best keep that 9-mm very handy, he's a shady bastard. It had crossed my mind before, but we don't know where the hell he is. Damn it all. Loose ends with a loose cannon. Not good, not good at all. Hayward had that on his mind the last time we spoke. After the drop, do they do the transfer on land or on water? If it's on the water, then Lance is probably using a different marina for his boat, or he has a cabin or something around these parts. Who knows? This isn't good. I should have been more prepared than this. Either that or Hayward should be providing me some backup. That's probably more like it. One-man show up here is what I am. This is what you wanted; this is what you craved. Well, you got it, all right.

My car's not parked here. Lance would have had to watch me walk in here and set up, and no one watched me set up. I made sure of that. The marina store closed at six, and Mackinaw City isn't exactly hopping tonight. He doesn't know me from Adam, but I can't be too careful. Well, that's it. The sun has set. Shouldn't be too long now. That freighter from Asia should be passing through anytime now. Look at them out there, freighter after freighter, passing through with God knows what in them. I can't believe someone didn't come up with this idea before the Pierson boys. But then again, I do have to give them some credit. Wait until I tell Hayward that I actually know where the freighter comes from. That will kill him. There's only one set of freighters from Asia using the Great Lakes this summer, and they have coincided with our wiretaps perfectly. Yep, just like clockwork. You had the phone-conversation tip, Hayward, but not the use of a freighter. Got ya there, Hayward. You overlooked the obvious. And look at the magnificent bridge, five miles long and suspended only by metal and air. Bring the drugs in on a seven-hundred-foot freighter and drop them off the side of the ship when you see the Mackinac Bridge. Make sure they float, and we'll take it from there. It wasn't brain surgery, but it sure would take some balls.

Should I call Hayward after this? No, it will probably be too late. Who knows how long it takes Frank to get the drugs, and who knows how long it takes him to do the transfer with his brother? Tonight should tell. I'll only call him if Pierson has a stomach full of lead, and I have about twenty pounds of heroin on me. Nope, that's not good either. Hayward would flip. Tonight is a stakeout only, and don't take a step on to a boat was his only instruction. Dark as hell is what it is already, and absolutely nothing is going on. Take a nap is what I could do, should have brought some coffee.

Look at the little red dot skimming across the water of Lake Huron. Just another unmonitored boat flying across the water. Just what I need. Not one car has pulled into the parking lot other than—Jesus . . . that red light . . . that boat . . . that's Frank's! Binoculars up, that is his boat. Yep, it's a DNR boat, all right. This is it. Hold still and don't move a muscle, fingers on the metal.

No wake my ass, huh, Frank? Look at you, pulling in here like you own the place. You probably think you do, don't you? Boy, he's no small man now that I have a better look through the binoculars. Yep, big dude, got an arrogant look about him too, still in uniform, you prick. You should be shot for that alone.

He's pulling into his slip—the DNR slip, that is. Time for a photo or two. Thank God for infrared technology, no flash on this baby. Smile, Frank, the pieces are coming together. We'll get you the next time you do this. Parking the boat, looks a little nervous right now. Definitely having a good look around, aren't you? You're looking a little paranoid there, partner. Look how he quickly hops out and begins to tie the front of the boat up and then begins on the back set of ropes. Guy looks like a fullback with some height on him, makes that uniform look a little small. I wouldn't want to have to face him without a piece of iron in my hand; that's for sure.

That's it; he's done, leaving the slip—nothing on him, absolutely nothing, not even a bag. How can this be? He's reaching his right hand down to his weapon. Yeah, Frank, it's still there. Don't move. I'm in the dark, and he isn't. He can't see a thing.

The dope is either on the boat, or he and Lance have already done the transfer. How can that be? It doesn't seem late enough for that. That was quick, too quick. He wasn't gone for two hours. He's off the dock and into the parking lot, walking quickly and alertly. God damn it! This doesn't solve anything unless he left it all on the boat. But why would he do that?

"Remember, Deacon, you step on that boat and you're out of a job, not to mention the Pierson boys will show you just how deep Lake Huron really is." Fuck this! I'm checking that boat. I'm checking that boat as soon as Frank gets here and his truck out of viewing distance. If the drugs are on the boat, then he's fried. I'll call Hayward then, we got him, and I've got the pictures to prove it. We'll wrap up this baby tonight.

C'mon on, Frank. There you go. Start that truck and get the hell out of here. Time to gather up, foods in the pack, camera, and binos. No trace of me being here. He's leaving the parking lot; it's time to move.

There he goes, brake lights well off into the distance. Make this quick. Very quick. Should I run? Yeah, step it up. Check the boat and get out of here. No! Stop. Look around—nothing and no one. Hurry it up. Let's go, down the dock. Yep, this is the boat. No, nothing there, nothing on the back. Hell, there's not even room to hide a bag, a lot of water on the floor. He pulled something out of the water tonight. How about the front? Hop on, don't touch anything, no finger prints. The boat starts to slowly rock back and forth. Nothing, absolutely nothing. He didn't leave the dope on the boat. They did the transfer. They already did the fucking transfer. But how? Had to have been on the water. Had to be.

Chapter 34

Plinking the Beav—

He'll see me smiling. Yes, he will—just like the smile that I'm wearing today. He will see my movements if only for a very brief moment, all right. He'll see me precisely as our eyes meet, and I plunge a knife into the thick of his neck. And after all of the wriggling and bleeding is done, I will dismember the parasite's body and hide it in a very specific place where it will never be found. I shall not hesitate to use the initiative. I pity him—you, Frank Pierson—for it is now far too late.

I was probably at home during the attack on my mother, but who knows? Possibly out drinking with Billy, but probably not. Asleep, upstairs, in the safety of my own home as the engagement began. She said no and you said yes, and then your newfound history began. And now she's gone. See you soon, Frank, very soon.

Drunk was he, Aunt Mary? Does that help things? Does that assist you? Is that how you help yourself sleep at night? *Is it?* Whatever it takes, Mary, whatever it takes in your pathetic state of mind. That state of mind that yields nothing but knows something. I am different, Aunt Mary. I'll act. I will act even if it locks me up forever. My mother meant the world to me, and I will remedy this situation. I promise this to you.

But I do want to thank you, Aunt Mary, and I want to thank you from the very bottom of my heart, you useless piece of shit. You missed the funeral, called constantly, your hands shake, and you absolutely demand my attention. I would like to offer my sincerest gratitude for leading me down the road to my drive to Detroit. Poor Billy, he had to drive, didn't he? He is always there—always—isn't he? But you, Mary, far more importantly provided that elusive missing piece of the mystery that my mind, body, and soul craved. I desperately needed this knowledge, and in life's strange way, it was meant to be. And now you can die someday too having given it your all with nothing else to provide.

Plink goes the 22-caliber rifle held steadily in my hands across the clear water of the beaver pond. *Plink, spat, plink, plink* again, *splat,* as the beaver's oily brain matter sprays across the water. Tomorrow is the first day of July, and I've been hunting these industrious creatures for almost a month now. They swim with their heads and beady little eyes held just slightly above the water. Their demise is a critical part of the plan, unfortunately. For I have nothing against this great animal of the earth, but I am required to evacuate them as I need their home. I must, at least, have this specific beaver house that sits less than a hundred yards from me now in the middle of this pond. It is a massive structure—one of the largest beaver houses I have seen in my short nineteen years, nearly the size of a shed or large vehicle. But far more importantly, this particular beaver house lies less than a quarter mile from Mr. Frank Pierson's bear-hunting stand. He's hunted in this platform for as long as I know as I've seen this stand in the woods for years, but that is irrelevant. He'll be here shortly. As a matter of fact, he's already visited twice. I've seen his bait pile, and I've seen his truck that leaves a certain kind of tire tracks—and it won't be the last time.

I studied wildlife biology in high school and have read many, many books, and they are all wrong—there are far more of these animals per square mile than what is written. I've taken numbers 22 and 23 today, and there are far more to kill. But I have taken out all of the animals that used to call this pond and beaver house home. It is their relatives who now visit looking for their former connections and now swim this pond wide-eyed. I'll kill every beaver I see until I put that miserable parasite's body into this now-empty beaver house.

I've done the exterior measurements and by my calculations this beaver house is approximately four feet wide on the interior, and who the hell is going to be poking around the inside of a beaver's house within the Deadstream Swamp? There are very few souls who know the geography of this massive piece of sunken land like I, and fortunately, most are no longer alive. He'll fit neatly within his little new home, fed on by insects and whatever else decides to gain oxygen within these confines. I've seen pictures of the interior in books, and it couldn't be built better for the purpose of hiding something. Busy as a beaver, they say? How about as busy as a son's mom who has been raped? I wouldn't compare my mind-set with much of anything really, but that's just me. A mound of mud and sticks configured by nature's best, they'll never find him. And that's a promise.

He'll consistently rot is what he'll do, and after that, I will be an extremely free man. A piece-of-shit officer of the law that has somehow disappeared? Where did he go? Does anyone know? Not me, not you. Oh, what a shame. Who will care? No one—absolutely no one.

Who would have thought that all I really needed are a swimming mask, fins, and a small rifle to do the job? The perfect murder committed by the perfect predator.

How does one get a rather large human body into the inner confines of a beaver house? There lies the most important question I may ever face. The several entrances of the beaver house are provided by tunnels that start under approximately six feet of water. These tunnels seem to be no larger than three feet across from what I have read and seen so far, but that was only a preliminary glance. Can I fit a grown man's body through and up the passage and into the house? And more importantly, can I fit my own body? It's time to find out.

The water, as usual, is very cold. A spring fed kind of cold. It is as clear as it is cold, gin clear. I painfully bring my face down into the water and peer through the mask—the dark backs of brook trout dart left and right from the murky bottom of the pond. A mere twenty feet down, it is littered with sticks and logs that the beaver seemingly didn't think were adequate for the building of the house or the dam that holds the water of the pond in place. The house seems to be strategically located in a shallow portion of the pond so that the tunnel-like entrances almost touch the bottom of the pond. That area of the pond cannot be more than six or seven feet down; the shallowness should help my cause. I am up and into the clear blue sky, take a deep breath, lungs full of air, and I am down.

The water feels much colder as I gain strength and head down into the darkness. It is absolutely freezing as I gain momentum and reach the bottom. I need to make this quick—very quick indeed. For God's sake, this pond must be entirely spring fed. Ice cold—there it is. I don't have the breath. Just do it and hold it. Just another second, yes—yes, look at that. Looking up, I see a dark tunnel built entirely of sticks that lead up into the behemoth of this house, black as night. That's it. Gotta get up and up—oh, God, bring me up. Up, bring me up.

I exhale and spit into the hot air. What a wonderful sensation. As I thought, there are only three tunnels that lead into the house. Typical, at least from an academic standpoint. That one didn't look too bad, wide enough, it was. Worse case I could peel the layers of sticks off of it and shorten the length of passage. Yes, I could do that if I had to. I could start that job today. That is a brilliant idea. I could even strip the tunnel away to the point where it joins the house itself. A body would definitely fit into the house then, or at least pieces of a body.

Devil's advocate—what if he proves to be too large? He could hit the two-hundred-pound mark even after I empty him of his guts. I could always dismember him and litter the bottom of the pond with his pieces—arms, legs, and torso. They won't last long, will they? The fish and the otter will have a field day and have him gone in no time. But they could be found, feasibly. If they look for him, they could see this, especially if someone somehow learned to step into my skin and think like me. The body must be perfectly hidden; nature will do its work from there. Yes, the inside of this beaver house is the obvious choice. He will not be found there—ever.

He'll see my eyes, yes. He will see my eyes just as the blade of my knife begins to feel the sting and resistance of his spinal cord. My smile will be the last thing he remembers—forever. Please be quick. My God's a little sick.

Chapter 35

Healthy Habit

It's been ages since I have even heard a single word about that boy, thought Dr. Sharon Jury. *It seems like it's been months. What can he be doing with himself? Out there holed up with a bottle of morphine that I somehow indirectly provided him. Oh! What was I thinking? Don't fret and don't worry; the Lord won't let him go that way. No, he can't. I must think about something else.*

Trent won't even return my phone calls these days. I wish he would. I miss the sound of his voice. I miss seeing him, and he probably thinks I'm off my rocker. Nancy's not coming back to him by the sounds of it. He has probably started to notice my feelings towards him. Could we ever be together?

Even Shirley Kudray had an edge to her voice the last time I called to speak with Billy. I am starting to think I must annoy the heck out of everyone. I think everyone is very ready to put this whole situation behind us, but it's just not that easy. Everyone's life turns on a dime over the sound of a shotgun that no one even heard.

"Dr. Jury," Cindy says, through the phone on her desk, "your 1:00 p.m. is here. Martha Gladstone just pulled in."

Oh well, time to listen to another person's problems. Oh, the constant problems. They come in here and dish their immense issues with life and typically leave in a much better mood than when they arrived. I am sick of listening. I am sick of all of this. When is someone going to listen to my problems? When?

"Hi, Martha," the doctor says, as the large woman waddles slowly into the office, "please take a seat. How you been?"

"Oh, OK, I guess. Work's just been so busy. I'm not sure I can take it anymore."

"Yes, I remember you saying that last time," the doctor says. *I'm sure the library is really crazy, isn't it? Sounds like total chaos, anarchy at its finest, can hardly get a parking spot over there, right, Martha? I'm not sure I can sit through another meeting without telling her she needs to go on a diet.*

"I just came from there, couldn't wait to leave that library today, let me tell you," she says, with a sigh. "I did see that poor young Brendon Castleman today at the library, you know, the one whose mother killed herself?"

"What?" the doctor says. "Who?"

"Brendon."

"You saw Brendon . . . Brendon Castleman? Today? At the library?"

"Yes, it was him," she says, attempting to find comfort in the chair. "We chatted for a few minutes. Such a nice young man, and I absolutely adored his mother. She was so pretty, wasn't she?"

"You're kidding. I've been looking all over for him," gasps the doctor. "How did he . . . how did he look? I mean how did he seem?"

"OK, I guess. He doesn't look healthy, to be honest," she says, scratching her chin. "I think he may have lost some weight. God knows he didn't have any to lose."

"What was he doing there? At the library?" Dr. Jury says. *This is a good sign. He's at a library. That's semisocial, isn't it? He's reading; that's a healthy habit. Maybe he's becoming well-adjusted already. Oh, I always knew he was strong. There is hope—there is always hope.* "Martha, was he alone?"

"Doctor, we are here to talk about me, aren't we?"

"Yes, of course, Martha, I'm sorry. This session is free, on me. It's just . . . I treated Maddie, and I'm really worried about Brendon," the doctor stammers. "I hope you understand."

"Oh, I'm sorry, Doctor. Yes, of course, of course, I knew you were close to Maddie. He was alone; he knew exactly what he was looking for. We chatted for a few minutes while he checked out his book."

"He was there to get a book? Good, good, he just seemed to disappear as of late. I just don't think he has anyone right now."

"Yes, I'm sure he's been someplace that, fortunately, most people never have to go. But I see he's still interested in wildlife biology."

Well, he could surely be doing something worse than visiting our local library. Looks like I'll have to start spending more time at the library. "What was that, Martha? I'm sorry, my mind wandered."

"He checked out a book on beavers, said he'd read it once before for a class he had. I'll tell ya, Doctor, if it makes you feel better, he did smile a few times. He was very polite; his manners are impeccable, just as he's always been."

"Oh, thanks, Martha. That does make me feel better. I just feel like I failed on that one—him, I mean. I just couldn't break the walls down," she says, lightly dabbing the tears from the corner of her eyes.

"Do you think he'll still go to college?" Martha asks. "I hope he hasn't given up that dream now."

"I don't know," the doctor says.

"That would be a shame if he didn't," Martha says, looking at the floor and toward the feet that she cannot see, "very intelligent boy, that one."

"Now, Martha, let's talk about you. We are here to talk about you."

Chapter 36

You Know What They Say?

"Sadie," the sheriff says, "I've got Brendon Castleman coming in any minute. Just send him in when he gets here."

"OK," she answers.

"I don't want him waiting."

"Sheriff, how is he doin' lately?" Sadie asks.

"I don't know, to be honest, part of the reason I want to sit down with him. Kid's been to hell and back lately, ya know," the sheriff says. *Ya need something to chew while you're at the salon, don't ya, Sadie? Everyone is so damn interested in that boy, and very few actually give a flying fuck about him. I should cut the doctor some slack on that front; she does care for the boy. I should probably return one of her phone calls too, but then, she always goes off the deep end after about thirty seconds. Yeah, screw it. I ain't callin' her, not today, not unless I get a little loose beforehand. Speaking of which, I should probably get a swallow in or two before I see the boy.*

"Sheriff, Lawrence called this morning and said he wanted to speak with you about extending his vacation. He said something about using it or losing it."

"What? I gave him the week off. What the hell else does he want?"

"He said he's accrued three weeks, says he has to use it all or he will lose it according to the state's vacation-time rules."

"Three weeks in a row? What the hell does he think this is? Some sort of fucking health club I'm running here? You know the last time I had a week off, Sadie?"

"I know, Sheriff, I know," Sadie says, as the phone rings again. "Houghton Lake Sheriff's Department, how can I help you?" she says. "Oh, yes, Lawrence, he's right here," she says, eyeing the sheriff.

"Oh yeah, I'll take this in my office, God damn it," the sheriff says, stomping down the short hallway and into his office. "Lawrence, this is Trent. What's goin' on?"

"Well, Share'iff," Lawrence says, in his slow drawl, "I just wanted to call you considerin' this is the first day of my vacation. I was a checkin' the manual here, see? And I need to take all of my vacation time, or I lose it."

"Lawrence, I gave ya a full week off. You can't take any more. I need you in here, and you know that," the sheriff says. *Jesus Christ, he's yanking my chain, as usual. I gotta hire someone and get this fucking hillbilly out of my office.*

"Well, Share'iff, I'm gonna have to use it."

"Lawrence, you take a full three weeks off and there isn't any use in you coming back. You hear me?"

"Don't get all mad and such, Trent."

"Don't tell me what to do."

"Ah, Trent, that ain't nice."

"Fuck off, Larry."

"You know what they say, Trent, don't you?"

"No, what do they say?"

"Women don't leave men to be alone."

"What did you just say?" he screams into the phone. "You motherfucker, I will fucking ruin you the next time I see you, you motherfucking piece of shit!" shouts the sheriff as his voice reverberates through the open door and into thin walls of the building. *Dial tone! The fucker hung up on me. That motherfucker, I'll fucking kill him. I knew you were sleeping with her, but now you gotta wave it in front of my nose. You will pay, Lawrence. You will pay. He doesn't even care about this job; that's obvious.* "God fucking damn it!" he screams again, slamming his fist into his desk.

"Hi, Trent," Brendon says, coyly from the doorway. "I think maybe this isn't the best time, ay?"

"Oh Jesus, Brendon, I'm so sorry. Oh geez, you saw me at my worst. This is a case I'm working on, oh, anyway. Hey, sit down and relax," he says, with a huff. "I'll be right back, Brendon. Gotta hit the bathroom, and I'll be right with you," he says, quickly exiting his office and down the hallway into the men's bathroom. *Oh, that's it. That's better. Cold water on the face, cold water, wash it away, wash it all away. Don't let him get to you, no, not now. Now it is time to concentrate on Brendon's welfare. Lawrence is fired, and that's that. He's out of my life for good now. I'll have Sadie place an ad today. She can also call Lansing and see if one of those young guys wants to get out of the big city. That's it. Lawrence is out of here, what a relief. Now, I know I had one up here,* he thought, reaching his hand up and onto the top of the medicine cabinet in the bathroom. *It was a pint or maybe a half pint? I just hope I didn't kill it one of those times, one of those times I can't remember. Nope, here it is, yes. Hell, this is a freshy. Look at this little beauty, almost full. What a find. This little guy will get me till five. Everything is going to be all right, all righty indeed. What comes around goes around, Lawrence. You'll get yours, you fucking Southern hillbilly. I'm going to beat the shit out of that man someday. OK, where were we? Oh, Brendon, Jesus, he's in my office.*

"Sorry about that Brendon, how you been?"

"Oh, OK, I guess."

"I'm glad you got my note, and I'm even more glad you called me. I've stopped by the cabin a few times, but you weren't there. What have you been up to?"

"I've been very, very busy, actually. Spending a lot of time outdoors, catching a lot of trout—it's been nice."

"You been working at all?" the sheriff asks.

"I've been working, all right, working on getting better."

"Good, good, you seem better. Time heals, kid. Keep your chin up."

"Yep, things are making a lot more sense to me now, Trent."

"Well, good, that makes me feel better. We all love you, Brendon; and people like Billy, me, and the doctor—we want to be here for you. I hope you understand that."

"Oh, I do. I just needed some time to deal with this on my own. It's really all I asked from all of you."

"True, true," the sheriff says. *Jesus, he is doing better. Oh, what a relief. I knew it would just take some time; that's all the kid needed. OK, OK, this is good.* "Hey, I gotta be honest with you, Brendon. I talked to the realtor, and there hasn't been much interest in the house lately, but it will sell if we give it some time."

"I would imagine that word is out about what took place there, the reason that it's for sale. Would you buy it?"

"Well, I don't think that's it. We just need to give it some time."

"That's too bad. It would be nice if it is sold," Brendon says, glancing out the window.

"Well, it will. I was thinking. You still planning on goin' traveling to Europe and meeting up with Scotty Buzzon? It's July already; you'd better go if—" the sheriff says.

"No, I'm not going now. I've reconsidered."

"Well, I hope it's not because of the house. I mean I can help you out financially until it is sold, if necessary." *Boy, my wife will be really happy about that, she's already starting to talk about money.*

"No, Sheriff. Thanks though. I am OK right now. I think everything is going to be just fine."

"Good," the sheriff says, with a nod of his head. "I got to thinkin' you might want to go over there and see that English girl," he says, with a laugh as Brendon smiled. *There he goes, smiling and everything. He's in a lot better shape than the last time I saw him. Billy's right, though; he does need to get some sun. White as a sheet.* "You want to marry that girl, kid, or what?"

"I suppose things could be worse if I did," Brendon says.

"Why don't you just find a woman you hate and buy her a house?" Trent says, with a sly smile.

"That's a good one, Sheriff. I'll have to remember that one."

"Just a joke, Brendon. You know me."

"Yes, Sheriff, I do. You know, Trent, I've made a decision—either life goes on, or it doesn't."

"Yep," the sheriff says.

"And I've chosen for it to go on," Brendon says.

"Son, sometimes the right decisions in life are, by far and away, the hardest ones to make," the sheriff says, as their glassy eyes met. "I hope that makes sense somehow."

"Oh, it does, Sheriff. Loud and clear."

Chapter 37

See You Soon

Well, that was easy, a walk in the park is what it was. I knew I could rely on my friend the sheriff—he just wants everything to be ok so there aren't any worries on his mind. He wants to see me succeed in life. And how about 'the right decision can be the hardest one to make' part? Oh how succinct . . . But, in truth, I disagree, my drunken friend—the decision that I have made is also a walk in the park. I'll end that parasite's life if it's the last thing I do. Stamp out that little insect's life for the good of this world.

I need to get out of my cocoon of a cabin and start making trips into town more frequently, I actually should be more visible in regards to taking out Frank, if only from a strategic standpoint. As a matter of fact, I should probably be seen directly after the deed is done, just in case . . . just in case I need an alibi. But, they could never decipher that I was somehow involved in the disappearance of the miserable piece of shit, could they? How would they? No one is aware of the true reasons behind my Mom's actions, no one but Mary . . . she could prove to be a loose end. But no one is going to talk to her. And if they do . . .

Over the past few weeks I've been to the library and now to the sheriff's office and the people of this town are obviously nothing to be worried about. After all, what is more nerve-wracking for some than a visit to a sheriff's office? Nothing, for most people. I've got that man set deeply in my back pocket and he may prove to be a very important piece of the puzzle. You know what, what the hell; I don't feel like going back to the cabin yet. I'm going to get a cup of coffee and enjoy myself, it's time to get out and talk to some people. And it's ok that I can already sense their nervous smiles and hellos, it's about time to get over all of this with these people. My Mom's gone and I didn't have anything to do with it—someday everyone will realize this.

Ahhhh . . . this feels good, not being afraid, this feels wonderful. My time spent at the cabin has been therapeutic, but now it is high time for a change. I can't spend the rest of my life out there, not if I plan on living very long, that is. Who would have thought a donut and a cup of coffee could provide so much enjoyment, yep, I need to start spending more time around the people of this great Earth. An earth that will be a much better place, very soon.

I've got to stop by and see Billy and his mother, I need to thank them for all of their heartfelt and much needed help and support during that awful first month of hell. Those poor people, they didn't have anything to do with this, they didn't want to have to deal with this. I haven't even stopped by since I left, not to mention it was an awkward leaving. I damn near climbed out the window of Billy's bedroom by the end of my stay—how many times did that cross my mind?

Oh God, no—this is it, unbelievable. Look who's pulling into the parking lot, speak of the devil, what timing this is. Oh no, this isn't good. This is far too soon. Is he alone? Yes, he is and of course he's parking right next to my Jeep. Frank must not have his thinking cap on today, either that or he no longer recognizes my vehicle. He's out of his truck quickly and around the back of the building, picking up donuts are we, Frank? Getting ready for a trip out to the Deadstream, are we? Time to bait your stand, is it? Time to whisper in your ear, is it?

I need to get out of here, feel like I'm in a fucking closet. I knew I shouldn't have come in this place. And I knew I should have kept a gun in the car. Look at him, back again, miserable piece of shit. I could take him out right here, or at the very least, when he leaves this place. Should have brought a fucking gun, I knew I should have relied on my gut. Pull up next to him outside of town and blow the side of face all over the inside of his truck. Put another one in his stomach for good measure, he'd know why . . . He'd know exactly why I did it. I'd love to see the surprise cross his face as he saw my smile before I pulled the trigger. He'd think, how? How did you find out about what I did to your mother? Oh, but how?

No, no, and no—stick to the plan, the plan is perfect. Stick to your plan and keep your eye on the ball. Catch the walking parasite in the woods and gut him like a pig. No distractions and no witnesses. I'll unzip your stomach Frank, yes—that's what I'll do. Now he's back, back at his vehicle. Ah what the hell, it's time to get a good look at Frank Pierson.

"Thanks for the coffee, keep the change," I say, opening the door into the warm air. "Little early for baiting, isn't it Frank?" I say, to the uniformed broad back in front of me.

"Brendon, oh my God, you surprised me," he says, spinning around and taking a quick step back providing distance. "You shouldn't sneak up on someone like that."

"Oh, I wasn't sneaking, just having a cup of coffee and a donut."

"I, I haven't seen you in a long time," he says, breaking eye contact. "I, I'm so sorry about your, the loss of your mother, I—"

"That's ok, Frank. I've come to the conclusion that it didn't really have anything to do with me. Know what I mean?" *Enjoy that one, Frank.*

"Frank, I wonder what could have driven her into that state of mind?" I asked.

"I, I just—"

"I'll see you soon, Frank. Soon," I say, hopping into my Jeep and putting the keys in the ignition. *Look at him, absolutely bewildered, standing there absolutely clueless to the future. Scratching his head, holding onto a bag full of day-old donuts . . . Enjoy the oxygen while it lasts, Frank. Enjoy . . .*

Chapter 38

T Minus One and Counting . . .

Oh, God, this is it. This COULD be it, that is. I never thought it would be like this, this stressful, thought Deacon. *Keep your cool, gotta stay cool on this one. Jesus, I'm sick of living in this trailer, mosquitos up here the size of small birds.*

Oh well, Hayward better have his shit together or I'll give him an earful, his fax said he didn't know if he could make it and was working on sending me resources after we speak today. After the wire, that is and it's almost time. Watch this be the one that they don't do, or decide to do on another day—wouldn't that be a nightmare?

And how are they doing the transfer? Not to mention Frank Pierson's gloomy figure rising up from his boat the last time I saw him . . . I've been dreaming about that asshole, I need to get him out of my head. There is something about that man, something I can't quite put my finger on, but I do know he's dangerous, very. Just the way he carries himself and that cocky swagger with his head quickly moving and pivoting to each side. He almost looks overly alert, as if he knew that we were on to him and he didn't even care, 'Come and get me guys, I'm ready . . .' Strutting around in a uniform of the state and doing what he's doing, it's going to be very nice seeing him behind bars.

Ok, it's money time, it's almost four. Come on, guys, don't let me down this time. 3:59 and counting, there's the metallic jingle of Frank's coin's, just like clockwork they are, let's hope they're the same way again with the drop.

"Hello."

"Hey, Frank, it's me," says Lance. "How are you today?"

"Fine, I guess."

"You ready, everything all set?"

"Yeah."

"What's wrong, brother? You sound a little off."

"I'm fine, fine."

I think you're right on this one, Lance. Frank has a little different tone this time, there's no confidence in that voice.

"I can tell when you're fine, tell me what's up."

"Nothing, don't start."

"We don't speak but once a month and we can't even fucking see each other until this is done," says Lance with a laugh. "What's on your mind?"

"It's just, well—"

Cough it up, Frank, what's goin' on? Silence, c'mon Frank, speak.

"I bumped into that boy today."

"What?"

"Maddie's boy, you remember me telling you about Maddie?"

"What boy?"

"You remember Maddie?"

"No, what are you talking about?"

Maddie's boy? Where have I heard that name before? That's odd, I know I have . . . I don't like the sounds of this, no, I don't like the sound of this at all. I don't need something new, not now, in the tenth hour.

"I'll tell you, tell ya when—" Frank mumbles.

"Listen, Frank, does this have anything to do with the drop tomorrow night?" Lance says.

"No, no, not at all. I'll tell you about it the next time we get together, it's nothing anyway."

"Ok, so we're on for tomorrow?" Lance asks.

"Yes."

"I'm going to park a little closer to you this time and I'll be on the binoculars as usual, just in case someone is on to us. My source said this may be the last one."

"What?"

"Frank, are you listening to me?"

"I'm sorry, my mind drifted."

"Pay attention, will ya? This could be the last one."

"Ok, good. I'm ready for this to be the last one. We're all set, I'll be up there tomorrow night a little after dark. I'm going to bait one of my bear stands and then head up."

"Yer baiting already?"

"Yep, have been for over a month."

"Ok, see you then."

"Bye."

Dial tone, they were on the phone no more than two minutes . . . damn, they are good. They've never been on more than two minutes and I know the thought of the phone calls being traced has crossed their minds, at least Frank's. Jesus, this could be the last one, the last one? Damn, this is it. It is time to spring. No ifs ands or buts about it, Hayward. The time is now. He'd better pick up, c'mon Tom, c'mon, answer the phone.

"Hayward here," answers the voice on the phone.

"Hayward, it's me, Deacon, we need to talk."

"Go ahead, I've been waiting on your call, I've got no more than five minutes."

"Listen, this is it. Just got off the wire, it sounds like it could be the final drop. If we don't act now this could be a wasted effort."

"Ok, ok," says Hayward, "did Lance say that?"

"Yes. When are you coming in, the drop is tomorrow?"

"I'm not, I can't make it."

"What?" says Deacon, "why not?" *This is unbelievable.*

"Deacon, you have no idea, I'm up to my fucking ears down here and things aren't good."

"What's goin' on, where are you?"

"Chicago, Deacon, as we've spoken about, I've got backup on the way for you, but I cannot be there. You need to understand, that I can't be there."

Who gives a fuck if you're here? I don't, I'll take down these fucking scumbags myself if I have to.

"One of my best, he's in intensive care right now at Rush Presbyterian. He got ran over by a car last night. We were doing a drug buy on the south side and the seller got edgy and ran him over, twice. It was a mess. I feel that I am responsible for this. He's always done whatever it takes and it all went wrong. I'm not sure what to say right now."

"Oh, Jesus, I'm sorry to hear about that, but you know—" Deacon says, in a raised voice.

"Deacon, get off my ass—this is how things really work in our world. I've got three agents, good agents, driving to meet you right now. I have them converging and staying in Gaylord. Now, can you take the sheriff?"

"Well, yes, I'm sure. He hates Lance Pierson with a passion. I'll just have to keep those two apart. Trent will shoot him if he gets the chance," says Deacon.

I'll have to have him sober . . . that may not be a good idea on second thought.

"Ok, good and yes, do keep them apart considering their history," says Hayward.

"That gives you five guns, that should be enough. Do you agree?"

"Yeah, we can do it with five, now, who you sending me?"

"I've got two guys leaving any minute out of Flint. Good, solid guys that are used to this kind of heat. I've worked with them for years. As a matter of fact,

Roy McCalister helped me on the original case against Lance Pierson. They're kind of doing me a favor on this one."

"Ok, keep talking."

"I've got an agent out of Green Bay who can be there in less than a day, she's a solid individual and we used to work together on drug-related homicides in Denver. I'll tell you this, you can rely on her in a pinch. The woman can shoot like no one alive, shoot a fucking crow out of the air with a pistol. My people in Detroit, as usual, are buried. And Chicago is a mess."

And you call this a small army?

"You're sending me a woman out of our Green Bay office?"

"Yes, I am and don't say it like that."

"So tell me about her."

"Sandy is a lifer, just like her dad was. She's actually started her "own thing" within the Bureau."

"What do you mean by, own thing?"

"Necrosearch, believe me, you'll hear all about it."

"How do I get a hold of her?"

"I just talked to her, she's driving across the Upper Peninsula right now, and she'll be in Gaylord by dawn."

"Ok."

"She'll call you, I gave her your info."

"Alright."

"Oh and Deacon, one more thing, get this—you were right. We finally got Lance's old cell mate that's still in Jackson Prison to break; they are bringing the drugs in on freighters. Giant, freighters all the way up through the St. Lawrence Seaway."

"I know, Hayward."

"There is only one freighter line out of Asia using the Great Lakes this year and it's out of—"

"Let me guess," Deacon interrupts."Burma?"

"I see you've done your research?"

"Yes, as a matter of fact, Hayward, only about 10% of the freighters using the Great Lakes are ocean going, most are American and Canadian, mostly bulk carriers, ore, grain, limestone and such. This one is out of Burma and is supposedly delivering textiles to Gary, Indiana."

"Well, I'm sure it is, but that doesn't mean they can't throw a huge bag of heroin off the side of the boat."

"Exactly and according to the taped conversation that I just listened to, tomorrow may be the last shipment."

"Deacon—I will never say this to you ever again, but do what you have to. Take these fuckers down. We know what they're doing, we have the wires and pictures, and one of them has a record, just get fucking cuffs on their hands. That's it. Got it?"

"Absolutely, Hayward, I will get the job done."

"I know you can do it, I'm confident, now remember—if you do have to throw a little lead try and take them down but keep them alive. Shoot for their upper right shoulder or in the thigh or something. I want them alive."

"Ok, got it."

"And keep an eye on that sheriff, he shouldn't even be there technically."

"Yep."

"And I hate to preach, but keep the fucking Canadian authorities out of this, they can't learn about this until it is too late to matter. Huge chip on their shoulders every God damn time. They are absolutely miserable to work with, trust me. They seem to think that they're as important as us, but they're not. Got it?"

"Absolutely."

"We're awfully close to the border on this one, makes me nervous. And make sure you get the gear in the process. We do need a very large bag of heroin on this, I know you know this, but—"

"Hayward, I got it. We're going in during the drop, I know how they're doing it. They do the drop at the bridge, that's their marker. And after that, Frank hands it off to Lance on the water."

"Deacon, listen, I'm at the hospital, he's coming out of surgery, I gotta go, ok?"

"Yep, good luck. I'm sorry to hear things are so bad down there."

"Me too, good luck and goodbye."

Jesus fucking Christ, this is unbelievable. Here we go . . . So, I'm going in with three agents I've never met and an alcoholic sheriff. This should be good. This is awful. This isn't how I imagined it. He mentioned helicopters before, there aren't any fucking helicopters. Who else can I bring? Lawrence maybe . . . God no! Trent will put a bullet in him and act like it's a mistake. A massive steel bridge where Lake Huron and Lake Michigan meet and let's not forget the 740 foot tanker out of Burma. What could go wrong?

"Sadie, Special Agent Deacon here—where is the sheriff?"

"Well, he's in his office, but he's got the door locked."

"Sadie, get him on the phone immediately. Sorry about the tone but this is important."

"Ok, ok, one moment."

Oh, what am I doing? Let's go, Sadie, it's been two minutes already . . . Trent's probably surrounded by empty fifths and asleep on the floor. I cannot believe I'm bringing him in on this, but I need the manpower, no question about it.

"Deacon, what's going on?"

"Trent, Trent, I'm glad you're there. Hey, it's time to put these scumbags away and I need your help."

"What can I do this time?"

"I need your backup and I need your gun. Tomorrow night, we're meeting around four to go over everything."

"Where?"

"Gaylord, just north of you."

"Yeah, I know where Gaylord is. What's the story?"

"I'm going to need you all day and probably well into the night, so try and have a clear head if you know what I mean?"

"Yeah, I know what you mean."

"This is it Trent, tomorrow is the night that both brothers go down."

"Sounds good, I'm in if that's the case. Speaking of which, I haven't seen Frank or his truck at all lately."

"Well, you're going to see him tomorrow night. Speaking of which, you were right; he is breaking the law. Bear baiting doesn't start until August 10th, he's early. I checked the fish and game laws."

"Frank has no regard for the law."

"Yeah, not that that's relevant. Hey, while I'm thinking of it, how is boat traffic on 4th of July weekend?"

"Awful, the lakes get real busy."

"Great, glad I asked."

"Are you talking about the Great Lakes?"

"Yes, I am."

"Oh, don't worry about that. They're too big, shouldn't be an issue, I was talking about the inland lakes. We gonna be on a boat?"

"Yes, probably well into the evening. Bring some backup too, whatever your comfortable with, not just your pistol. Something that will do the job without having to aim too much."

"I'll bring my sawed off twelve-gauge, don't even need to aim with that, shoot first and ask questions later."

"Yeah, that will do the trick. Thanks for being there for me, I really need the backup."

"Hey, thanks for including me."

"Holiday Inn, room 124 at 4:00."

"See you then."

God, I hope the weather is reasonable. Well, here we go. This isn't how it always works, is it? It can't be, this is the FBI. This is it, time for a steady hand. Time to rely on the people around me and get the job done. God damn it that makes me nervous.

Chapter 39

Bleed the Freak

This was a mistake, this whole elaborate plan of catching him out here . . . sitting out here in the middle of nowhere since almost noon. I knew it was a mistake from the beginning. I shouldn't have approached him at the coffee shop, that was definitely a mistake. What if he's on to me? What if he sensed my animosity? What if I have spooked him? He never really liked me anyway and he obviously knows what took place with him and my mother. Yeah, I've fucked this up too.

This is the last day of waiting, waiting for him to arrive—I promise you that. I'll step things up tomorrow, I'm going to start hunting the piece of shit like I should have done from the beginning. I could have killed him after he left the coffee shop for Christ's sake. What's the difference if I blow his head off while he's driving down the road or whether he disappears in the Deadstream Swamp? God knows they will find his truck after a while . . . that should only take a week or so. I'm not messing around with his truck—where would I hide it? And if I'm seen in it I'm definitely screwed. And so what if he's gone? And so what if no one knows why?

I'm not the only one around here who thinks he's a piece of shit, the guy doesn't even have any friends, not that I know of. Damn mosquitoes, I'm so sick of sitting out here everyday, alone, waiting. It will be nice when the first frosts arrive, but we are a good month or two away from that. It will be dark in a half an hour, he's not coming, this is it. Give it another ten minutes, just in case. He's not going to be out here this close to dark, that's for sure. Oh God, that almost looked like something or someone. That is a vehicle, yes—just a slight glimmer, but it is a car, it's got to be him. No, that's a truck and yes, it's him alright. Running a little late are we, Frank? This is it, grab the paddle, time to get this canoe in gear and mobile. I got him, I got you now, you worthless fuck. Keep paddling, almost to the edge, I'll be within 100 yards of his stand when we land. Listen, yes listen, there it is—a car door slamming. Yes, Frank, you are now mine. I'll shed my skin tonight, one can only hope. I will handle this the only way I see fit.

This is perfect. The tip of my canoe slips quietly into the cattails that rim the piece of high ground where Frank's bear stand sits waiting for us both. Time to park the canoe. I slip into the small grove of cedars that line the water's edge. Time to make some decisions, the time is now. I'll get him after he dumps the donuts, it will be darker then. Oh shit, what to do? Do what feels right, get in there and get set up. He won't know what hit him, won't have a clue. Time to get set up, this is it, be quiet. Take your shoes, off, yes this will help. Let's go, find that patch of tamarack just east of his stand, he'll walk within twenty-five yards of me on his way in to the stand. Here they are, same place they were the last fifteen times I've been out here. Lay down below the largest one, he should be through soon. I give him about five minutes, I wonder how quietly the piece of shit can bring himself through the woods? He's a woodsman, let's see what you got Frank—you any good? Look for his legs and his feet, that is all that will be visible from this angle, deep breaths, stay calm. He'll be through soon. Slow, deep breaths are all you need now. I've got the knife, I've got the towel and I've got a rope and axe for the after kill. Come on, Frank, get along now. Where is he?

A full moon begins to light up the woods as if it were almost daylight, good, my eyes are adjusted. I'm ready for you, I can see everything.

Waiting for movement . . . waiting for any movement. What was that? The woods are quiet at dusk, but that wasn't. That was a twig, a twig breaking. He's close and he's on the deer trail as expected. He's close, there's a leg and foot, there's another. He's no more than 20 yards, now. He's stopped, he's stopped dead in his tracks, he must be listening—no movement, maybe he's nervous? He should be.

Be patient, let him dump the donuts and come back by, stick to the plan, I only need another 20 seconds. C'mon Frank, get a move on, there he goes, and he's mobile again. He's walking quickly now, keep it up. I pump the muscle and tendon in my forearm, yes, the knife is still there. Just do it now, don't fuck around, just get the job done. There are his feet and legs again, he's close, time to stand up, there are enough trees between us . . . I can move, stop. Move again, he's moving, closer, closer, too close now. I've got him, I'm right behind you now, Frank. Can you hear me? No, you can't, do you feel my hand above your shoulder? Do you hear this wind like movement? His large body stops and his head turns to face me as I tap his shoulder. I feel the ferocity of a thousand hours worth of pain flash into my arms as the edge of the blade catches him squarely in the neck and my knees bend as I pull my weight down hard, lifting myself almost off of the ground, click goes the knife as it connects with bone. You're done now, Frank, nobody's coming back from that one. Hold still you fucking piece of shit, writhing, flopping around, hold fucking still. Moisture, moisture everywhere as I have him held solidly on the back of his heels against a tree. He's a lot bigger than I remember, as you our eyes meet—built like a horse. A heavy black fluid rolls down my arm in the moonlight and towards the leaf covered ground. Look at me, Frank, look at me. It's me, Frank. See? Do you know who has a knife held deep within your jugular vein? He wriggles slightly as we stare and his entire body begins to once more shudder uncontrollably. Oh my, Frank, what's that I smell? Have we pissed our pants? Yes, Frank, I think we have. You know now, don't you? Yes, he does, look at him, you know it's me, don't you? Look at your alert blue eyes flicking wildly . . . It's me, Frank. Yes, it's me . . . Maddie's son.

"Hello, Frank," I whisper lightly into the meat of his ear as our eyes meet again, "I told you, now didn't I? I told you I'd see you soon. How does that feel, Frank?" I say, as I rotate the knife lightly and hear the clicking of his spinal cord chipping away. *Fingernails on a chalkboard? His hands grab the belly of my shirt. I am in, just hold it, he doesn't have another minute in him, he's lost far too much blood. I may have to come out here tomorrow and clean this place up a bit in the daylight, Jesus, what a mess. No, too risky. Especially with his truck parked out on the road. Just hold him, he's not going anywhere. He huffs up his neck and chest as blood bubbles begin forming from his nostrils, he's done. That's it, you're done, Frank. Goodbye Frank.*

Jesus Christ he's heavy, this isn't good, I don't want to have to gut him here, that needs to be done in the water or canoe. If I slide him it will leave a trail in the leaves to the water. With the amount of blood on the floor it won't matter—if someone comes upon this mess it will be obvious something died. But what?

Wrap the towel around his neck and twist, we don't want too much blood on the ground. C'mon, up you go and onto my back. He stinks of death, what a miserable human being. Up you go, one more time. C'mon Frank, keep your arm over my shoulder, don't be difficult now. There's no use in that, almost to the canoe now. One more push, let's go, one more set of steps and there you go. You're down, lay down Frank, it's time for a rest, then its time for the disembowelment.

Oh, I was worried about this. Should I gut him in the water or in the canoe? Gut him in the canoe and all of the innards are centrally located, this is imperative. I can then flip the canoe in the middle of the pond and get rid of everything. If I gut him here in the shallows it is more likely to be found, gotta think. Gotta think like they're on to me—yes, gut him in the canoe while standing in the shallows, I always knew that would work, no footprints in the bottom of a pond. I can stand outside the canoe while I do the job. Ok, up you go one more time, Frank. Get in the canoe, Frank, there you go, big guy. Alright—this can't be much different than a deer. Let's see here, if I make a cut around his belly button then we can get started. You're a hairy fucker, aren't you Frank? I slip the knife into his lower belly very easily as the stink and gasses erupt, yes—this is just like gutting a deer. A foul stench of guts and life continue to float up into the moonlight. His neck is still bleeding, look at how effective that first cut was. Amazing—now that was a sound decision. I shivered him right in his tracks with that first cut, he wasn't going anywhere, I may very well have scared him to death at that exact moment. Imagine having someone approach you from behind and touch you on the shoulder in the woods after dark? Imagine hearing someone throw a bladed hand through the air? He knew he was gone and he knew who it was, oh what a wonderful day this has been. I may have to do this again, someday. Oh, what a thrill.

Ok, guts are nearly out, he'll be much much lighter now. Time to go, there's the paddle. Time to move, can't wait to take a swim and clean up. Now the real work begins . . .

Chapter 40

Awry

"Alright everyone, listen up and welcome to Gaylord, Michigan," Deacon says, glancing at the white walls of the hotel room. "Tonight's a big night and I, we, have a lot on the line. John and Roy, I really appreciate you driving up, and Sandy, I can't thank you enough for your midnight drive. Now, this is Sheriff Trent Mayfair whose county I've been working in since April. Trent's going to be riding with me tonight so I'd like to get down to the micro of your assignments," Deacon says, pacing around the room of the hotel. *Did that sound too official? Feels like it . . .* "Anyway, please refer to the maps I have provided."

"Hey Joe, no offense, but how long you been working in the field?" John asks.

"Long enough John, now—"

"And Hayward has you in charge of this one, the entire case?" he says, prodding some more.

"If you really need to know, he's in charge of the case and brought me in on it in April, he's got a lot on his plate. Is that alright with you?"

"Relax Joe," Roy McCallister says, "this is just part of John's act, he gets bored on the job, this is his way of having fun."

"You won't be bored tonight, I assure you," Deacon says.

"You need to learn how to take a little ribbing," John adds, "if you're going to last at the Bureau."

"Why don't you guys shut the fuck up and listen and give the kid time to explain what we're doin' tonight; I for one would like to know," the sheriff says, uttering his first words of the meeting.

God damn it, I told him to arrive sober, Deacon thinks, *that can't be a sober statement. He doesn't even know these guys and they outrank him, for Pete's sake.*

"I agree with the sheriff," Sandy says, "tell us what we need to know, from what I've heard; this one could be a little interesting."

Boy, am I going to like her, Deacon thinks, *drove over from Green Bay on a minutes notice. Cute as a button and she can shoot a pistol according to Hayward. What a combination.* "Thanks Sandy, ok, here we go. I'm not saying tonight is going to be simple, but our plan is . . . Sandy, you are going to be covering the marina in Mackinaw City where Frank Pierson keeps the DNR's boat. Watch him park his truck. Standard state issue, green with a gold emblem on the side, from a distance. And watch him board the boat and go. You should never see him, without cuffs on his hands, ever again. We're all on radios so we will be communicating as to when he arrives, etc. And don't worry about the radios, no one else can pick up our signal, so use them. That really should be it, we'll have him after he picks up the drugs. Trent and I will be on our boat and arrest him when he picks up the drop. As soon as he picks up the package, we go in. Sandy you stay at the marina in case something goes awry."

"Got it," she says with a smile.

"Now, there are a group of trees, the only ones around, to the left of the marina as you face the water. Set up in the there with your binoculars and your gun, after he leaves, just in case."

"Now, John and Roy, you're going to be monitoring the marina in the Upper Peninsula that Lance is using. This could be a little slippery, remember, I only figured out where he stores his boat three days ago . . . Quite frankly, I don't have the prep you need, which is why I want two of you there. Just try and be covert and look like fisherman if you happen to have to speak to someone. Lance should never see you, there is a gas station about a quarter of a mile from the marina; it's on your map, watch him through your bino's park his vehicle and board the boat and leave. Then move in, this is where it gets a little tricky. I'm betting that he's going to come back into the marina hot after he figures out that his brother Frank isn't there for the transfer. When he rolls in, tell him to put his hands in the air and arrest him."

"What if he flees and doesn't come back to the marina?" Roy asks.

"My guess is that he will come back to the marina, but—"

"Sounds like a guess," John grunts.

"Listen—we'll have the big fish in Frank, he's an officer of the law. We'll get Lance one way or another. Now bear with me; if Frank decides he's not going to give up, we'll put a bullet in him, if necessary. But, I need him alive. Lance, on the other hand, shoot to kill if necessary if you see a gun. This guy is as dangerous as they come; Roy, I think you've had first-hand experience with that?"

"Yeah, I worked with Hayward on that one. I remember him, should have had a longer prison term if I remember correctly."

"Not to mention he has nothing to lose and I'm sure he doesn't want to go back in the pen. Guys, when he comes back into the marina, don't be afraid to knock him down. He should come back to the slip and park the boat, but we don't know what he'll do from there. But, he's probably going to try and get in his car and go. What concerns me is that he said on the wire recently that he would be close enough this time to Frank to watch him get the drop through binoculars. He's gonna be in an awful hurry when he rolls back into the marina, keep that in mind. I would set up right next to his slip and show him a gun as soon as he parks the boat, but that's just me. Any questions?"

"Hey, we've all got radios," Sandy says, "sounds like a plan to me."

"Boys?" Deacon says.

"Let's do it," Roy says.

"John, Roy—you've got the farthest to drive to Cedarville, should probably get a move on, everything will go down an hour or two after dark. Enjoy the drive across the bridge, that thing is amazing."

"What is?" John asks.

"The view," Deacon says.

"We'll see about that," John says.

"Anyway, Sandy; you're setting up in Mackinaw City, same exit that Trent and I will be getting off at."

"Ok, I'll follow you until we exit, by the looks of this map," Sandy says, tucking her dark black hair behind her ear.

"Perfect."

"By the way," she says, "How far is it between these two peninsulas?"

"Well, the bridge is five miles long—fresh water oceans is what they are. Plenty of room to drop something off the side of a freighter and not get noticed. Trent's very familiar with the area as a local, he said there will be a few fisherman and some boat traffic, mostly tourists getting ferried back and forth to Mackinac Island. Oh yeah, there are only three freighters scheduled to pull through, ours is the last and only one headed west. It should be about an hour after dark and that's when the Pierson boys move in to get the drugs."

"Ok," Roy says.

"Alright, remember radios on."

"Let's do it," Sandy says, as they all begin to arise.

"Trent, ya ready to do some fishing?" Deacon asks.

"Always ready to do some fishing," the sheriff says.

"Nice meetin' ya, sheriff," John says, with a straight face.

Look at Trent glaring at him on his way out the door, glad those two aren't going to be working too close together tonight, that wouldn't be good, Deacon thinks. *No, let's go, none of this nonsense now.*

"Sandy, this is us, just follow us until after we get off the exit," says Deacon.

"Sounds good," she say, with a quick smile.

"Trent, let's get on the road and get on that boat."

"No offense, Deacon," the sheriff says, closing the door of the car, "you think it's a good idea havin' a woman out there, for Christ's sake? She seemed nice, but, you know what I mean?"

"Hayward said she's one of the best, someone I could rely on."

"Ok, it's your case."

"Yes, Trent, it is."

Thanks for the reminder sheriff, God damn it I wish Hayward was here, this is bullshit. If something goes wrong, at least we all know whose ass will be on the line. Anyway, I need to concentrate on the task at hand, not worry.

"Trent, whatever happened with that suicide case you had on your hands?" Deacon says.

"Why?"

"Maddie something or other?"

"Deacon, knowing you, you're up to something; why do you ask?"

"Oh, I was just thinking about it the other day, you know, thinking about this summer—this case. I was in your office when you got that call. Just sounded like, like maybe it was a bit personal for you."

"Oh, it was, to be honest. I went to high school with Maddie and I've known her son Brendon for a quite a few years. He's was my Dad's duck hunting guide for the last five years or so, until he passed."

"Oh," Deacon says.

"Such a shame, ya know? Leaving him with all of this. Great kid, not a mean bone in his body. His grandfather is sort of a local legend around Houghton Lake. Back in the 20s and 30s when Mickelson had people living in it, there were farmers trying to raise cattle and sheep on the edge of the Deadstream Swamp. Well, the bears would come in after dark and eat the livestock; these people were living day to day, hardly getting by, not to mention the noises after dark scared the hell out of them. Art Jackson, Brendon's grandfather, was the local hunter and trapper, he was the professional. He'd hunt and trap the bears so that the people could actually subsist, ya know? He was a hero to those people, helped them survive, but anyway, I'm ramblin' here, what were you asking me about?"

"Oh no, please do, this area fascinates me. Anything to get my mind off this case for a minute or two, Trent. To be honest, I'm a little nervous."

"About tonight? Don't be, we got five guns to their two; we'll get this done."

"Yer' right, I just have a lot ridin' on this, Hayward will flip if anything goes wrong."

"Sounds like we know what they're doin' and how they're doin' it. You mentioned wires earlier, is that how you've been listening to those two? Over the phone?"

"Yes, it is. Hayward got clearance for the wires about the time they shipped me up here. They have worked well for us, thank God for that. The Pierson boys are very careful, never seen in public together and only talk via that one payphone, as far as we know."

"Where is the pay phone?"

"Right next to I-75 in Roscommon."

"That's right next to Frank's office."

"Yep."

"Well, we're almost here, Mackinaw City. There is Sandy, right behind us."

"Yep, there she is, pretty little thing."

"We'll wave goodbye from here."

"Trent, you good with a boat?"

"Yeah, grew up on one, if that's what you mean?"

"Good, you're driving tonight; I'll be up front with my binoculars."

"And pistol," the sheriff adds.

"Yes, and pistol. Glad you bought that shotgun, if you're driving, you might not have much time to take aim, know what I mean?"

"Yes, I do."

"Ok, this is it, this is where our boat is."

"Who's boat is it?"

"It's a rental, I have it for the whole week, fast as hell. Four Winns Liberator with twin 454's in the back. Lance is using a Boston Whaler and Frank's boat can't be faster than this. Hopefully we won't have to find out how fast this thing can go."

"You're taking away from the excitement," the sheriff laughs.

"I don't need any excitement, I just want those two in cuffs."

"Take a deep breath and relax, Deacon, everything is going to be just fine."

"You're probably right, I'll feel better when we get out there and get set up."

"Well then let's get set up."

"Put that blanket over the shotgun case, don't need anyone raising an eye at us."

"Got it."

"Which boat?"

"That closest one, blue and white," Deacon says, walking down the dock with an armful of gear.

"Keys in it?"

"Yep, should be."

"Got it, ok, let's get these ropes off and get out there," Deacon says, as the vessel begins to rumble.

"Starts up nicely," the sheriff says, over the noise of the engines.

"Yep, now," Deacon says, as they move around the small dock, "take us out and to the north end of the bridge, we'll get set up right in front of St. Ignace."

"Alright, hang on," the sheriff says, as the wind grows louder and the boat begins to plane out.

We should be out here plenty early, much earlier than Lance and Frank. Just keep doing what you're doing guys, just one more time is all I need. Trent looks good, minus his speaking at the meeting. Hey, someone needed to shut John up, should be thanking Trent is what I should be doing. I'm glad he's here, minus the drinking, he's about as solid as they come. Guess everyone has a weakness.

Look at that magnificent steel structure of a bridge and imagine the balls it took to come up with this plan and try it for the first time? Just throw the drugs off the side of the freighter when you go under the bridge that is five miles long—unbelievable. Well, this is it, he's slowing the boat down, time to sit and wait. Won't be long now, Frank should be arriving at the marina soon.

"Far north pylon, Trent, right over there, that one. Try and get us behind it, so they can't see us," Deacon says, above the waves and hum of the engines.

"I know, Joe, I know," Trent says, with a smile.

He's mocking me, just need to relax, we can hang out here and we shouldn't be seen and if anyone does see us we'll have the rods out. Ok, this is it, right about here, perfect. Sun is starting to go down, crunch time.

"Trent, is that shotgun loaded?"

"Not yet, will do now. Is this the spot?"

"This will do, perfect."

"Deacon," says the walkie-talkie, "it's Roy, come in."

"Gotchya, Roy, go ahead."

"All is well on our end, Lance just got in his boat and left, squirrelly lookin' guy, I'll tell ya that."

"Ok, good, good, right on time," Deacon says.

Wow, I hope he doesn't decide to get too close to Frank on this one. He sees us come in and arrest Frank through his binos and he will really flip out. Trent looks like he's handled that shotgun before, but I'm sure all these hunting types know their way around a piece of iron.

"Joe, come in," the light voice says over the walkie-talkie.

"Go ahead, Sandy," Deacon answers, "Loud and clear."

"There is no sign of the perp yet, figured he'd be here by now, just wanted to let you know, it's getting kind of dark."

That isn't good, he should be here by now, should be getting to the marina soon if he plans on seeing that freighter . . . well, time to check the horizon.

"Just hang tight, Sandy; he'll be there soon, trust me, he won't miss this."

"Ok," she answers, "I'll let you know when he pulls in."

"Trent, can you see those lights off to the east?" Deacon says, pointing a finger and binoculars to his eye.

"Nope, nothing."

"Well I can, that's our freighter, be here in about twenty or thirty minutes, a little ahead of schedule," huffs Deacon. "God damn it, Trent, something doesn't seem right."

"Relax, Joe, we still got time, Frank might just zip out when he sees it getting close to the bridge, would only take him a minute or two, it's not that close yet."

"Yeah, you're probably right."

"Joe, hope ya don't mind, I need a nip," the sheriff says, with a wink.

"Do what you need to," says Deacon, "just keep those hands steady, we may need them."

"Patience young Joseph, patience," the sheriff says, offering the pint to Deacon.

"No thanks, I'm not a pro like you."

"Suit yourself."

"Roy, come in."

"We're here, what's up?"

"Can you, by chance see Lance out on the water? Any idea exactly where he's parked?"

"As a matter of fact, John's looking at him now—he went out about a mile and a half or so and is just sitting there."

"Good, good, let me know if and when he moves, that's good—he's a long way from us," says Deacon, setting down the walkie-talkie. "Thank God for that, Trent; Lance is too far from us to see us, he's just waiting for the freighter and his brother."

"Yeah, well he's not the only one."

Hayward said I'd be up for some vacation time after this and he knew I'd be ready for it, he was right. Can't wait to look that scumbag in the eye after he's got cuffs on, c'mon Frank, you better be getting close by now.

"Sandy, any sightings?"

"No, Deacon, not at all. I think something's wrong."

"Why?"

"I can see the freighter from here, he's going to miss it if he doesn't show up soon, this is our freighter, correct?"

"Yes, Sandy it is," Deacon says, releasing the button on the radio. "Shit, Trent; she's right, look at that. That boat will be here and under the bridge and past us in no time, maybe fifteen minutes."

"Frank still has time, it's not time to worry yet," says Trent.

"What if he's on to us? What if?"

"Joe, you're not thinkin' straight—if Frank knew we were on to him, Lance wouldn't be sitting out there ready to do the transfer? Got it?"

"Yeah, you're right, good point. But, if Frank's using a different boat, we could be screwed, don't know why he'd do that now."

"Frank could pick up the drugs well after they drop it, supposed to have a light on it and it's not going to float too far."

"Yeah, different boat could mean he'd be coming from a different direction, keep our eyes peeled, there aren't shit for boats out here now."

"This is it, they're going to throw the drugs off within five minutes, seriously."

"Good, we can watch."

"Not too sure which side they throw them from though, if we're on the wrong side we won't see a damn thing. Remember they used a green light last time. Frank said he could see it fall from the sky."

"Luck's on your side, Deacon," Trent says, looking through his binoculars. "There is a new, mind you, green light on the south side of the freighter. That wasn't there two minutes ago. Look."

"Where?"

"Right on the front, yep, just moved, there it goes!"

"Holy shit, you're right," says Deacon.

Look at that—wow, falling, falling—

"Boy," says Mayfair, "It took a while to hit the water, didn't it?"

"Sandy, come in, please tell me you see Frank."

"No sign, nobody, not one person. Sorry, Deacon."

"Just hang tight, Sandy, just stay there," Deacon says, "Jesus Christ, Trent, what now? I mean, the drugs are in the water and no Frank."

"Keep it together, Deacon, keep your eyes peeled, he's got to be using a different boat."

"Deacon, it's Roy, come in."

"Go ahead."

"Lance is on the move, just fired up his boat, he's heading right at you guys, we just lost his lights because of those islands. He's headed west, right at you."

"Trent, you hear that? Maybe Lance is doing the pick-up, but that's not what they said on the wire."

"Relax Joe, my gun's ready, but I can't see anything yet," Trent says, looking through his binoculars.

"There he is, Trent, I can see his lights, he's a little more north than I figured. He's coming at us and he's clipping right along. Move the boat, Trent, now. Get behind a pylon, let's surprise him if we have to. Keep the lights off, he won't see a thing."

"You sure?"

"Yes, hurry, it's dark enough. He's still a mile out or so, get on it, just throw in reverse and keep us there."

"Can you see the drugs, the light?"

"Yep, it's just south of us and has moved a little to the west, current must be pretty strong."

"How we gonna do this?"

"Jesus, I don't know. Let him go for the drugs, he'll see the light."

"You want me to hammer it if he reaches the drugs?"

"Yes, that's all we can do, right?"

"I guess, where the hell is Frank?"

"I don't know, fuck!" Deacon says, under his breath. "He's probably looking for Frank too, ya know? Making a quick transfer. Keep it steady, right here. I can see Lance and the drugs. We got about two minutes, Trent."

"Stay down, keep your head down," Trent says, motioning with his finger.

Ok, there he is, silhouette, he's looking, looking all around through his binos. You're looking the wrong way, Lance, the drugs, there you go. They're right over there.

"He's seen the light," whispers Deacon, "get ready."

"Should I let him pick them up? I think we should," whispers Trent. "He'll be preoccupied pulling that out of the water."

"Good idea, he's back on the move, yep he's going in, he's going directly to the light. He just turned the lights off on his boat off."

"OK, I can still see him, give him about 20 seconds after he stops, then hammer it."

"OK."

"He's stopped."

"Can you see him through the binos?"

"Yep, I got him, he's leaning off the side, hammer it."

The boat rose quickly out of the water as Deacon felt the grated steel handle of his 9—millimeter.

Yep, the lights are off, good Trent, here we go. Time to rock and roll. The spotlight is right there, gotta be ready, gotta be ready to pull this trigger.

"Take a quick pass by, Trent, go by fast in case he's ready to shoot, do a quick circle and we'll come in."

"Can't see him, Joe, he's hiding, get ready."

"OK," Deacon says, looking back at Trent as the sound of rankled metal singed his ear and fire shot out of the end of a gun in the darkness.

Pop, pop, pop, went the bullets into the back of the boat as Deacon fell to one knee and faced Lance's boat.

"Jesus, Joe, you hit?"

"I'm fine, shoot Trent, shoot."

Pop, pop, went Deacon's 9-millimeter as he saw a shadow rise from the boat no farther than 50 feet away. Pop, pop, went Lance's gun returning fire.

"Trent, use that shotgun," Deacon shouts, lying on the bobbing floor of the boat, "light him up, the whole boat, do it now. Trent?" *Oh shit, where is he? He's down, fuck no, no,* Deacon thought as he crawled down the floor of the out of control boat.

"Trent, speak, can you speak?"

"Yeah, I got hit in the shoulder, I'm ok, though, just, just get me some water."

"Fuck, he's moving, Lance is—"

"Go, go," huffs Trent, "it's only a flesh wound, follow him, God damn it!"

"Roy, come in," Deacon says, slamming the boat into gear and follows the now disappearing Boston Whaler.

"Go ahead Deacon."

"Things went bad, get ready, gunshots, several. Trent's been hit, we got a man down, we got a MAN DOWN!"

"Oh shit, where's Lance?"

"I'm right behind him and he's hauling, headed right to you guys, be ready. Light him up as soon as he pulls into the marina," Deacon shouts, over the wind, "Just fucking light him up!"

"Sandy, come in," Deacon screams, into the walkie-talkie.

"Go ahead."

"You get me an ambulance at the marina where Roy and John are asap. Tell them to wait there if I'm not there yet and that we have a gunshot wound. Prep them for the possible need of a helivac. Trent took a bullet."

"Ok, will do. Still no sign of Frank."

How did this happen? How? This couldn't be worse. Look at the sheriff, good—his eyes are still open.

"Trent, how ya feelin'? I'll have you in to an ambulance in no time."

"You just catch that fucking boat in front of us, I'll be ok, just—"

"Roy, you guys set up? I'm right behind Lance, he's hauling ass and headed right at the mouth of what must be the marina."

"We're set, ready. He's ours."

Just hang in there, buddy, hang in there . . . C'mon boat, I've got it down as fast as it will go, Lance is getting smaller, he's going faster than we are. How can that be? C'mon boat, c'mon. Trent's moving, he's motioning . . .

"Trent, just hang tight, I'll have you to land soon."

"You," gasps Trent, "you have to trim the prop, we're not planing out, trim the prop."

"Trim the prop, what?" Deacon says, staring down at the lever and steering wheel. "What?" *He's fading, his eyes are closed, oh not now, Trent, keep them open. Lance is way in front now, we should be near the marina.*

"Deacon, it's Roy, come in."

"Go ahead."

"He passed the marina, he's not coming in, he's on to us."

Shit no, God no.

"Stay there for now, I'll follow him. Sandy, come in."

"Go ahead."

"Did you call an ambulance?"

"Yes, one on the way."

What now, what now? Gotta make a call, follow Lance? And lose the sheriff to loss of blood. Oh no, look at that, the floor is black, he's lost more blood than I thought, shit, slow the boat. Pulse, Trent, c'mon wake up, wake up. He's got a pulse, but he's starting to turn gray, he's unconscious.

"Sandy, get me an ambulance where Trent and I launched, it's closer. Do it now and meet me there."

"Ok, got it," Sandy says.

"Roy, call the Royal Mounted Police immediately, tell them that Lance just passed Mackinac Island and he's headed north," he says, reaching down to the map. "He's headed north to either Canada or Drummond Island."

"Joe, I lost you, what did you say?"

"Tell the Mounties that Lance is headed north towards Canada and he just passed Mackinac Island. Put out an APB, he is armed and very dangerous, already shot a cop. He's on the run."

"Where will he land, Joe?"

"I don't know, no idea, just tell them to look at a fucking map," Deacon shouts, clenching his teeth.

This couldn't have gone worse and if I lose Trent—don't say that, just don't even think that.

"Trent, we're headed in, going to get you to a hospital."

Just hang in there, Mayfair, just stay awake. Have you to the medics in fifteen minutes.

"Sandy, I'm turning around, Trent doesn't look good, we'll be there in about ten minutes."

"Ok, the ambulance is on the way, do you want me to call Hayward?" she asks.

Had to ask me that, didn't you? God damn it, Hayward.

"No," he says.

No, not at all.

"I should be the one to explain this to him."

"Joe, it's Roy," says another voice, "it's starting to rain pretty hard over here, looks like it's moving east."

"Ok, ok, I should be off of the water in a few minutes. Roy, you and John get over to Sandy and back her up if she needs it."

C'mon boat, give me all you got, hope those lights are the right ones . . . Can't lose Trent, no, this is the right thing to do. We'll get Lance, we'll get him, can't hide forever. But, where in the fuck is Frank? And if he was on to us, how come he didn't let his brother know? Shit, hope those are the right lights for the marina, they sure look it from here, yep, that's gotta be it, that's an ambulance. Hold on Trent, hold on buddy. Jesus he's gray, doesn't look good at all and his eyes are shut. God damn it, Trent, hang in there. No wake zone, my ass. Ok, ok . . .

"Sandy, have them at the front dock with a stretcher, I'm here," Deacon says into the walkie-talkie.

"We see ya, Deacon. They're right there, ready for you to unload the sheriff."

"Time to park, or just get this thing sat down," Deacon says, slamming into the dock, "Ok, guys, we got a man down, right here," he screams. "Get him out of the boat and into that ambulance, pronto. Gunshot to the left shoulder."

"Here," the medic says, "you get his feet, up we go and over. Strap him down, we got him from here."

"Here's my card, you get him in the ambulance and to the nearest hospital. Call my car phone when he's admitted."

"Got it, looks like he's lost a lot of blood."

"I know, I know, go, go, go."

"Jesus, Joe, you alright?" asks Sandy.

"No, fuck no. This case just went down the drain. We have no drugs, no Lance or Frank and Trent took a bullet. Fuck!" he shouts. "I told Hayward I didn't have enough coverage for this, God damn it!"

"Think, try and concentrate, what can we do from here?" she asks.

"I don't, I just don't know."

"Where are the drugs?"

"I don't know, I don't even know if Lance got them into his boat, it was dark, it happened so fast. He was shooting at us the moment we got near him, the drugs could still be out there floating around for all I know."

"I'll call the Coast Guard and let them know what to look for."

"Good, good thinking. Tell them that the package had a green light on it. Then call John and Roy and let them know what happened, there's nothing they can do now."

"What are you going to do?"

"I'm going to call Hayward, then I'm going to go to the hospital, wherever they took Trent."

"They said it would probably be Traverse City unless he got real bad on the ride there, then they might have to go to Gaylord."

"Ok, thanks Sandy," Deacon says, burying his head into his hands on the top of her car.

"Deacon, you need to get out of here."

"What?" he says.

"A van just pulled in, they have a camera, someone must have called the press."

"What, how can that be?"

"I'll take care of them, Joe; get in your car and drive, call Hayward, it's all you can do."

"Are you sure, I—"

"Yes, I'm sure. We'll get these guys, just not the way you envisioned. Now, stand strong with Hayward, we, you did what you could. Now go, get out of here."

Maybe she's right, time to call him, but first time to get in my car and get to the hospital. Keys in the ignition, she was right, that's a reporter, Jesus H. Christ, time to go. What could have I done differently? Nothing, Frank was supposed to be here and he's not. Call him, just get it over with.

"Hayward, it's Deacon."

"I've been waiting for this call, tell me the good news."

"There isn't any."

"What do you mean?"

"It couldn't have gone worse."

"Don't tell me, don't tell me this, Deacon. What—"

"Frank never showed but the drugs did. Lance came in because Frank didn't do the pickup, Trent and I moved in on him when he came in to grab the drugs."

"And?" Hayward says, gruffly.

"And Lance started shooting immediately, the sheriff took a bullet."

"Oh shit, is he gonna make it?"

"On the way to the hospital right now."

"Where's Lance?"

"He got away, I chased him for almost three miles, had to turn back because of Trent's condition."

"He was headed towards Canada on the water the last time I saw him."

"Oh no."

"Oh yes."

"And Frank, where is he, Deacon?"

"Your guess is as good as mine right now, he just didn't show. It was unbelievable."

"And the drugs?"

"No idea, it all happened so fast, Lance started shooting, we don't know if he got them into his boat or if there still out there bobbing around someplace."

"What? No, drugs, no Frank, no nothing?" Hayward screams.

"That's what I said, didn't I?"

"Deacon, do you know how much of my budget is wrapped up into this case? Do you?"

"Well obviously not enough considering we were out there understaffed and *my* guy ended up taking a bullet."

"Don't talk to me that way, you—"

"You should have been here, Hayward. You know that, I was understaffed and the whole thing went wrong."

"Oh, I'll be there alright. Already booked my flight, be in Traverse City tomorrow at noon."

"It was a mess, Hayward, I did everything I could."

"The sheriff wasn't even technically supposed to be there!"

"I know, I know."

"Have you called the Canadian authorities?"

"Sandy did as soon as we lost Lance."

"Oh Jesus, what a mess."

"I did everything I could."

"You best find him and you best be the one who picks me up at the airport, got it?"

"I'll be there."

"I think you and I need some windshield time to get a few things straight. Deacon, where the fuck is Frank Pierson?"

"As I said, we don't know."

"Do you know where Lance Pierson is?"

"As I said—"

"Call me if you get any news, I don't care if it's late."

"I'm headed to the hospital right now."

"This is a fucking mess, Deacon, do you know that? Do you?" Hayward says, hanging up the phone as the dial tone returned once again.

Fuck you Hayward, just fuck you—

Chapter 41

Conceal

Look at the parasite, empty of his guts in the bottom of my canoe glistening in the gorgeous moonlight. The foul smell of death and my new life rises into my nostrils. How do you feel, Frank? A bit empty perhaps? Yeah, I know the feeling—I took you down, I took you out, don't ever forget that my newfound friend.

Are your eyes still open? Yes, they are—perfect. And if you close them again I'll open them again, remember this, Frank. Oh, what a glorious evening. I'll never forget this, Frank, I owe you for all of this glory.

Back to the task at hand—I must park the canoe, yes, we are here, this is it. Tie the canoe to the beaver house, there is my stick. Steady, steady, now. Don't move, Frank; you'll rock the boat. Hah!

There we go, yes, there we go. Ok, time to get wet, time to wash this filth off of me. Time to strip off, I don't need the added weight, clothing will be heavy, especially when wet.

The July water is already warm, much warmer than the silky evening air. Time for my mask, but no, not the fins. Not the fins if I'm going inside this time. Ok, time to find the orange tag, it's down there, submerged at the entrance of the beaver house that I have prepared. Stay right there, Frank, and don't move a muscle.

Up and into the starry moonlight and down, into the darkness. There it is, an out of place unnatural piece of ribbon. Good, it's here, back up, back up into the oxygenated light of night. Hands on the edge of the canoe, hi, Frank—yes, it's me again. Where's my rope, there it is. Time to rock and roll, kid. Time to tie this rope around my ankle and actually go into the bowels of this amazing natural structure.

Knots tied snugly around my ankle, big deep breath, just like we practiced, keep them coming. The rope is tied, inhale, deep, we go on three—two, exhale, inhale and three. Down, down we go, hold steady, ok, we're here, time to go in. Damn it, I knew I should have gone in before now, up, ouch, that was sharp, shoulders fit, don't stop, not now, can't get stuck. Up, up and in, reach and pull. Oh fuck, my lungs are hot, kick, one more kick.

Go, go, no breath, my hand, my hand feels dry, or is it? Hurry, this, this is it. This better, be, oh, air, oxygen, oh, thank God. Thank you God, thank you—I'm in.

Dark as night and I am in; this is it. Feel, feel around. No, relax, try and relax and catch my breath. The rope, is it? Yes, it's still there, around my ankle, good. Relax, relax and untie the rope. Must relax and focus . . . There we go, come off now, the knot is tight from the water. Damn it, I need a light, I need both hands for this, there we go. I lean on my elbow, this feels like mud. Feel this, feel the inside of the darkness, it's all mud in here, reeds and mud. I need a light, I knew I needed a light. No, it's ok, I can do this with instinct, I can. Got the rope off, alright. Where to tie it? I need a stick, or something stable I can rely on. Only mud in this darkness, mud, smelly mud. Try the ceiling, yes, try the—yes, there we go. That's a good strong stick, pull hard—this will do. I can tie a knot in the dark, can't I? Prop me up, I must sit down, rope in mouth, up we go. Ouch, damn, sharp stick to the forehead. Well, now I know where the ceiling is within this darkness. Feel around, arms widespread, nothing. This house is plenty big for the two of us—at least temporarily.

I must go out face down, watch that sharp stick from the way up. Time to go, turn around, I'll have to be on my side, yes, deep breath, time to go down, slide into the water of the tunnel. Grab and pull, grab and kick down, pull and I'm out—kick, kick, up and up and into the moonlight. Much easier on the way out and down with the help of gravity. Yes, that's it, bright and above me. The water is warming, air, my beloved and necessary air. I must rest, I must rest for a bit, that was a lot. Grab the edge of the canoe, just lay here on your back in the water and rest.

Ok, Frankie my boy, time to move. You've enjoyed the comforts of my canoe for far too long. C'mon buddy, got ya by the ankles, out, out and onto the beaver house where you can be prepared. There you go big guy, oh—you look like you're smiling. Yes, Frank the moonlight is very bright. Do you like the moonlight, Frank? Yes, how could you not? Arms behind your back Frank; you have the right to remain silent Frankie boy, this being the only right you have. We don't want any snags in the tunnel, now do we? Arms are tied. Now for those big feet of yours, don't want one catching something, now do we? Let's take these water-laden boots off for Christ's sake, must be at least ten pounds right there. I'll have to sink them to the bottom of the pond, no evidence, Frank, none. Tie the rope around his body, we need to keep everything tight, Frank, you need to fit into that tunnel like a glove. The rope is tight, now you have your own rope coffin. Don't fret, the rope is only a tool, your true coffin is made of wood, sticks, and mud. And now it's time to slip down into the inky black water. You're floating, Frank; this is no time for silly shenanigans, time to get that chest cavity full of water, every nook and cranny. Yes, there we go, sink, sink and sink some more. He's under, God I hope this works, if he doesn't fit, I'll have to hack him into bits—that would be disgusting.

Now, should the other connecting rope be tied around his neck or his feet? What do you think, Frank? No help as usual . . . How will he best fit through the tunnel, feet first or head first? Yes, around the neck, obviously. Sorry to do this Frank, but it is necessary, need to tie this one very tight. Hold still buddy, we're almost ready.

This is obviously going to take several trips; first I must submerge him and tie his body to the bottom of the entrance. Once that is done, I can then come back up for air and go back down in order to finish the job. The rope that is around his neck is connected to the inside of the beaver house, not bad kid, not bad.

I'll enter the house again and hopefully won't become entangled on the rope that is tied on the inside of the house and around his neck. And from there I must pull him up the tunnel and into the beaver house. God help me if he gets snagged on the way up into the tunnel to the house, that's my only way out, the only tunnel I have cleared. Down you go, Frank, down you go. There, stay right there for a second; three or four feet down will help you become full of water, stay down, I just need to keep my foot on his body and balance myself, stay down, there we go. Yes, he's not moving, he's submerged. Time to put the mask on, time for three deep breaths. Up, look up, the moon is still there, big breath and down, down, down to the entrance, got the rope, time to pull him down. His feet point upwards towards the bright moonlight as I pull him down headfirst to the entrance. Good, Frank, you're here; time to set you under the entrance so that you don't move or drift back up to the surface, that should do it. That should do it. Stay Frank—stay right here, I'll be right back, time for more oxygen.

Ok, this is it; this is when things get serious. Time again to hang onto the side of the canoe and relax for a minute and catch my breath. One more final step—get his body into the inside of this beaver house and I am out of here. After this is finally complete, it's time to go home and rejoice. And more importantly, it's time to get high. It's time to go to that plane, my plane, where only angels dwell—I've seen them. But, how can I get any higher than the last two hours of my life? How? There is time for this sort of pondering after the job is done—it is now time to take the final step.

Rope tied on the inside of the house, check. Rope tied around his neck, check—deep breath, one more, focus, I'm going in. Down again and away from the moonlight, there you are, Frank. Haven't moved a muscle, have you? Hopefully your waterlogged body isn't too heavy and won't create any problems when pulling you up and into the house. For once that is done, you are lodged forever. You'll enjoy your new home, as the insects, otters, and muskrat pick at your flesh whenever they feel necessary. It's ok though, nature wouldn't have it any other way. Will the beaver mind that someone's grave has overtaken their carefully built home? Will the muskrat that decide to reside here because the beaver are now gone? They'll get over it, Frank, don't you worry. Up and into the entrance and up, I can feel the rope, don't knock it, kick and kick, almost there now. Up and air—I'm in, once again, I'm in and breathing again. Reach up, where, there it is. The rope is still tied to the invisible stick, it is still pitch black inside the lodge of the beaver. Time to get comfortable, comfortable enough to leverage this rope in order to pull a body up and into this beaver house. Need to be careful in the beginning, don't want him getting snagged in the mouth of the entrance. That could be hell—he stuck in the entrance and me on the inside. You'd be fucking me there, wouldn't you, Frank? This would become both of our slimy and watery graves . . . But, that won't happen, I'll see to it. Pull the rope slowly, just like ice fishing, every so slowly, there is his heaviness. I've got one on the line and he's moving, he's mobile.

C'mon Frank, don't be difficult, we just need to get your head and torso into the bottom of the entrance. Pull, but not too hard, give me some leverage. He's stuck? Pull, damn it, he's stuck, c'mon Frank, give it another tug, there we go, and he's moving again. C'mon Frank, come to Papa, up and into the house. Time to move, I need to be on my knees for this piece of the job. Time for a good strong pull, pull—he moved at least twelve inches with that one, another, pull up the slack, pull again, pull up the slack. Come on Frank, can't be long now. Pull—just how long is this rope? It's dark and it stinks and the oxygen is thinning. I'm working myself into a fervor now, stay focused, the finish line is almost here. Couple more pulls and I should have it. Reach down into the water? Is that, it is—a wet soaked head. He's only a few feet from his home. Almost there now, Frank, we're not worried about those big broad shoulders now, are we? Few more tugs, uh, there we go, his head is out, yes it is. Welcome! Welcome to the house and out of the stick-laden labyrinth. Stay there, Frank, I need to rest for a second or two. I can now pull on the other rope that is wrapped tightly around your body, yes, much better leverage. Get your legs and feet out of the tunnel Frank, it is now time for me to leave. There, sit there, right next to me, no—not on me, Frank, next to me. Wish I had some smokes, wish I had a light, wish I could show you around, but, I must leave you, forever. He's up and onto the ledge, get up there, head and feet, going to lay you on your side, Frank—forever. Hope you don't mind. There, he seems solid, he's not moving anywhere. Ok, down, need to get out of here, time to get wet again. Deep breath and head down into the top of the tunnel and water, time to go, Frank. Kick down and down and out, sorry to leave you, Frank, but I must. I have a life to live, a brand new one. Hope you don't get lonely, Frank. Take it from someone who's been there—it's an awful place to be.

Chapter 42

Desperate People

"It's about time, Sadie, you're late," Deacon says, pacing in front of the sheriff's station.

"Its 7 am, I'm early, actually, isn't Trent here yet?"

"No, he's not."

"Do you have keys?"

"Well, yes, of course, I'm sorry, I didn't—"

"Ok then, get them in the door, I need to get to work."

"Is everything ok? You look like you haven't slept?"

"No, I'm afraid it's not and yes—I haven't slept. Sadie, Trent's not going to be in for a while, he took a bullet last night working on one of my cases."

"What? He did what? Oh, is he, is he alright?" she gasps, almost dropping her purse.

"Yes, he's in stable condition, they removed the bullet this morning."

"Oh my, that's awful. Where is he?"

"Traverse City Hospital," Deacon says, breezing through the lobby and into Trent's office, "and put some coffee on, please."

Jesus, this desk even smells like alcohol, knowing the sheriff there's probably a bottle hidden around here somewhere. Oh my God, I hope he pulls through this one. An alcoholic with a gunshot wound, can't be good. And it was on my dime, fuck me anyway. Ok, gotta think, gotta rally. Trent's at the hospital and they successfully pulled out the bullet, nothing more there I can do. I've probably done enough already.

Hayward flies in at noon, what can I do before then? What good can I do before noon? Frank Pierson you fucking asshole, where are you? Guy up and disappears the day of the drop—unbelievable, but how? I listened to the wire on Thursday and he's nowhere to be found on Friday and I'm sitting here fucked on Saturday. How could he have known about us? He couldn't, I just can't believe that. But, what if he didn't? What if? What was different about the last wire? Think, he was different, Frank was different. Lance even called him out on it, he sounded worried, Frank was worried.

'I'm a little worried about Maddie's boy', a little worried, Frank? That could be something, but what? This is a small town, someone's gotta know something and I've got to start asking some questions, that and I'm going to need some help.

"Sadie," Deacon says, in a rush, "Here's the deal, I want you to call Lawrence and get his ass in here ASAP."

"He's not going to like the sounds of that, he's on—"

"I don't care Sadie, you tell him that it is a direct order from me, from the federal government, got it? Tell him the truth—Trent's in the hospital and I'm going to need some back up around here."

"Ok," she answers, lightly. "Mr. Deacon, do you think Trent is going to be ok? He's a good man, ya know?"

"Yes, I do think he's going to be ok."

"Good, this just worries me so."

"Sadie, I'm going to need your help as well. Is that ok with you?"

"Well of course it is, what, what can I do?"

"I need your help from an informational standpoint, quite frankly. What do you know about Maddie's boy?"

"Oh, Maddie's boy, you must be talking about Brendon. Terrible thing, her committing suicide and all that."

"I know about that Sadie, I was standing in the sheriff's office when you took the call, remember?"

"Oh, I forgot about that, yes."

"Well, what else do you know? I don't want to have to bother Trent with these questions, he hasn't the energy. This is between you and I and the fence post, understand?"

"Well, I knew Maddie, everyone knows everybody around here, small town. Well, there's been some talk around town lately. Ya know, everyone thinks the boy is gonna kill himself, too? I know Dr. Jury is awfully worried about him, she's been keeping an eye on him. Speakin' a which, I need to call her and cancel her meeting with Trent today."

"What does she have to do with it? This Doctor?" he asks.

I remember Trent bitching about a local doctor and it was a woman.

"Quite a bit, really. She treated Maddie, I do know that, and she was the doctor we had to call to pronounce Maddie dead. Trent didn't want to, but we didn't really have a choice with it bein' the weekend and all."

"What time is she coming in to see Trent?"

"In about a half an hour, I should call her now."

"You call her now and confirm that she is going to be here, please tell her not to be late."

"But, but why? Trent's not here and—"

"I need to speak to the doctor, Sadie. By the way, what kind of doctor is she?"

"Dr. Jury is a psychiatrist by trade, but she used to be a regular doctor, I think. She does some work for the medical examiner, which is why we had to call her that day. Choices are kind of thin out here, ya know? I've heard her call herself a Christian Psychiatrist before, which I thought was kind of odd."

Yeah, I agree, odd is right. Can't wait to meet this one, see what Trent was bitching about.

"And don't forget to call Lawrence, get his ass out of bed and in here pronto," Deacon says, stomping back into Trent's office.

I need to talk to Lawrence about the sheriff's drinking habits. The doctor calls on my car phone this morning and wants to know how much alcohol Trent consumes on a daily basis so that they can make up for it during his stay. How on earth am I supposed to answer that question? I don't know how much exactly, a lot . . .

The PA rings on the desk.

"Mr. Deacon, it's Sadie. Lawrence is on his way in right now, he said no problem."

"Good, send him in when he gets here, I need to speak with him immediately."

How are Maddie's boy and Frank Pierson related. Must be if Frank mentioned him? Sadie's been pretty chatty, why not ask her? All she can tell me is no.

"Hi Sadie, sometimes that PA is so impersonal," he says, stepping back into the lobby, "I've got one more question and this is entirely off the record, ok?"

"Sure."

"Do you know Frank Pierson? The DNR officer?"

"I know who he is, I don't know him though."

"Did he know Maddie? Brendon's Mom?"

"Yes, they dated for awhile. Never saw them together, but heard about it through the grapevine.

What the fuck? They dated, did they? Unbelievable—maybe there is some meat on this bone after all. I wonder what the doctor knows? Didn't Trent mention her being a bit gossipy, or am I making that up?

"Thanks Sadie, I heard about that too, but just wondered if you knew something I didn't," he says, with a charming smile. "Remember—you, me and the fence post."

What if this kid did have something to do with this mess? It's a stretch, but you never know? I need to move on this soon, I need to move on this right now.

"Mr. Deacon, Lawrence just pulled in."

"Ok, thanks Sadie."

I'll have Lawrence do a loop around town looking for Frank, check his house again. Then I'll have him go and pick up this kid, Brendon. I've got a few questions for him, might as well, nothing to lose. Maybe he has something to do with the drugs? Maybe he is a distributor? Maybe that is why he and Cliffy Stoink got into a fight? Have to bring Cliffy back in too.

"Mr. Deacon," Lawrence asks, standing in the doorway a bit taller than usual and dressed in uniform. "Can I come in?"

"Yes, Lawrence, thank you. I really appreciate you coming in, I need your help."

"I heard Trent's in the hospital, he goin' to be alright?"

"I think so, Lawrence, I think so. Sit down, I have some questions for you so that we can get to work."

"Yes, sir."

"What do you know about Frank Pierson?"

"The DNR officer, not much."

Ok, Lawrence, thanks for your honesty.

"How about his brother Lance, ever heard of him?"

"Yeah, I heard of 'em, ex-con. He was in town a few months back raisin' hell at the local country club. The sheriff seemed a bit rattled by him bein' here."

"Here's the deal—Frank Pierson has been under investigation for some time now, this is strictly between you and I," Deacon says, as Lawrence nodded. "Frank's missing right now and I need to know where he's at, immediately. He's not at home and his truck wasn't there either when I checked his house this morning. No tire tracks, no nothing, but we did get some rain last night. I need you to take a swing around town and look for him, you see him and you call Sadie immediately. Check his house again for me too, got it?"

"Yes, sir," Lawrence says, bright-eyed.

"After that, come back to the office and I'll give you an update on what we do next."

"But, Mr. Deacon, why is Frank under investigation?"

"Lawrence, I'm going to be candid with you—that's not something I can explain right now. But, you will be learning a lot more about this case over the next week or so. I need you to be my right-hand man; you're working for me now. How do you feel about this?"

"Mr. Deacon, I've been ready for this all my life."

"Good, I like your attitude, now please do that drive and get back here as soon as you're done."

"Yes, sir," Lawrence says, reaching for his hat and the door.

The PA screeches as Lawrence makes his way out the door and past the arriving doctor.

"Mr. Deacon, it's Sadie," she says, as Deacon rises from the desk and walks into the lobby, "the doctor just walked in."

"Hello doctor, I'm Special Agent Deacon with the FBI, please follow me."

"What, who? Where's Trent?" she says, without returning the invitation to shake his hand.

"I'm a good friend of the sheriff's, he's not in the best of shape right now, follow me and I'll explain."

"Is everything, ok? I hope—"

"It's going to be, c'mon we'll use Trent's office."

"But—"

"Please shut the door behind you."

"Excuse me, please tell me what's happened, I've known Trent for a long time."

"He's in Traverse City at the hospital and he's stable. He was hurt in the line of duty last night, I think everything is going to be ok."

"What was he doing, I mean—"

"That's not something I can discuss with you, doctor. I'm sure you care, I know you care about him and he's going to be ok."

"But, Mr. Deacon, that's not enough, I want to know what happened."

"Doctor," Deacon says, interrupting, "Do you miss Maddie Castleman?"

"What?"

"You heard me."

"Mr. Deacon, that is enough. What is this about? I demand an—"

"Dr. Jury, you aren't in a position to demand anything right now. You are a part of an investigation of the Federal Bureau of Investigation, my investigation," he says.

Choke on that one doctor, we'll see who speaks next. Silence doctor, how's it treating you? Fine with me, won't last long though. No, especially with an emotional psychiatrist.

"Well," says the doctor, "what can, what do you want to know?"

"Everything, absolutely everything."

"She was my patient, I have a patient to doctor confidentiality to acknowledge, even if she is gone."

"Were you two close?"

"Yes, she confided in me greatly."

"And how well do you know her son, Brendon?"

"Brendon?" gasps the doctor, "Is that what this is about, because if it is, I'll—"

"Just answer the question, doctor," he says.

Well, well, well—she's a little touchy about the boy, isn't she?

"No, I won't. Not unless you tell me what this is about," she says, "that poor young man has been through hell lately."

Hell—sounds like maybe he's desperate? Sometimes desperate people do desperate things.

"Sharon, you either answer the question or I'll have reason to believe that you're withholding pertinent information to my case," Deacon says, through a stare.

"Excuse me, what is this all about?"

"Doctor, answer the question."

"What question?"

"Tell me about the boy." *Come on, she has to know something, spit it out.*

"I have nothing to say about Brendon."

"Well, you can always stick around for a while."

"What? You'll arrest me?"

"Well, obviously I could, if I felt that—"

"You must be kidding?"

"Do I look like I'm kidding?"

"That's preposterous," she says, slapping her knee.

That's it; you're getting warmed up now, she looks frustrated. Nothing quite like getting them out of their comfort zone.

"Well, Maddie was my patient and after she left, I, I tried," she says, fighting tears, "I tried to help Brendon, I tried to care for him. But I failed."

"Where is he now?"

"I don't know, no one knows, living out in the cabin in the Deadstream probably," she says, "alone, all alone."

"When is the last time you saw him?"

"It's been ages, months, seems longer than that. After Maddie left, he stayed at the Kudray's for awhile, I saw him every day then."

"And?"

"And what?"

"And what aren't you telling me?"

"Nothing, honestly, I—"

"That's it Sharon, I'll be back, I'm going to let you think about this for awhile," Deacon says, standing up.

"Ok, ok, for God's sake stop!" she screams, "why are doing this to me? Why?"

"Sharon, I want to know what happened, I'm worried about the boy too."

"Well you don't sound worried, you sound—"

"Well, I am, now begin," Deacon says, still standing.

That's it, doctor, come on now, just tell me the way it is . . .

"The day that Maddie, ya know, Maddie's day—the day she left us, I was called in. I only live right down the street. Well, I absolutely lost it when I realized what had happened. It was awful—Brendon is the one who found her and that's so unfair. He was laying in the front yard after he found her and it looked like he was going to die himself, shaking uncontrollably. I had just come from an elderly patient's home who I'd had been administering morphine shots too because he was dying. I gave Brendon a shot to calm him down, I shouldn't have, but it did work."

"And?" *Get to the point, doctor, I don't have all morning.*

"And then it happened, we learned that someone had broken into the clinic and stole the bottle of morphine, I think, I know it was him. And this is something I created!"

"So he stole a bottle of morphine and?"

"And that's it, I didn't report that I knew it was him. I looked everywhere for him to try and explain how dangerous using this drug could be, but I couldn't find him. More like he wouldn't let me find him."

"So, he's probably in pretty rough shape right now?" Deacon says. *So, he uses drugs, I know that, but how can he be connected to Frank?*

"I'd say, I think he's probably walking through hell right now, but I'm the only one who feels that way. Trent and I haven't exactly seen eye to eye on this."

"Tell me about Frank Pierson, Frank and Maddie."

"Oh, well they dated for awhile, always was a sensitive subject to Maddie, one of the few things I think she never felt comfortable talking about in therapy."

Really? Is that so? Bingo, we may have something here. I wonder why, Maddie? What happened there?

"What about Frank and Brendon?"

"I don't know anything about that, I don't think Brendon really liked him, that is one of the few things Maddie told me."

"Doctor, I really need your help and I want you to be honest, if only for Brendon's sake. Do you think Brendon could be involved in selling drugs?"

"What? No, I don't think so, but I never thought he'd break into the clinic either, it pretty much had to be him," she says, clearing her eyes of tears. "Why don't you tell me what you're up to, you haven't told me anything and I'm trying to do everything I can for you."

"What I am up to is up to me, doctor."

"Whatever."

"How does he feel about Frank, anything there at all?"

"Just what I told you, he told Maddie that he didn't have any respect for Frank and didn't really like him being around. Why, I don't know."

So he didn't like Frank, didn't want him around, so maybe he isn't involved in the drugs? But, he uses drugs? This is all too confusing, I've got to talk to this boy. "Thank you doctor, thank you for your time."

"Well, I didn't really have any choice did I? Do you always threaten to jail people that you don't know in order to gain information from them?"

"Only when necessary, doctor, only when necessary."

"That's unacceptable, you should be ashamed of yourself."

"Enough, doctor, enough. Now, how can I reach you if we need to speak?"

"I don't think we need to speak anymore."

"What if it involves the welfare of Brendon Castleman?" Deacon asks.

"Well," she says, "then call me at this number," handing him a card. "Do you think I can visit Trent, he probably wouldn't mind a friendly face right now."

"Yeah, I guess, if the doctor will let him have visitors. Doctor, if I call you and leave you a message I will expect a phone call back very quickly."

"Understood."

The noise of the PA brings Deacon's focus back to the desk.

"Mr. Deacon, Lawrence just pulled back in, just wanted to let you know."

"Good, Sadie, send him in, the doctor was just leaving."

"Lawrence Vintage, huh?" says the doctor with a shrug, "good luck with that one."

Looks like the doctor is on Trent's side with that.

"Ok, doctor, speak with you soon and thanks," he says, to an unreturned smile as she passes Lawrence rushing into the office.

"No sign of 'em Joe—now what?"

"Give me a sec—I'm thinking . . . you got any smokes, Lawrence?"

"Yes, sir, I do. Here ya go."

"Mr. Deacon, it's Sadie again, you have a call."

"Who is it Sadie, I'm meeting with Lawrence now."

"It's a doctor from Munson in TC, he wants to know about the sheriff's drinking habits, some Indian fella."

Oh God, forgot to call him back. Not now, not now.

"Lawrence, how much do you think the sheriff drinks every day? I'm serious, they don't want him drying out while he's in the hospital or it will hinder his recovery. Any idea?"

"Well, hell yes. Me and Trent used ta booze all the time until recently, well he—"

"Mr. Deacon, sorry to interrupt you again, but I have a Mr. Hayward on the other line, he's screaming at me, he's making me uncomfortable."

Oh Jesus, what next? No wonder Trent had a nip on the job, sounds kind of good right now.

"Lawrence, talk to this doctor, give him the truth, sound advice as to what Trent's average day was like, ok?" Deacon says, looking into Lawrence's bloodshot eyes.

"Yes, sir."

"I'm going to take the other call in the conference room, be right back."

"No problem, Joe, I can handle it," Lawrence says, finally taking a seat at the sheriff's desk and picks up the phone.

"This here is Deputy Lawrence Vintage, what can I do ya for?"

"This is Doctor Sanjay Patel, can you help me with the assigned question?"

"The what? You mean how much booze the sheriff would put down every day?"

"Yes, the drinking, his average daily intake."

"He drank a fifth of Wild Turkey and a twelve pack of beer every God damn day."

"What? I believe sir, that is physically impossible."

"I ain't kiddin' ya thar' doctor."

"Sir, are you serious, who is this again?"

"This is Deputy Lawrence Vintage, like I told ya the first time. I'm the actin' sheriff now that Trent's down."

"Well, that is a lot of alcohol. I am surprised he has lived this long."

"Don' get me wrong, sometimes he'd skip the beer, but I tell ya what—he skips that whisky and he'd act like a fish outta water."

"Well, in that case, I will have to administer an IV for him with trace amounts of alcohol for our post-op. We must prevent any detox with this sort of trauma accident."

"Well, I don' know about all a that, doctor—you just keep him nice and oiled up in thar' so's that he can recover, ya hear?" Lawrence says, with his feet propped up onto the desk, noticing the shouting coming through the thin walls of the office.

That must be Joe in thar' talking to that Hayward guy? Boy, he sure does sound fired up. Need to stay on the good side of him if I'm gonna end up sheriff.

"Lawrence," Deacon says, skidding back into the room, "Is that doctor still on the phone?"

"Yup," Lawrence says, putting his feet back on the floor.

"Let me talk to him," Deacon says, grabbing the phone. "Doctor, this Special Agent Deacon with the FBI, put Trent Mayfair on the phone."

"Now is not a good time, sir."

"I don't care, put him on the phone, I need to speak with him."

"Let me see if he's awake."

"Ok, thanks and if he isn't, wake him. Lawrence can you give me a minute here, please close the door as you leave," Deacon says, as Lawrence ambles out with his head down.

"Hello," comes the raspy voice over the phone.

"Trent, it's Joe, how ya feeling?"

"I've been better, what's up?"

"Trent, Frank's still missing, nowhere to be found. Did Frank know Brendon Castleman?"

"No, not that I know of. Why?"

"Maddie used to date Frank, I'm sure they knew each other."

"What are you asking?"

"Well, I'm sending Lawrence over now to bring Brendon in for questioning, tell me what you know."

"Are you fucking kidding me? Lawrence doesn't even work there anymore, he's fired. And if he's wearing a uniform right now, he's breaking the law. I don't even want him in the building."

"Trent, calm down, you sound like you—"

"And you leave that boy out of this Deacon, I'm not kidding, I'll—"

"Trent, did you know that he broke into a clinic and stole a bottle of morphine recently?"

"What the hell are you, where did you hear that from? That's a bunch of bullshit."

"Dr. Jury just left, Trent. Get some rest, I'll keep you in the loop," he says, hanging up the phone.

That may have been too much, the guy took a bullet last night, need to keep him out of this for awhile, he's not going to help with the boy.

"Mr. Deacon, Mr. Hayward's on the line again."

"Ok, ok, I got it. Deacon here, what's up now?"

"I'll tell ya what's up, God damn it—the fucking Canadian authorities have called everyone from the Pentagon to the CIA, this is what these pricks do when they feel like they've been left out of something."

"Oh, Jesus."

"Oh Jesus, is right Deacon. Do you know how much of a mess this is for me now? Do you?"

"Oh no."

"They're calling it an international drug ring, Deacon."

"But it is."

"That's irrelevant, you fucking greenhorn."

"You know what, I'm sick and tired of you speaking to me that way."

"This was ours, all the credit ours. No one else was involved except for the Podunk sheriff. I am taking off for TC now, be there."

"Oh, I will, don't you worry," Deacon says, hanging up the phone and making his way into the lobby.

"Sadie, I need you to think, is there anyone else I'm missing? Brendon, Maddie, the doctor, anyone else?

"Well, there's Maddie's sister, Mary. She lives in Detroit though, but she did call a lot around the time of the funeral.

"Do you have her number?"

"Yes, I do."

"Remind me to call her when I get back, ok? I've got to run to the airport and pick up Hayward. Call me on my car phone if you need to. Lawrence, listen up—I need you to go and pick up this Brendon Castleman for questioning, understand?"

"Yes, sir," Lawrence says, puffing out his chest.

"Do you know where he lives?"

"Yup."

"Out in a cabin, I heard?"

"Yes, sir."

"Please don't call me sir all the time, ok?"

"Yup," Lawrence says, as the phone rings again.

"Mr. Deacon, I've got the *Detroit Free Press* on the line, they have requested to speak with you?"

"What? Me, by name? Are you kidding?"

"No, a reporter from a paper in Grand Rapids called earlier, wanted to know who he could speak to about the case."

"No, no, no comment, I'm out the door anyway. Don't tell them anything, Sadie, ok?"

"Ok," she says, as he went out the door.

"Never seen anything like that one, Lawrence," Sadie says, rising to glance at Deacon getting into his vehicle. "He's really fired up about all of this, I hate it when it gets this busy around here."

"Sadie, keep that call on hold, I'll take it."

"Oh, Lawrence, that's not a good idea."

"I'm a standin' in now for sheriff, Sadie. You might as well get used to it."

"Lawrence, I don't think that is what Mr. Deacon meant, seriously just do whatever he asked of ya and—"

"Quiet Sadie, I gotta take this call," he says picking up the receiver. "Hello, this is Deputy Lawrence Vintage, what can I do ya for?" he says staring at the ceiling with one hand on his gun. "I see, you's a reporter and all. So, ya'll want a press conference?" he says, tapping his pistol with his index finger. "Yup, yer' talkin' to the right person, yup, I'll give ya'll a press conference."

Chapter 43

How the Hell?

As I again lay my head on this tear stained-pillow, I am now starting to realize the full impact of the last forty-eight hours and my now transcendent existence. I watched the sun rise this morning and will again later gaze at its setting. What a wonderful world I now live in. For, time—time is now on my side. And this is my time—I will spend it however I see appropriate. And what is wrong with this? I am not bothered—I am numb and have very few visitors. And what is wrong with that? After all, who ever said there is something wrong with a room full of emptiness?

Footsteps outside, can't be, never had that before. My hermit-like existence has me now hearing noises that aren't really there. What, the front door is—

"Brendon, it's Lawrence, need ta talk ta ya," the southern accent says, "I know yer' in there."

"Jesus, Lawrence," I say, jumping out of bed, "whatya' doing out here?"

"I got orders to pick you up, it's best if ya come down to the station on yer' own accord."

"What?" I say, peeking around the corner in disbelief, "what are you talking about? Why didn't Trent just come on his own?"

"He's a little tied up right now."

"Where is your car at, Lawrence, did you walk here?"

"No, just parked down the road a ways—in case you didn't feel like havin' any company today."

What the hell is that supposed to mean? And how on earth would he have thought of that?

"Didn't know you was a trapper?"

"What?"

"Those beaver pelts you got hangin' in the back yard, season ain't even open yet, is it?"

"Oh, those are some old ones I, I've had in the freezer, just stretching them out now."

"Oh?"

"Yeah, saw some article on a guy who makes them into furniture."

"Hmmm," Lawrence nods with a wannabe tough guy look.

What was I thinking? I should have never of kept those hides, I just didn't want to be wasteful. They can't be on to me already, no they can't . . . Picking me up the day after the event, this isn't right, this can't be? How did this happen? How? How the hell?

"Let's get a move on, kid, I got a lot ta do today."

"Ok, ok, let me grab my wallet and stuff. Lawrence, what's this about, seems kind a odd?"

"You'll be findin' out here soon, now let's a hop to it."

"You mind if I drive and just follow you in to town? I got a bunch of stuff that I—"

"Nope, yer ridin' with me, boy. Don't need any funny business either."

"Funny business, what the hell are you talking about?"

"Brendon, let's go."

"Ok, ok, calm down."

"Don't tell me what to do, boy, just follow my orders."

Where the hell has this attitude come from? Always was an odd duck, but now this? Who the hell put him in charge of anything? Wouldn't have been Trent, I do know that. There must be a reasonable explanation for this—maybe the house sold? But Trent wouldn't send Lawrence out to pick me up for that—something's up, something's not right.

"Lawrence, you sure I can't drive my way into town, I—"

"Yes, I'm sure."

"Ok, you got any smokes, Lawrence? That is one of the things I wanted to buy in town."

"Yeah," he says, sheepishly, "I got some in the car."

"Ok, let's go," I say, as I shut the door and began to follow him down the dirt two-track of a road. "How was your fourth of July?" *Gotta get him talking.*

"Ok, I guess, supposed to be on vacation, but things got real busy. How 'bout you?"

"Great, best ever."

"Whatya' do?"

"Nothing, absolutely nothing. Just fished, it was great."

"Yeah."

"How far is the car?"

"Right there," he points. The cruiser is parked off of the main road hidden slightly into the woods.

"You sit in the back," he says, sharply as I open the front door of the cruiser.

"Oh, ok, Deputy Vintage, whatever you say. How about that cigarette?"

"Here ya go," he says, passing the lighter back.

"Ya know Lawrence, I haven't seen you since that day you were standing over me chain smoking cigarettes."

"What?" he says, looking back into the rear view mirror.

"You know, the big day?" I say, with a straight face.

The only way I'm going to get anything out of Lawrence is if I play this card, he's acting awfully strange today. And today, the day after, I don't need anyone acting strange.

"Oh, well I didn't know you was awake that day?"

"Yep, I was."

"Well ya sure didn't act it, by the way, we's all real sorry about what happened that day, ya know? Very sorry."

"Yeah, we're all real sorry, aren't we?"

"Yep," he says, nodding his head.

Why on earth can they be bringing me in today. . ? Come on, there must be a legitimate reason, must be. But, your timing is terrible, hell I still probably smell like Frank Pierson. Need to relax; this is Trent's office, after all. Just relax, can't be acting all nervous, not now. Almost there now and Lawrence obviously doesn't feel like talking, that's ok. Trent can explain things. Well, here we are, time to find out.

"Follow me, Brendon," Lawrence says, now donning his metallic aviator shades.

What has gotten into this guy, you'd think he was sheriff of this small town. Come on anyway—let's get this over with already.

"Hi Sadie," I say, holding up my hands acting as though I were cuffed.

"Oh hello, Brendon," she says, looking alarmed until realizing I was only joking.

"Brendon, you follow me, I need you ta hang out in the conference room for the time bein'."

"Nice sunglasses, Lawrence," Sadie says, with a smile.

"Thanks," he says, nearly bumping into me.

"Just have a seat, we'll be with you shortly."

"Who will be?"

"We will be, you need something to drink?"

"No, I don't," I say, as he nods and shuts the door.

How in the world did this happen? I'm at the sheriff's office one day after I take out that miserable piece of shit. . ? And they have me in the conference room without explanation? Where is Trent? He wouldn't approve of this, hell no. At least I have a window, or do I? Let's see here, yes, we do have a window—look, it doesn't even have a screen. Well, that may come in handy if need be. Just relax, not climbing out a window, not yet, at least. Need to concentrate, need to focus, gotta think, what is this all about? C'mon, need to listen, need to listen, that's them talking, Sadie and Lawrence, what are they saying? There's a good inch or two under that door, should be enough—

"Lawrence, before you leave, one of the state boys called a few minutes ago," she says, lowering her voice, "they saw Frank Pierson's truck parked out in the Deadstream Swamp."

"No shit," Lawrence says, excitedly, "who else knows?"

"No one, I guess, we put an APB and they got it."

"Deacon will be happy about that," Lawrence says, ripping off his sunglasses.

"Maybe you should go and take a look at it?"

"Good idea, I will, just in case, ya know? Hey, where's that number for the reporter that I gotta call?"

"You took it into your office the last I saw. They've been callin' all morning, by the way. Don't do anything stupid, Lawrence."

"Zip it, Sadie—I got a job to do here," Lawrence says, heading past the conference room and to his office.

"You know what I mean, I'll call Deacon about Frank's truck bein' found."

"Ok," Lawrence says, closing the door to his office.

"Hi, Mr. Deacon, it's Sadie."

"Go ahead, Sadie," Deacon says.

"A state boy called in here earlier—he happened to drive past Frank Pierson's truck this morning and had heard we were looking for it."

"What? Are you . . . where is it?"

"Out in the Deadstream Swamp, he said it seems to be deserted."

"Oh, Jesus Christ, Sadie—thank you! Where's Lawrence?"

"He's here, on the phone, gettin' ready to leave and go look at the truck."

"Ok, good, you have him radio in to you when he gets to Frank's vehicle, ok? I want you to call me as soon as he radios in, got it?"

"Ok, got it," she says, twirling her hair.

"What about the boy, Brendon?"

"Oh, he's here too. Lawrence just brought him in."

"Good, good. Didn't Lawrence pick him up out by that way? In the Deadstream? He lives out that way, where Frank's truck was found, doesn't he?"

"Yeah, I guess, he's been staying out there lately, from what I heard."

"Thanks Sadie, I'm still in TC, Hayward's flight was delayed. You've been a great help. See you shortly."

"You're welcome, sir," she says, smiling.

"I'm outta here," Lawrence says, grabbing his hat as Sadie hangs up the phone.

"Ok, Lawrence. Hey—did you talk to that reporter?"

"What's it to ya?" he says, sharply.

"Well, Lawrence, don't exactly think you should be doin' any press conferences."

"Done'm before when I worked down south, you stay outta this, me and the Federali got this one under control," he says, opening the door to leave.

"Ok," Sadie says, glancing at a shadow below the door of the conference room.

"Sadie," I say, opening the door with my nicest smile, "can I at least use the phone?"

"No, that's not a good idea, Brendon."

"But, there is one in here," I say, pointing, "it's a conference room, Sadie."

"Please don't use it, Brendon, no. I can tell if you pick it up, a light goes off on my phone, ya know? Yer puttin' me in an awful difficult situation here. Lawrence told you to sit and relax, please just listen to him."

"Where is Trent? Either charge me with something or—"

"Trent's in the hospital Brendon, he got shot last night, I know it sounds awful, but they said he's going to be ok."

"What?" *Shot? Trent was shot? Lawrence was lying—lying the whole time—I knew something was off by the way he was strutting around. This isn't good—may be time to rally.*

"Then why am I here?"

"I don't know, Brendon, just sit tight. Lawrence will be right back."

"Ok, Sadie, but you have to admit this is kind of odd."

"Hey, I just work here," she says, tilting her head to one side with a smile.

"Can I at least get something to drink?"

"Sure, just grab something out of the break room and get back in that conference room before you get me in trouble."

"Ok, one more thing—do you have a cigarette I could bum?"

"I got some out in my car, but—"

"Please Sadie, c'mon," I say, pleading.

"Ok, ok, I could use one too. You go sit down, I'll be right back."

"Thanks Sadie, I owe you one. I'll be in there," I say, pointing to the conference room—*the room with a view and a window.*

"Ok," she says, going out the front door of the building.

C'mon, phone dial, c'mon, pick up, pick up, if you've ever picked up, just this once . . .

"Hello," says the cheerful voice of Shirley Kudray.

"Mrs. Kudray, it's Brendon, I need to speak with Billy immediately," I whisper.

"Oh, Brendon, we miss you so, how have you—"

"Please put him on the phone, now. It's an emergency."

"Oh, ok, I hope everything is ok, one sec."

"Hello."

"Billy, it's me, Brendon—I need your help."

Chapter 44

A Little Tough on You

Oh, if I could only sleep, thought the sheriff. *Just an hour, just a minute for that matter. I've taken a bullet and am doped up and still can't sleep. That motherfucker Lance Pierson—I have a new job in life, as soon as I get out of this hospital, I'll hunt him down like an animal. A carpet knife, stitches and now this? Not to mention my marriage hasn't been the same since one of his cronies threw a brick through my front window ten years ago. What a crock of shit—this is life? This is my life? This is pathetic.*

The phone rang next to his bed as he began the slow but steady motion in order to reach it.

"Hello," he whispers.

"Trent, it's Sadie, how are you?"

"I'm ok, I guess, just wish I could sleep some."

"When are you coming back, we miss you, it's just not the same."

"As soon as possible, I promise. Trust me, don't exactly like it here."

"I was just calling to say hello, ya know?"

"C'mon Sadie, I can tell by your voice that's not why you're calling."

"No, I—"

"Spit it out, Sadie, what's going on?"

"Sheriff, I hate to tell you this over the phone, especially in your condition, but we got reporters from all over the state calling in here. The *Chicago Tribune* called about ten minutes ago, it's makin' me nervous."

"Oh Jesus, really," he says, looking up at the ceiling, "shouldn't be a problem, Sadie. Just don't tell them a God damn thing."

"That's not the worst of it, Trent—Lawrence has been talkin' to one of 'em and now he's talkin' about doin' a press conference."

"What?" the sheriff says, with a raised voice. "He's fired, Sadie, you know that!" he screams, grimacing at the pain it caused. "You tell him, you tell him

I'll put a fucking bullet in his head if he even so much as talks to the press, I'm not kidding, Sadie."

"Oh, Trent, please calm down, this can't be good for your condition. Ok, I will stop him, I'll try, I—"

"I'm not kidding Sadie, tell him exactly what I said, I'm not—"

"Ok, Trent, I knew I shouldn't have called, you get some rest, ok?" she says, hanging up the receiver.

"Tell him he's fired, Sadie. Did you hear me?"

Shit, she's hung up the phone already, should probably call her back. God damn that man, gonna put me in an early grave, I tell ya. I knew he'd find a way to fuck with me while I was in here. What a boat ride that was last night. Thought that was it, thought I was done for. Saw my life flash right before my eyes, life through the end of a bottle. The face on Deacon you would have thought I had already left, kid looked like he was looking at a dead man. That sounded like a knock, now who the hell is it? Let me guess—another foreigner looking at me like I'm a caged animal or crazed mental patient.

"Hi, Trent," Doctor Jury says, bashfully, "it's me, is it ok if I visit?"

"Yeah, Sharon, come in."

"Oh, Trent, you look so tired, I'm so sorry, I heard you were shot," she says, smiling weakly, "it absolutely took my breath away."

"Oh, Sharon, thanks for coming," he says, returning the smile in the dimly lit room. "I think, I think I kind of owe you an apology, Sharon. I've been a little tough on you to be honest."

"Thanks, Trent, we have been a little at odds," she says, placing her hand on his.

"But, why didn't you tell me, Sharon. That was a mistake."

"About what?"

"About Brendon breaking into the clinic?"

"I'm so sorry," she says, "I didn't know what to do, when they told me what was gone, I knew it was him. I knew it was him immediately, I am so sorry Trent, I should have told you, I should have confided in you."

"Yes, you should have. I would have gone out there and grabbed him and locked him up myself if I knew he was using drugs," he says, weakly.

"Oh, Trent, darling—you look like you should sleep."

"Darling? I kind of like that," the sheriff says, through tears, "I am so tired, I've never been this tired in my life," he says, closing his watery eyes. "I just can't sleep."

"I think I can help, Trent," she says, rising to turn down the lights. "Please just relax, Trent," she says, sitting back down and pulling the chair closer to him. "Just relax, Trent," she whispers into his ear carefully placing her hand on his forehead. "Just try and relax, Trent, just relax. Shhh . . . Everything is going to be ok," she says, staring into his eyes as his breathing deepens. "Trent, would you mind if I were here when you wake up?"

"You know what Sharon, I never thought I'd say this, but there is nothing I would like more."

"Goodnight, Trent, my darling," she whispers, into his ear, "you sleep now."

CHAPTER 45

PC

"Now, ladies and gents, I wanna thank ya'll fer comin' all the way up here to Roscommon County, my county," Lawrence says, tilting his chin down, "I knows yer' as interested in this here case as I am, but I can't tell ya'll everythin' on account of the fact that this here is an on goin' 'vestigation, see?" he says to click of flashbulbs.

"Deputy Vintage," says the voice of the female reporter, "we've heard that a sheriff, your sheriff, is currently in the hospital due to a gunshot wound, is this true?"

"Well, now, ya see, ya'll gettin' ahead of me here, but yes, he is in the hospital and more importantly I'm the actin' shariff' now. So, that's just the way that it is."

"Is it also true," whines another voice, "that he was involved in the investigation of an international drug ring that was using the Great Lakes?"

"Well, now, I can't talk about that right now, I'm a still learnin'—"

"What kind of drugs were they shipping, Deputy Vintage?"

"I can' answer that one either, God damn it!" he says, tilting his hat back.

"Come on, deputy, you've got to give us something here, the Canadian papers are already reporting more than what you're giving us. What about Lance Pierson, the fugitive?"

"Come on now, ya'll know I can't be revealin' that sort of information," Lawrence says, finally taking off his aviator shades and pulling out a filterless Palm Mall.

"You might as well spill the beans, sir," the female reporter says with smile.

"Well, ok then. Let me start off by tellin' ya'll little about myself here . . . Give ya'll a little bit history about myself and all, well . . . did I ever tell you folks about the time I get arrested at the border for impersonating a police officer?" he says, with a chuckle, "now that was a humdinger!"

"WHAT?" the reporter says.

Click, goes the flashbulbs, click, click . . .

Chapter 46

Reincarnation

There will never be another day that passes when I won't visit the day that my Mother chose to leave me. I cannot pretend to have walked in her skin and made the decisions that she was forced to make. I love her deeply and I always will—and that is the end of the story.

Everything that transpired this past spring and summer is irreparable and I truly feel that I have done all that I can. From a wise man that is very few on years—these events only prove that the purest elements in life are also the most fragile.

Just like there will never be a day that I don't envision the beautiful blond English girl asleep in my arms that warm and soft summer night, sleeping she was. There isn't a day my heart doesn't find her—she's out there, floating somewhere, one must only reach—just a little farther, right around this next bend—

It's been just over twenty-four hours since I erased that parasite's heartbeat and took him to another place. Upon my determination, I may never be welcomed back, here—but things could be much worse, for I have been there before. I will miss my swamp and I will miss Billy—even if his incessant tears finally forced me to pick up my bag and make this final walk down a narrow corridor. Everything from this point on is going to be all right, for I own what has happened to me, just as I now own my sins. Someday, I will be wonderfully clean of all of this filth that covers my mind, body and skin. But, if only out of pure honesty I may make one final and decisive point—never, ever underestimate the power of denial.

As I take my seat, there is now a black haired woman around forty years of age walking a perfectly and perpetual straight line in front of me dressed in a tightly pressed uniform. She has a permanent smile and is now finally making her way to me. She arrives as the engines below me begin to rumble.

"Seat belt, sir," she says, red-lipped, like a wet painting, "please."

"Ma'am—can I get two Jack Daniel's on the rocks and after that can I get two more?"

"Oh, now," she smiles with eye contact through pursed lips, "we don't want to be hung-over when we arrive in LA, now do we?"

"Oh, I'm not going to LA," I answer.

"Well," she says, leaning over with a wag of her head, "then where are you going?"

"Bangkok."

"Oh, Thailand—any specific reason?"

"Yes, I'm going to see a girl."

"She must be a pretty important lady?"

"You have no idea—"

Houghton Lake Resorter

Area's master woodsman died 37 years ago this month

By Glenn Schicker

He died 37 years ago this month, but you might still see his picture displayed on the walls of Houghton Lake's older sports shops and resorts. Why would an unassuming woodsman, who spent much of his life living in the wilderness of the Deadstream Swamp, warrant so much attention? He was even the subject of a 1945 feature in Outdoor Life magazine.

His name is Art Jackson, and he was probably the most famous hunter ever to stalk the woods of Roscommon County. Jackson bagged his biggest trophy in the Deadstream in 1943. Jackson had trapped a smaller bruin, and discovered the larger animal eating the carcass. Jackson followed the bear's trail and was able to take it by surprise by a leaning a cedar tree.

A shot in the head brought the big bear down. Jackson trekked several miles to Houghton Lake and returned with four friends. All five men were unable to lift the animal. The returned the next day with block and tackle to finish the job.

Laurence Dayton, state game manager, measured the beast at 6 feet, 6 inches long and 5 feet, 7 inches in girth. The animal was never weighed. Estimates ranged from 500 to 935 pounds. Jackson's 1947 Resorter obituary said the bear weighed 873 pounds.

The kill became somewhat of a legend. The Resorter said, "Pictures of the giant bear are displayed at practically every place where sportsmen congregate in northern Michigan.

Jackson died at his home in Lyon Manor Jan. 16, 1947, at age 1976. His Resorter obituary listed among his survivors, "hundreds of sportsmen friends who respected his talents as a master woodsman."

The Houghton Lake Resorter
SECTION TWO — PAGE ONE
THURSDAY, JAN. 5, 1984

JACKSON'S BIGGEST BRUIN
Art Jackson poses with the biggest bear he harvested during a 70-year hunting career. He bagged the animal in 1943 in the Deadstream Swamp. It weighed an estimated 873 pounds.

I would like to thank the following people for their friendship, love and support.

Louise Deeley, Donna and Bill Oliver, Lynda Stuck, Elmer Tews, Jerry Tews, and Barbara Porterfield.

Josh, Nicki, Hudson, Emma, Debra, Bill, Donna and Kenneth Platt, Diane Dozer, and Janet Ryan.

April, Scott, Jeffrey, Randy, Michelle, Brownie and Mary Stuck, Joyce and Charlie Webber, Robert and Gertrude Briggs.

Bill, Irene, Chas, Bertha, Charlie, Alex, and Julia Lilley, Amy, Mike, and Sam Powell.

Dan and Sarah Draper, Brian and Krista, Tera and James, Kim and Rob, Mishelle, Bob and Sherron Garrow, Peter Ginopolis, Scott Gorgacz, Ken and Jen Hartman, Aaron and Emily Hoiles, Brett Hoover, Art Jackson, Jason and Amy Kudary, Kevin and Martha MIller, Justin Nalley, Eric and Monica Noonan, Brian Price, Ken Shtino, and Brandon Warson.

Special thanks for your advice from a technical standpoint: Will Byington, Jerry Cleaver, Eric Hamp, Aaron Hoiles, Jean-Francis Lafontaine, Julia Lilley, Dave Mertz, Glenn Schicker, Kristi Schroeder, Ken Shtino, Randy Stuck, Helen Valenta, Peter Virginelli, and the Houghton Lake Resorter www.houghtonlakeresorter.com.

Printed in the United States
43525LVS00006B/199